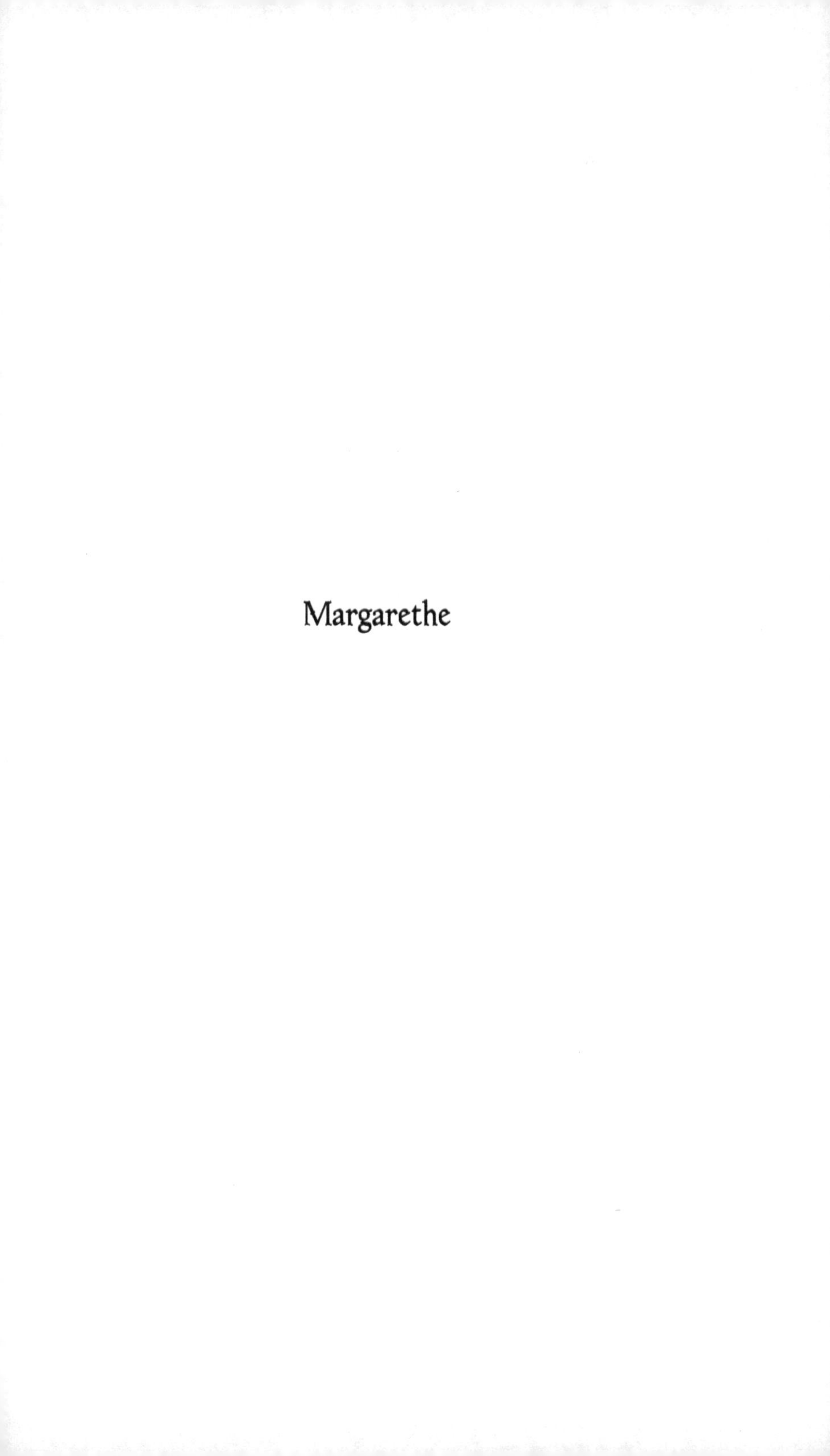

Margarethe

Emma Leslie Church History Series

Glaucia the Greek Slave
A Tale of Athens in the First Century

The Captives
Or, Escape From the Druid Council

Out of the Mouth of the Lion
Or, The Church in the Catacombs

Sowing Beside All Waters
A Tale of the World in the Church

From Bondage to Freedom
A Tale of the Times of Mohammed

The Martyr's Victory
A Story of Danish England

Gytha's Message
A Tale of Saxon England

Leofwine the Monk
Or, The Curse of the Ericsons
A Story of a Saxon Family

Elfreda the Saxon
Or, The Orphan of Jerusalem
A Sequel to Leofwine

Dearer Than Life
A Story of the Times of Wycliffe

Before the Dawn
A Tale of Wycliffe and Huss

Emma Leslie Church History Series

Faithful, But Not Famous
A Tale of the French Reformation

Daybreak in Italy
A Story of the Italian Reformation

Margarethe
A Tale of Luther and Zwingli

Constancia's Household
A Tale of the Spanish Reformation

At the Sign of the Golden Fleece
A Story of Tyndale and the English Bible

The Hermit of Livry
A Tale of the Days of Calvin

Lady Cecily
A Story of the English Reformation

Luther Nailing His Theses on the Church Door

Page 96

Emma Leslie Church History Series

Margarethe

†††

A Tale of Luther and Zwingli

BY

EMMA LESLIE

Illustrated by
FELTER

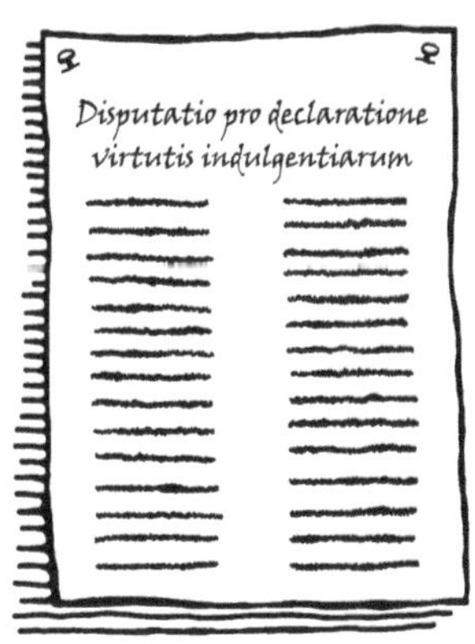

Salem Ridge Press
Emmaus, Pennsylvania

Originally Published
1879
Phillips & Hunt

Republished 2012
Salem Ridge Press LLC
4263 Salem Drive
Emmaus, Pennsylvania 18049

www.salemridgepress.com

Hardcover ISBN: 978-1-934671-46-7
Softcover ISBN: 978-1-934671-47-4

PUBLISHER'S NOTE

There have certainly been many important times in the history of the Church, but the time in which *Margarethe* is set may be one of the most pivotal. The events that Martin Luther and the other reformers set into motion changed the Church forever and ended the Roman Catholic Church's near monopoly on the Christian religion.

While Martin Luther was only able to correct some of the abuses that filled the Church of his day, the work that he and other reformers like Zwingli began continues to this day. Now it is the responsibility of each one of us to continue this work and to make sure that every aspect of our lives is based upon the inspired Word of God!

Daniel Mills

May, 2012

PREFACE TO THE 1879 EDITION

I shall say but few words by way of preface to this, the second volume of this Second Series of Stories of Church History.

The period chosen is the most wonderful in the history of Europe, or of the world; and was, indeed, the dawn of a new and brighter day: for this movement, both religiously, politically, and socially, cannot be traced to one man, or society, or nation; but, like the coming of day, stole upon the world from various points in the heavens almost simultaneously, although Germany was, undoubtedly, the glorious East from which the sun arose that was to lighten all the nations around. Luther was, undoubtedly, the reformer pre-eminently; but Luther could not have done the work he did but for those who had preceded him by a few years, and were his compeers. Reuchlin might fairly be called his forerunner. Then, too, the wonderful invention of printing, which was now making its way in the world, and the revival of learning in every country, so materially helped forward the Reformation, that the times of Huss and Wycliffe, compared with those of Luther, sink almost into insignificance.

All these various influences, combined under the one grand name of the Reformation, I have tried to portray in this story of Margarethe; but the redundancy of the materials, and the difficulty of choosing among so much that was important in its bearing upon the whole, has rendered my task a most difficult one; and I can only hope that my readers, after perusing *Margarethe*, may feel so dissatisfied with the necessarily scanty historical information conveyed in it, as to study the subject more thoroughly in larger and more pretentious works. I am very greatly indebted to D'Aubigné's *History of the Reformation*, as well as to Anderson's *Ladies of the Reformation*, Ranke's *Lives of the Popes*, Roscoe's *Leo the Tenth*, Luther's *Table-Talk*, and other volumes.

As my readers will perceive, this story closes almost at the beginning of the Reformation. It could not be otherwise in the limited space at command and the crowd of events that marked that time. In my next volume I hope to trace something of its progress, and the efforts made to suppress it in every country.

That these volumes may be blessed to the reader is the earnest prayer of the author!

Emma Leslie

HISTORICAL NOTES

Several important historical figures from the sixteenth century A.D. are mentioned in *Margarethe.* Here is a brief summary of some of these people:

Martin Luther: Born in 1483 A.D., Martin Luther studied at the University of Erfurt and then entered law school. Following a near death experience, Luther abandoned his study of law and entered a monastery. As a monk, Luther tried in every possible way to free himself from his guilt and sin, often imposing strict fasts and punishments upon himself. At last, through his study of the Scriptures, Luther recognized that forgiveness is a free gift of God and cannot be earned through human effort. Luther never desired to overthrow the Roman Catholic Church, but his work and teaching led to the Protestant Reformation and the founding of the Lutheran church.

Johann Tetzel: Johann Tetzel was a Dominican friar chiefly remembered for his sale of indulgences in Germany. These indulgences promised the owners complete forgiveness of sins, past, present and future, and immediate access to heaven upon their death. As a Doctor of Theology, Tetzel defended his indulgences against Luther's criticism, but died shortly thereafter in 1519.

Historical Notes

Ulrich Zwinglius: Zwinglius, more commonly known as Zwingli, was a priest in Zurich, Switzerland for many years. In his preaching Zwingli placed great emphasis on the Scriptures as the foundation for all of life.

Emperor Charles V: In 1519, when Charles was appointed Holy Roman Emperor at the age of 19, he was already ruler of the Netherlands and King of Spain. Although he opposed the Reformation, Charles was unable to force his German subjects to return to Roman Catholicism.

Count von Sickengen: Along with his friend, Ulrich von Hutten, von Sickengen attempted to overthrow the Roman Catholic Church by force. He was killed in 1523 during a battle with the Archbishop of Trier.

In 1517 A.D. Martin Luther nailed his **95 Theses** to the door of the Wittenberg church. These ninety-five statements laid out Luther's opposition to the sale of indulgences and invited readers to a debate on the topic.

During the Middle Ages, and throughout much of history, men have attempted to predict the future using the positions of the sun, moon, planets and constellations. This study, commonly known as **astrology**, is clearly condemned in the Bible.[1]

[1] e.g. Isaiah 47:13-14

IMPORTANT DATES

A.D.

1508 Martin Luther is appointed a professor of theology at the University of Wittenberg

1516 Johann Tetzel begins to sell his indulgences in Germany

1517 Martin Luther Nails his *95 Theses* to the door of the Wittenberg Church

1518 Ulrich Zwingli begins to preach in Zurich

1521 Luther refuses to recant his doctrine at the Diet of Worms and is excommunicated by the Pope

1531 Death of Ulrich Zwingli

1534 Publication of Luther's German Bible

1546 Death of Martin Luther

Germany in the 16th Century

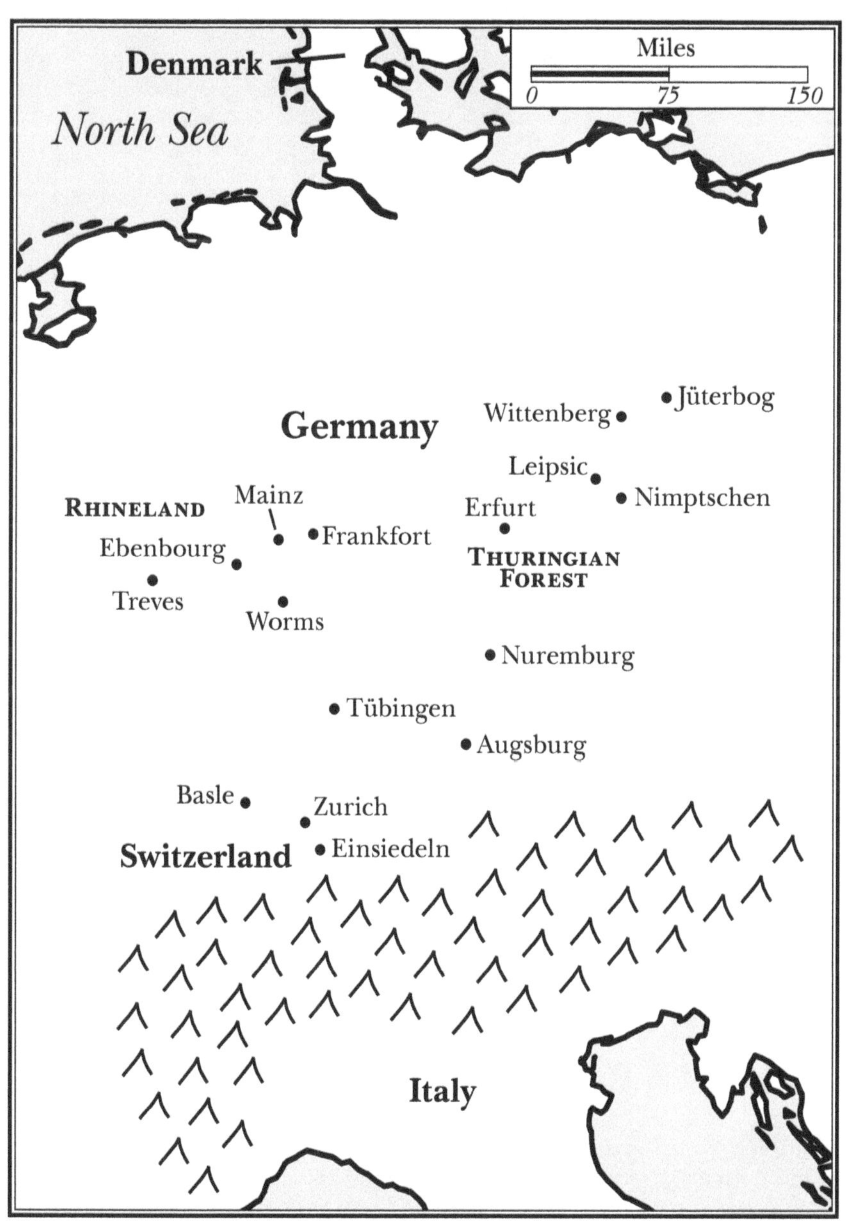

CONTENTS

CHAPTER | PAGE

ILLUSTRATIONS

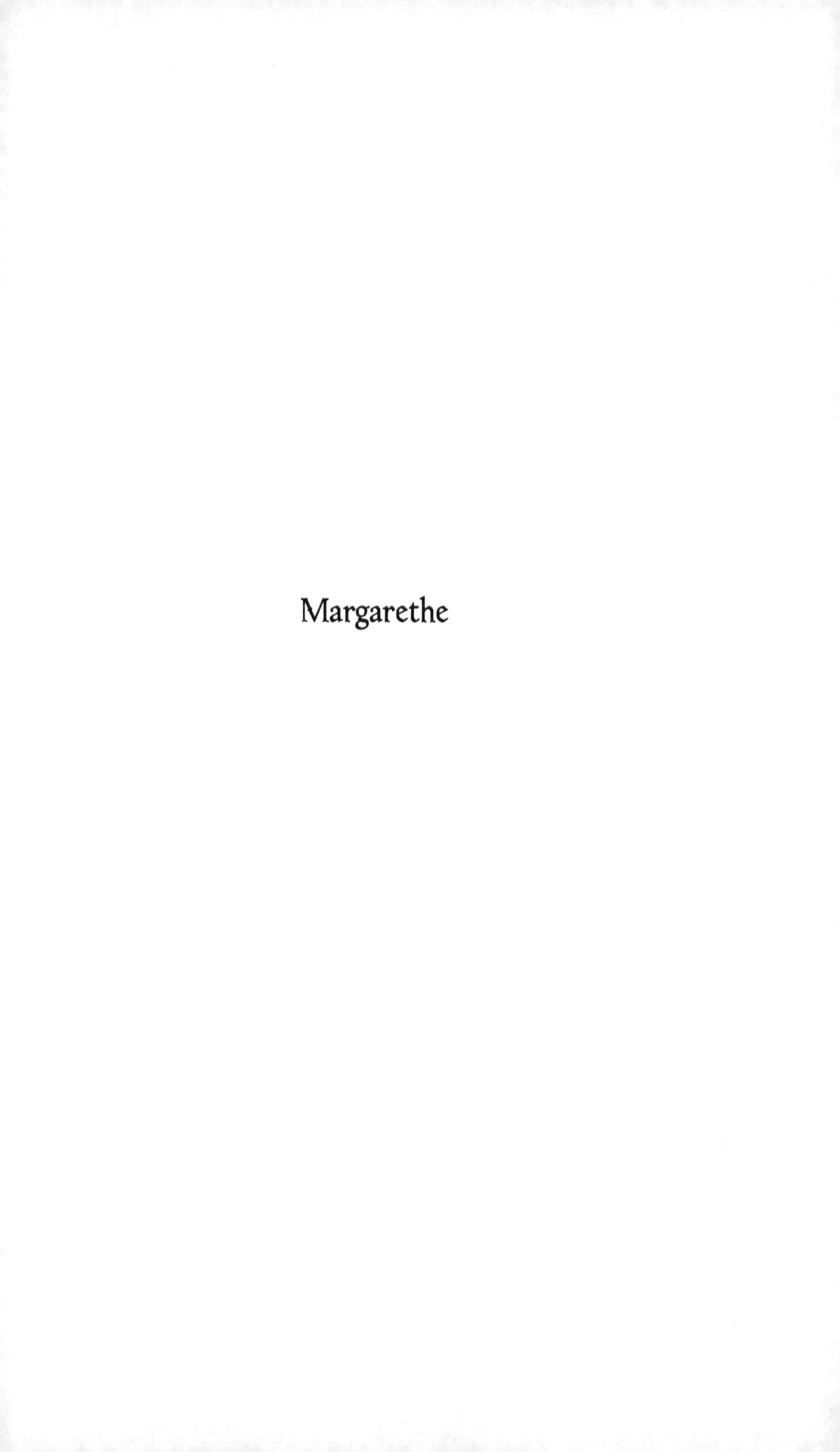

Margarethe

Margarethe

Chapter I

The Sisters

SPRING sunshine was gilding the tops of the tall pines of the great Thuringian forest,[1] and penciling streaks of gold here and there on the soft velvet turf below. The turf had been well cleared of sticks and pinecones; for in the valley a little lower down was nestled a tiny village of peasant huts—the houses of the retainers who served the knight living in the grim-looking fortress that crowned the hill.

From the castle terrace one could look down upon the tops of the swaying pines, and they effectually hid the little cluster of cottages, and even the thatch-roofed church, from the eyes of its lordly owner, who thought little and cared less for how his peasant retainers might fare, so long as they served him faithfully.

[1] A forest in central Germany

RETAINERS: *servants*

Today two young girls were walking here on the terrace, and looking down upon the road that wound its circuitous way between the pines up to the castle gate.

"Fritz said he should be home today; that he would come early, too. I do hope—" and there she stopped.

"What is it, Else, you are afraid of? for I can see you are afraid of something," said her sister, turning upon her rather sharply.

"Nothing, only you know the burghers of Erfurt might hinder him, Margarethe."

"Those miserable burghers!" stamped her sister impatiently. "But I do not believe they would dare to rob and murder a knight," she exclaimed the next minute.

"O, not murder him! of course not; but I heard my father say—" and then again Else glanced at her sister hurriedly, and stopped.

"Well, what did our father say?" asked Margarethe, with a little more color in her cheeks.

"Only this, dear, that he wished the time had come for me to go to the convent, and he might make himself strong enough to punish these upstart burghers."

Margarethe started, and her checks flamed, and her dark eyes flashed. "He may punish these burghers if he will—burn their town and university, if he likes; but, Else, if you are sent to the convent he shall never join hands with Count von Schonstein through me."

CIRCUITOUS: *round about*
BURGHERS: *the inhabitants of a borough or town*

"O Margarethe, you do not know; it is not so terrible for me to go to the convent. Of course I shall miss you, and—and I am afraid it will be a long time before I can leave off loving you so much, and thinking of you as my beautiful clever sister Margarethe, as Father Sebastian says I must; but then, you know, he says my heart will be so filled with the ineffable love of the spouse—the Church and all the saints, I suppose he means—that there will be no room in my heart for any earthly love."

Margarethe looked rather hurt. "O Else, do you think you can leave off loving me like this? Why, we have been all the world to each other, and I-I couldn't, I wouldn't, leave off loving you. O, how I do hate religion and everything about it! I am glad I have no vocation, and—"

"O hush! hush! Margarethe; do not say such dreadful things," said Else, the tears welling up to her eyes as she spoke.

Margarethe looked down into the gentle blue eyes, and kissed her sister passionately. "It is cruel, cruel," she said, "and I hate it all. I am not a bit religious, I know, and, of course, God hates me; but I don't care; no, I don't care! I will love you, and, Else, you must love me, even though they do take you away to the convent."

"Yes, yes, dear, I will—at least I will pray for you always, and perhaps by and by God may give you a vocation; and then if you come to the convent we can love each other again, because we shall be sisters again, you know."

INEFFABLE: *impossible to express in words*
VOCATION: *calling from God to the life of a monk or nun*

But Margarethe shook her head. "No, no; don't pray for me to have a vocation and come to the convent; because I hate convents, and priests, and even the Holy Father at Rome sometimes. There is no religion in the world for me. I wonder almost that God let me be sister to such a dear, gentle, patient girl as you; only, of course, He always meant you to be a saint, and to take you away from me just when it was like taking my heart out of my body, that He might punish me. But it doesn't seem quite fair that He should begin to make me as miserable as He can here when He knows I shall go to endless misery when I die."

"O Margarethe, don't," said Else pleadingly, "pray don't talk so dreadfully."

"Dreadful! But it's true; you know it is; and I say it isn't fair. I wouldn't do it, I know, not even to one of those Erfurt burghers whom we ought to hate, it seems, as our hereditary enemies. If I knew I could make him miserable by and by, I would let him have a little peace now, and not watch for every little chance to make him unhappy, as God watches everybody that doesn't have a vocation. I wonder whether there is anybody else in the world as wicked as I am," concluded Margarethe in the same defiant tone.

"O don't say any more: think what you will have to tell Father Sebastian the next time you go to confession, and what a hard penance he will give you."

HEREDITARY: *passed down through the generations*
CONFESSION: *private confession of sins to a priest*
PENANCE: *punishment for sins committed*

"I don't care for the penance; but I don't mean to go to confession anymore," boldly avowed Margarethe, and her color brightened as she spoke.

"Not—go—to—confession!" slowly uttered Else, as though she thought that for her sister to absent herself from that sacrament of the Church was a depth of wickedness she doubted even in her with all her daring.

"No, I don't mean to go again," Margarethe coolly avowed. "Father Sebastian asked me some questions which I told him no maiden would ever answer, the very last time I went;" and at the recollection Margarethe drew herself up with dignity and walked away.

Else noticed the proud carriage, and thought she could guess what the questions had been. At least she would try to save her sister from the commission of such a great sin as absenting herself from the confessional; and as she walked along the terrace she slipped her arm within Margarethe's, as she was about to turn in her walk.

Looking up into the dark, flashing eyes, she said, "I believe you are of our mother's family, and more a Bohemian than a German, although you were born in this German forest, Margarethe."

"Perhaps I am, little sister," she said rather sadly.

"And the Bohemians are proud—prouder than the Germans, I think I have heard," said Else, again glancing up into her sister's face.

"Perhaps they are," again assented Margarethe.

"Yes, I think they must be," said Else, rather timidly; "and that is why you feel so hurt at Father Sebastian's questions. Of course you cannot help being proud, dear Margarethe, but—"

"But I never mean to answer such questions as Father Sebastian asked," interrupted her sister. "He said I was proud, and that such pride ought to be humbled and mortified; and—"

"O Margarethe, I was sure that was how it was, and you—you will go to confession again, I am sure you will," said Else.

"I am sure I will not. I tell you, Else, he had no business to ask a maiden such questions. Of course he has not dared to ask you such. You are but fourteen—two years younger than I. But if I thought he would—" Margarethe stopped suddenly and clenched her fist. "I wish I were a man, like Fritz," she abruptly added.

"That is an old wish, Margarethe. But look! look!" and Else pointed to a distant opening in the forest glades, where two or three horsemen were seen rather wearily wending their way up the road toward the castle.

"It is Fritz—Fritz has come at last," exclaimed Margarethe joyfully, and everything else was forgotten for a time; and, after giving due notice of the approach of the travelers to those within the castle, the two girls took their places to watch the cavalcade as it slowly wound round the steep, circuitous road.

WENDING: *making*

"I wonder whether Fritz went to the great fair at Nuremberg, and what he will bring us? He always does bring us something, you know, Else."

"Yes, perhaps he will bring you a new velvet bodice," said her sister.

"And you some wonderful toys, or one of those mirrors of the new Venetian glass that he was talking about when he was at home before," said Margarethe.

But Else shook her head. "He knows that toys and mirrors will be of no use to me in the convent," she said.

"O dear! that dreadful convent! it rises up like a ghost every time one speaks. I don't think I shall be greatly disappointed if I don't go to heaven, but to the other dreadful place instead," concluded Margarethe.

Her sister looked up, shocked and pained. "I mean to help you get to heaven; and that is why I am glad sometimes that I am going into the convent so soon, that I may have time to collect a store of good works."

"I wish you would not, then, for I am sure I should never be happy in heaven, where, of course, they are all monks and nuns, living something as they do in their convents here, only the walls being of shining gold, instead of bricks and stone, must make one's eyes ache sooner. But there! we will forget there is such a thing as a convent, or religion either, now that Fritz has come home. We'll listen to the glad, merry birds as they sing to their little ones in the tops of the pine trees; and go down to the valley, and see how many dear little babies have come to live there during the winter, and how all the old folks are; and we'll tell them about Fritz and his long journey to Italy, and listen to their stories about mother and father when they were young. But I wonder what Fritz will bring us?"

"I don't know. He will bring Aunt Ermengarde a book, perhaps, from the elector's new printing-press," said Else.

Margarethe turned up her nose. "I hate these printing-presses," she said, "for I heard Father say if it were not for this new fashion of multiplying books, and making learning cheap and common, the burghers of Erfurt would not be so upstartish and troublesome as they are."

"But our grandfather says it will be good for the world by and by."

"It will not be good for me if those tiresome burghers and students of Erfurt get everything their own way," objected Margarethe.

But now the cavalcade that had been hidden from their view during the last few minutes again emerged from under the brow of the hill, and now they could see one of the horsemen had taken off his plumed cap and was waving it, in token of his recognition of them.

Margarethe and Else were not slow to return the greeting, and when the horsemen again passed out of sight they ran down to the great hall to be in time to greet the travelers. They had not long to wait before the horn at the gate was sounded, and the next minute the clatter of horses' hoofs was heard in the castle yard; and then Fritz, looking every inch a knight, as Margarethe whispered to Else, was led into the hall by his father, while the old count, their grandfather, met the lad with tears of gladness and exultation.

Margarethe and Else kept modestly in the background, but their turn for greeting their much-loved brother came at last, and Margarethe contrived to draw him into a little nook and extort a promise from him that he would join them on the terrace as soon as he had seen his aunt; for Dame Ermengarde rarely left her own room now, and his father would be occupied for the next half hour with some of his retainers, who had been sent to meet Fritz.

"Well, little sister, you are still our little German blue-eyed Else," said Fritz, as he stepped out into the terrace, and then he bowed in mock reverence before Margarethe.

"Be quiet, Fritz; I am not in the humor to be teased," said his sister laughingly.

"What may it please your ladyship to command her loyal knight?" asked Fritz, with a merry smile.

"O don't tease. Have you been to the Nuremberg fair to buy Else some of the wonderful toys they sell there?"

"And to buy Margarethe a new velvet bodice?" interrupted Else.

"I have been to Wittenberg, but not to buy a velvet bodice," said Fritz.

"Wittenberg! That is where the elector's new printing-presses are set up. I hate them!" exclaimed Margarethe.

"Then you shall not be troubled with them, my lady sister. But while I was at Wittenberg I heard of one Dr. John Tetzel, who was at Jüterbog, a place close by, who had come from Rome with merchandise that could not fail to please my sister Margarethe, seeing that Lent, with its fasts, is ever such a sore trouble to her."

Margarethe laughed, "You will never forget how I cried for meat once, it seems."

"My sister has little love for religion at all, I fear," said Fritz, in the same mocking tone.

"I don't like it a bit. I hate it!" said Margarethe hotly.

"Well, it seems you are not the only one in the world, and doubtless someone must have told the Holy Father at Rome how many people there were who hated to keep the fasts of the Church and keep various commandments besides; so, to accommodate these, he has most obligingly invented a new kind of religion—just the sort of religion to suit you, Margarethe."

"I don't believe it," said his sister; "there is no kind of religion in the world, nor ever could be, that would suit me."

"O don't say that. Just listen now." And Fritz drew from his pouch a slip of parchment sealed with an

LENT: *the forty days preceding Easter*

Fritz Reading the Pope's Indulgence

enormous seal, and looked quite business-like and official, as he solemnly proceeded. "Listen now: 'I absolve thee, Margarethe von Ranitz, from all the excesses, sins, and crimes which thou hast committed, however great and enormous they may be; I remit for thee the pains thou oughtest to have to endure in purgatory; I restore thee to participation in the sacrament; I incorporate thee afresh into the communion of the Church; I re-establish thee in the innocence and purity in which thou wast at the time of thy baptism, so that at the moment of thy death the gate by which souls pass into the place of torment shall be closed for thee, while that which leads to the paradise of joy will be open to thee; and if thou art not called to die soon, this grace will remain unaltered. In the name of the Father, and of the Son, and of the Holy Ghost.'"

REMIT: *pardon*
PURGATORY: *a supposed place of punishment where the dead pay for their sins before going to heaven*

Chapter II

Dame Ermengarde

AS Fritz finished reading the parchment he held it toward Margarethe. "It is for you," he said, laughing.

"You are certainly very clever, Fritz. This is some of the new Italian learning, I suppose," said his sister.

"Italian learning! No, it is an indulgence. What! have you not heard of the indulgences Dr. Tetzel is selling everywhere in Germany? See, this is duly signed. Friar John Tetzel has signed it with his own hand. I will not tell you how many guilders I had to pay for it, Margarethe."

"Did you really buy it?" asked Else, venturing to touch the piece of parchment, and trying to read it for herself.

"Yes, I really bought it in the church of Jüterbog. In the church a great red cross was erected, with the crown of thorns and the spear and the nails hanging to it. Beside the cross is a pulpit, where Dr. Tetzel preaches; and in front stands

GUILDERS: *gold coins*

two great chests, one containing the indulgences granted by the Pope to all who like to buy them, the other for money that is paid for them. I heard the sermon, too, and can remember part of it, I think; so you may be quite sure this is a valuable document. As soon as Dr. Tetzel mounted the pulpit he told the crowd that filled the church that he had letters of indulgence, signed with the great seal, for all sorts of sins, even to lying, stealing, and murder; for the sins they should desire to commit hereafter, as well as for sins past. 'Nor do these indulgences only secure the salvation of the living; they equally insure that of the dead,' said Dr. Tetzel; 'At the very moment when the piece of money tinkles on the bottom of the box the departed soul for which it is paid takes its departure out of purgatory, and directs its free flight toward heaven.... For twelve pence you may redeem the soul of your father out of purgatory; and are you so ungrateful that you will not rescue your parent from torment! If you had but one coat, you ought to strip yourself instantly and sell it in order to purchase such benefits.'"

"If I were the Pope I would give the indulgences to those who are so poor that they have but one coat, instead of robbing them of that," said Margarethe.

Else still looked doubtfully at her brother. "I never heard of this new religion before," she said.

"That is because you are living here in the forest, where you rarely hear of anything going on in the world. If you had been living at Jüterbog now you would suddenly have heard all the church bells ringing one day, and if you had gone into the street you would have seen a long procession of priests and monks carrying banners, and chanting hymns, and after them the magistrates and burghers with their banners and music, all marching toward the entrance of the town, and you would have heard that Dr. Tetzel was coming, and that this procession was going out to meet and welcome him."

"Then, of course, it must be true," said Else; "only I cannot quite understand how it is that the Pope can give people leave to commit all sorts of sins, and promise they shall not be punished. If I do but forget to recite one of the prayers, Father Sebastian says I can never be forgiven unless I do penance for it."

"I cannot understand it either," said Margarethe, still looking at her expensive piece of parchment, that had cost so many guilders.

"I don't think there is any need for you to try. The Pope does not require people to understand, but to buy the indulgences." And Fritz walked away, while a smile of merriment that provoked Margarethe lurked about the corners of his mouth.

"Else, what does it mean—this new religion?" she said, turning to her little sister.

A CONVENTICAL LIFE: *life in a convent*

But Else could only shake her head. "I am sure I do not know, but Father Sebastian will be sure to understand all about it, and I will ask him when I go for my instruction tomorrow;" for Else was being taught all the legends of the saints, and the blessedness attendant upon a conventical life, by a family confessor.

But Margarethe felt rather impatient, and could not wait until the next day. She was not at all sure that Fritz was not imposing upon her, and so she went to sit with her great-aunt, the lady Ermengarde, who had come to live at the castle when her niece, Margarethe's mother, was married; and who, since that lady's death, had been as a mother to Margarethe and Else.

"Aunt, have you ever heard that there was more than one religion in the world?" asked Margarethe, as she seated herself on a low stool at her aunt's feet.

If Margarethe had been looking at her aunt's face instead of at the rushes and sweet buds strewn on the floor, she would have seen a faint color steal over it, and a look of trouble in the bright dark eyes. "Who says there is more than one religion in the world? who has been telling you of what is dead and—and almost forgotten?"

Margarethe looked up quickly, for there was a quiver in her aunt's voice. "Then there were two kinds of religion once! Was that when you lived in Bohemia, Aunt?"

CONFESSOR: *a priest who listens to the confession of sins committed and then grants forgiveness*

IMPOSING UPON: *deceiving*

"Hush, hush, my Margarethe. Have I not told you that Father Sebastian hates the name of Bohemia?"

"And I hate Father Sebastian," Margarethe boldly rejoined; "so tell me, please, about Bohemia and the other religion that used to be there. Did you like that other religion, Aunt Ermengarde?"

But for answer the frail old hands were lifted deprecatingly, and Margarethe was almost frightened at the look of horror that her words had brought to her aunt's usually calm face, as she said, "O, is the trouble never to die? Is that awful time coming back again to the world?"

"O Aunt, what is it? what have I done? You know I would not bring trouble to you or anyone." And Margarethe put her arms around the old lady's neck, and kissed the dear, troubled face again and again.

Dame Ermengarde was very fond of her grand-nieces, especially Margarethe; for she reminded her of some of their ancestors; and now, as she looked into the brave, dauntless face, she wondered whether it would not be better, after all, to tell her the truth about the trouble that had driven her noble ancestors from Bohemia, and which had also tended to increase the poverty of the von Ranitz family; for her mother had come a dowerless bride to the castle, which had greatly displeased the old count at first, until his heart was won by the gentle patience of the

DEPRECATINGLY: *in protest*
DAUNTLESS: *fearless*
DOWERLESS BRIDE: *bride without a dowry*

young Bohemian heretic, as he had at first called her.

But the word "heretic" had long since been forgotten by all but Dame Ermengarde, for no one called the lady "heretic" after the birth of her son Fritz, and so neither Margarethe nor Else had ever heard it or anything about their ancestry, except that their mother was of a noble Bohemian family.

Dame Ermengarde felt now that the time had come when Margarethe, at least, must be told something of that terrible past that had driven from Bohemia some of her best and noblest sons for it might be that Fritz had heard something of this from their enemies, who would be sure to misrepresent them. "Sit down, child, while I tell you something I have heard from my father, who was your mother's grandfather, you know. Only you must promise to keep the matter a secret from Else, and also from Father Sebastian."

"I will not tell anyone—not even Else," promised Margarethe solemnly.

"Well, my child, I will trust you, because I believe you will be as true as your grandfather was to John Huss and Master Jerome of Prague. You asked me just now if there had ever been another religion in the world besides that which the Pope and the Church teach. Well, my dear, there was. About a hundred years ago, or rather more, a noble and reverend doctor and priest, Master John

HERETIC: *someone who rejects Christian doctrines*

Huss, found out that the Church and the Pope had been making a mistake about many things, and teaching the people what was wrong, and he tried to show them this, and to teach them the better way. But the Pope was offended, and declared Huss to be a heretic; and he and his friend Jerome were burned at Constance. But although they burned Huss they could not destroy his teachings, for many of the Bohemian nobles had learned to love the doctrines he taught, and they would not give them up, even to please the Pope. Then a terrible struggle began. My father, as well as many others, lost all his property, and at last had to leave Bohemia and settle down in Moravia, after fighting nearly forty years for the truth that Huss and Jerome taught."

"And what was this new religion?" asked Margarethe anxiously.

The old lady glanced around the room cautiously. "My dear, I have forgotten much that my father strove to teach me when I was young, for I have lived in troublous times. Sometimes we were hiding in the road and forests, and sometimes flying for our lives from city to city, until we found a resting-place in Moravia, and settled there with some people[1] who had come from the valleys of Piedmont,[2] and whom the Pope hated and persecuted as much as he did the Hussites."

"Then this new religion was a bad one," said Margarethe.

[1] Most likely Waldensian Christians

[2] A region in northwestern Italy

But at that the old lady's eyes flashed, and she said quickly: "No, no; I have heard people say that if men would but believe the truth John Huss taught, and live the life he lived, the world would be a better and happier place than it is."

"And you forget all about this truth?" said Margarethe, rather reproachfully.

"I forget many things, but to me the great difference in the teaching of the Church and the teaching of our Bohemian reformer, as he was called, was summed up in some words I learned when I was a child: 'God so loved the world, that he gave his only begotten Son, that whosoever believeth in him should not perish, but have everlasting life.'"[1]

Margarethe's eyes opened very widely. "But—but God hates the world," she said.

"God hates sin—but He loves men. This was the new religion Huss taught," said Dame Ermengarde with energy.

"And now there is another new religion invented by the Pope for everybody who is dissatisfied with the old one. See what Fritz brought me;" and Margarethe held out her slip of parchment.

"What is this, my child?" asked the old lady

"A letter of indulgence from the Pope himself whereby he gives me free permission to commit any sin I please, even to murder, and remits all the punishment afterward, both in this world and the next."

[1]John 3:16

Margarethe spoke quite coolly, wondering what her aunt would say. Dame Ermengarde looked horrified, and dropped the parchment as though it had stung her. "Where did you get it, my child?" she asked.

"Fritz brought it. He knows, as everybody else does, that I am not at all religious, and so he thought this new religion might suit me."

"But, Margarethe, you cannot think that God, who is pure and holy, and loving to all men, would have you commit sin, as this indulgence teaches you may without fear of punishment."

But Margarethe only shook her head sadly. "I am not wise and learned, like the Holy Father at Rome. Of course, I do not understand it; but, then, I cannot understand anything, hardly, that is religious, except that God delights in making everybody miserable."

"That is a mistake, Margarethe, for God, who loves us, desires to make us happy."

"Why, then, does He make us so unhappy? Why does He watch us so closely that if we get a little bit of happiness He may snatch it away from us? I suppose He wants to see us all monks and nuns, and if we could be happy like that we might; but I can't, and I am not going to try," said Margarethe, with something of the old defiance in her tone that Dame Ermengarde remembered so well.

"Margarethe, my darling," said the old lady, smoothing the soft glossy hair. "I wish I could remember more of what I have learned; and then I am sure I could show you how you have made a mistake about this—for it is a mistake, I am sure; for I have heard many times that God loves us like our father and our mother. And think, dear child, He has given us the bright sunshine, and the merry birds, and the beautiful flowers in which you delight so much."

Margarethe started; but presently she said, slowly and sadly, "If He made these things He hates them, and does not like to see us glad in them, I am sure."

"O Margarethe!" and tears welled up to the old lady's eyes as she looked into the sad, defiant face of the girl.

"Of course, it must be so, for does He not love grim monastery walls better than happy homes, and monks and nuns better than little children? I shall keep this letter of indulgence, for, although the Pope says nothing in it about laughing and loving little children, these things cannot be worse than lying and stealing, and so I have the Pope's permission now to enjoy myself without doing penance for it; and there will be no need to go to confess to Father Sebastian again, for Fritz has bought me the Pope's pardon for all the sins I have committed, or ever may commit!"

"Margarethe, I wish I could make you understand," said her aunt tenderly.

"I do quite understand now, and this new religion is just the one for me, although it seems to be different from the one my ancestors learned in Bohemia and suffered so much for, which seems rather a pity, for—"

But there Margarethe stopped, for she could see that Dame Ermengarde felt pained by the light, flippant tone in which she had uttered the last few words. She resolved to say no more about the matter just now, and to forget it entirely, if she could; and so, tenderly kissing the thin, faded face, she left the room and went in search of Fritz and Else.

Her brother was still engaged with his father, she heard, but she met her sister on the stairs leading to the turret-chamber that had once been their nursery, and was now their private sitting-room.

"Margarethe, I have been talking to Father Sebastian about the letter of indulgence that Fritz brought you, and he has made it all quite clear."

"Well, what is it? Let me hear at once, and then we won't say another word about this tiresome religion for a month, for you know how I hate it."

"Yes, dear," and Else reached from a higher step and kissed her sister. "I am so glad," she said, with a little coo of content as she took her sister's hand and drew her into their chamber.

"And what has made you so glad, little sister?" asked Margarethe.

"Because Fritz brought you this precious letter of indulgence instead of a velvet bodice."

Margarethe sniffed rather significantly; but she only said, "Now tell me what Father Sebastian said, Else."

"I cannot remember everything, but I'll tell you all I can. He looked quite sharply at me when I asked if there were two religions in the world, and asked who had been teaching me heresy; but when I told him about Dr. Tetzel's letter he smiled, and said it was not a new religion at all, only the Pope made a discovery a few years ago, by which he has been able to save more souls than even St. Peter himself. He found out that there was a great store of good works left in the treasury of Christ, which might save many poor souls if they would give their money to help build the new church of St. Peter at Rome; and so, in his compassion for those who had no vocation for religion themselves, he sent Dr. Tetzel to proclaim to all men that they might partake of the benefits of this store of good works—of which the Pope alone has the control—if they would purchase a letter of indulgence."

"Then, Else, if it were not for the hateful question of my dowry—or if we were not so poor—you need not enter the convent," said Margarethe quickly.

But Else shook her head. "Father Sebastian explained that there is more need than ever for holy nuns, whose good works may help to replenish this treasury if they more than sufficed to save themselves and their kinsfolk; so you see I must go. It is necessary that one in a family should have a vocation, especially now; and besides, you know, my father says he cannot give us both such a marriage portion as becomes a noble, so that there is still the double reason why I should devote myself to a religious life."

Chapter III

Else's Departure

MARGARETHE was standing before a large oaken chest—her "treasury," as she called it—but she was looking rather discontentedly at the odd collection of treasures lying before her. The first thing to be lifted out was a ragged bird's nest, over which she had cried for nearly two hours when she was a little girl, because the eggs were all broken when Fritz got it, and the poor old birds had fluttered about the spot in such distress at the loss of their home that she and Fritz had quarreled, until at last he promised he would never touch a bird's nest again. Then came a bunch of faded flowers, which she had gathered years before in the woods surrounding the castle of their kinsman, Franz von Sickengen, who lived in the Rhineland. A gold reliquary with a hair of Saint Elizabeth was rather slightingly tossed aside; but a tiny leaden crucifix, which had been brought from Rome, and specially blessed by the Pope, was looked at rather critically by the not very

RELIQUARY: *a small box containing supposedly holy objects known as relics*

CRUCIFIX: *statue of Jesus on the cross*

devout Margarethe, who laid it aside with something of a sigh as she said, "I should think that would do. Poor, dear Else could not wear gold or jewels at the convent, but a little leaden thing like this she might wear on her rosary, and O, I do so want her to remember me! O, my darling, darling Else, I shall break my heart pining for you!" and poor Margarethe sat down on the floor beside her chest and gave way to her grief. She was alone in the turret-chamber, and so she could give way to her emotion unchecked; for Fritz had gone on a journey to Wittenberg, and Else was at her daily study with Father Sebastian.

After some sad reflections, and replacing her treasures in the chest, Margarethe went downstairs to her aunt's room, to learn, if possible, what was the cause of her father's unexpected haste in sending Else away; but Dame Ermengarde knew nothing more than she herself had been told; and although the old lady deeply sympathized with her in her sorrow, she seemed so occupied in reading over and over the pamphlet Fritz brought for her when he first came home, that Margarethe grew rather impatient about it.

"What is that book, Aunt?" she asked a little petulantly; "I never come to see you now but I find you reading it."

"Yes, my dear, it is the one my Fritz brought me from the new printing-press at Wittenberg, and so, of course, I value it," said the lady.

ROSARY: *a string of prayer beads*
UNCHECKED: *unrestrained*
PETULANTLY: *irritably*

"But what can it be about that you are always reading it?" asked Margarethe.

"It contains sermons preached by a very learned monk of Wittenberg, the good Friar Martin Luther."

"O, I hate monks, and all their books and sermons," said Margarethe scornfully.

Dame Ermengarde looked at her niece sorrowfully, and then glanced at the book she held in her hand. At length she said, rather timidly, "I think you would like to hear this monk preach, Margarethe. He is not at all like any monk I have ever heard of before."

"O they are all alike; they all try to make the world as miserable as they can. But now, do tell me why Else is to be sent to the convent so soon? And how long Fritz will stay at Wittenberg?"

But Dame Ermengarde had only heard vague reports of trouble having befallen their young kinsman, Ulrich von Hutten, through some writings in which he had held priests and monks up to ridicule; but how this could be connected with Fritz's visit to Wittenberg and Else's hasty departure for the convent she could not tell, only she feared that the old standing quarrel with Erfurt was likewise connected with it.

The last evening that the sisters were to spend together came all too soon for both of them, and though Father Sebastian had painted in glowing colors the joy and peace which could alone be found within the convent walls, Else was almost as sorrowful as her sister.

"If you could only come with me, Margarethe, my joy would be full; but now—"

"I know what you would say, little sister; this parting seems as though it were for all eternity," put in Margarethe, "and I cannot help it. You are leaving me in the world, and I shall always be of the world—one of those who must be lost, or, at least, have to spend so many years in purgatory that one can hardly hope for anything else at all."

"But, my Margarethe, you have forgotten the Pope's precious letter of indulgence," said Else quickly.

"I don't believe in it," said her sister shortly. Else looked greatly shocked.

"O Margarethe! you have been listening to poor Fritz, and the evil things he has learned in Italy. My confessor questioned me closely about what we talked of in the forest, and I told the wonderful things Fritz had told us of, how through the great scholars and wise men coming from Constantinople, to escape from the Turks, many mistakes had been found out both in religion and the learning that used to be taught in the universities; and he said such learning was very bad."

"Of course, he did," quickly responded Margarethe; "an ignorant man never likes his ignorance to become known."

"But Father Sebastian is not ignorant. I wish you

would come with me and listen to his accounts of the saints," said Else.

"He can recite the legends of their lives, I know, and tell a story very well; but do you know, little sister, that some monks now are not only learning to read Latin, as well as perform mass, but are learning Greek and Hebrew too?"

"But Hebrew is the language of the Jews, and therefore, Father Sebastian says, no Christian ought to learn it, and that all books in that tongue ought to be burnt," said Else.

"Fritz says the monks are angry at Hebrew being learned, because the Bible is written in that language, and they know that if the people once had the Bible to read for themselves their power would be gone."

"O Margarethe, I do wish Fritz had never gone to Italy. I am afraid it is these unsettling notions of his that are making my father so unhappy as my confessor says he is."

"My father unhappy!" repeated Margarethe, "I don't believe it."

"He is hiding it from us, but of course it must be so if Father Sebastian says it is," replied Else.

Margarethe's face flushed. How she hated the name of Father Sebastian! "If there be unhappiness he has caused it," she said hotly.

But of course Else did not believe it. The bland, wily priest had gained such an influence over her, that she could not see anything to be wrong that

MASS: *the Roman Catholic church service*
BLAND: *smooth*

he did. But for the strong love she bore her sister he would certainly have turned her heart against Margarethe before she went to the convent; for his elder pupil had proved a most obdurate and intractable scholar, very unlike the sweet, gentle Else, who had been as wax in his skillful hands; and he now began to fear that Margarethe, having given up his teaching for herself, would turn her sister's mind against him too.

This was the secret of Else's leaving home so soon, and Margarethe began for the first time to suspect it. Her father had been persuaded to do this by Father Sebastian, to whom the knight very readily listened, as it also fell in with his own plans, and so all the arrangements were made before either of the girls were told of it.

"Now, Else, we won't talk of Father Sebastian again," said Margarethe, when she had silently listened to a long defense of him from her sister. "See, I want you to wear this on your rosary. This little crucifix has been blessed by the Holy Father himself, and it will help to remind you of lonely Margarethe."

Else took the little relic and looked at it fondly, but then laid it down again. "I—I am afraid," she said.

"Afraid, Else! But surely not even Father Sebastian could object to this."

"I am afraid it would be a temptation; and indeed—indeed I shall not need anything to

OBDURATE: *unyielding*
INTRACTABLE: *difficult to influence*

remind me of you, for O Margarethe, I am afraid I love you far too dearly," and poor Else threw her arms round her sister's neck, and burst into a violent flood of tears.

Margarethe was no less moved than her sister, and for a few minutes they could only hold each other in a silent, passionate, tearful embrace; but at length Margarethe managed to whisper, "My darling Else, my dear little sister, you must not forget me; you must love me all you can, for I am so sad and so lonely, and I cannot look forward to being happy in heaven, even if I ever got there; and there is no happiness for me here now you are to be taken away. O, Else, Else, it is cruel for the Church to take you away. There are hundreds and hundreds of nuns in the world; why could not God let me keep my little sister?" and Margarethe's tears broke out afresh.

Else tried to soothe and comfort her; but there was so little comfort—so few words—so little hope for them in their desolation! The most they could hope for would be the seeing each other in a formal manner in the presence of those who would effectually check anything like an affectionate outburst of feeling; and even this meeting, unsatisfactory as it would be, could only occur after an interval of some months. Margarethe began to talk of these visits, at last, with some degree of hope, and promised to keep an account of all that happened at home, that she might tell Else when she went to visit the convent; while Else was to learn all the recipes for making herb tea to cure the ailments of the peasants, that she might teach Margarethe how to cure old Dame Grimma's aches and pains.

The next morning, at day-dawn, Else and her father, with Father Sebastian and a few retainers in attendance, rode away through the forest toward Nimptschen.

Margarethe stationed herself on the terrace, to watch the travelers as they wended their way down to the valley, her eyes almost blinded with the tears that she strove in vain to repress. While she was still standing, watching the lessening figures, she was surprised to see standing near her a little page who was in her brother's service, and whom she supposed had gone with him to Wittenberg.

The lad bowed low as he came close to her, and said, "Has the Lady Margarethe any message for my master."

"Your master! Is not my brother at Wittenberg!" exclaimed the lady.

"Yes, he journeyed thither more than a week since; but he left me behind to take word to him when his sister, the Lady Else, was to go to the convent."

Margarethe looked as though she doubted the lad's statement, until he said, "My master has given offense to Father Sebastian, who approves not of the learning of Italy, nor of the books Master Fritz

DAY-DAWN: *dawn*

has brought back with him, and so he advised that he should be sent to Erfurt until the Lady Else was safe at Nimptschen; but my master had a mind to go to Wittenberg instead, and is also resolved to ride forward to see his sister before they reach the convent."

"Then you will have to travel quickly to Wittenberg, or your master will fail to meet the travelers."

"Never fear but I will be in time. I have a fleet horse here, that will soon leave Father Sebastian's mule far behind. Give me some word to carry to my master, and I will instantly depart."

"Tell him—tell him not to fail in seeing Else, and to return hither soon, as I may need his help;" for Margarethe had begun to suspect that, once Else was disposed of, some active steps would be taken for the disposal of herself.

Her anticipations of this were confirmed when, an hour or two later, she went to her great-aunt's room and found her unpacking a large chest that had belonged to her niece, and which Margarethe had been told was to be hers when she was old enough to wear dresses and jewels, such as her mother had worn.

"Aunt, what is it?—what are you doing?" asked Margarethe, as the old lady shook out a purple velvet dress with a stomacher of seed pearls.

But the sight of the well-remembered dresses had already caused the old lady to shed a few tears,

FLEET: *swift*
STOMACHER: *decorative panel on the bodice*

and now at Margarethe's question she fairly broke down. "I seem to see your mother again, Margarethe, in these things just as she looked when she came into this room leading you and Else by the hand."

"They were happy days! O Mother! O Else! you have both gone, and I am so lonely," sobbed poor Margarethe. Then checking her tears, after a minute or two she said, "But why are you unpacking these things today, Aunt?"

"Your father desired that they might be prepared in readiness for you."

"For me!" uttered Margarethe.

"Yes, my dear. Have you not heard the news, that Count von Schonstein is coming to pay us a visit in a few weeks—before the winter sets in, and makes the forest roads impassable?"

"That is not all you have to tell me, Aunt," said Margarethe in a cold, hard, constrained voice.

"No, my dear; you know it is your father's dearest wish that the powerful families of Ranitz and Schonstein should unite against the common foe—the burghers of Erfurt—and there is only one way in which this alliance can be made."

"By selling his two daughters! We, Else and I, are both to be sacrificed that the growing power and wealth and influence of these burghers may be checked—stopped it cannot be, I am sure now, after what I have heard about them from Fritz."

"My dear, I begin to think it was a great pity Fritz ever went away from home, since he has infected you with so many strange notions," said Dame Ermengarde, as she fidgeted with the pearls.

"It is not a strange notion at all, Aunt; it is quite a matter of fact. Else is made over to the Church, because my father is not wealthy enough to provide us both with dowries as befit our rank, or that would command our acceptance in powerful families, whose influence would be useful to my father in his various feuds with other knights and the burghers; and so, as two cannot be gained, one becomes the more indispensable; and so my younger sister is immured in a convent, that her share of the family property may be thrown into the scale with me, and be sold to the highest bidder."

"Margarethe, one would think you were a lowborn burgher maiden, to hear you talk of buying and selling," said Dame Ermengarde angrily; and yet, as she looked at the girl's flushed, resolute face, the daring deeds of her noble ancestors flashed upon her mind, and she wondered what the future had in store for her little grandniece, who seemed more like her great grandfather than any of his immediate descendants had been.

IMMURED: *imprisoned*

Chapter IV

Rebellion

ULRICH VON RANITZ, the father of Margarethe and Else, had devoted himself almost exclusively to the study of astrology—at this time so common—and the defending his ancestral rights against the encroachments of the neighboring nobles and of the burghers of Erfurt, against whom the knights, sinking for the time being their private feuds, would sometimes unite, as in opposition to a common enemy. Astrology was studied as a means for ascertaining how his enemies might be the more successfully baffled; and he devoted himself so entirely to this, when not actually engaged in offensive or defensive warfare, that he had little time to spare for his family. He was not an unkind father; but, of course, his children were his own property, like his dogs, horses, and retainers; at least, his daughters were, and that they should be disposed of so as best to further the main objects of his life was only to be expected.

Now, von Schonstein was a neighboring knight with whom there had never been any actual

ASCERTAINING: *learning*
AVERSE: *opposed*

hereditary feud; had there been, the family pride would have been up in arms at the idea of not maintaining it; but he had been one of those very disagreeable neutral neighbors, who, while taking good care never to help von Ranitz, was by no means averse to reaping a little benefit for himself out of his neighbors' quarrels. Had he been a friend, he would have been too powerful to be lightly offended; and so half the petty quarrels, fights and reprisals with which the life of Ranitz was harassed, would never have occurred. Lately he had shown some disposition to be more friendly, and Ranitz was eager not merely to accept his friendship, but to secure it as a possession; and as Schonstein had a son two or three years older than Margarethe the way seemed easy enough. Of course, Else must be relegated to the convent, that her dower might be added to Margarethe's, otherwise she would be no fit bride for a Schonstein, for it was not often that a knight married, as he himself had done, a dowerless bride, for her beauty and goodness alone.

That either of his daughters should ever think of disputing his right to dispose of them as he pleased never crossed his mind. Of course, he knew that Margarethe would miss her sister when she went to the convent; but they would have to be separated sooner or later, and so the parting might as well come at one time as another. This was the father's view of the matter; and when he rode away with Else, leaving his elder daughter overwhelmed

REPRISALS: *retaliations*
RELEGATED: *sent away*

with grief, he felt rather glad that he had arranged to go on to Grimma to transact some business there before he came home; for by this means he should escape any troublesome manifestations of sorrow from Margarethe, and when he came back she would be quite reconciled to the change, and doubtless be glad to welcome the bridegroom he had provided for her.

He had given orders to Dame Ermengarde to make the necessary alteration in the dress of Margarethe, for hitherto the sisters had been treated as children and dressed accordingly, no change being deemed expedient, as Else would retire to the convent so soon. When, therefore, von Ranitz returned, and saw Margarethe still wearing the plain stuff petticoat and jacket that scarcely distinguished her from the peasants, he said rather angrily, "How is it you have not been dressed as I commanded?"

"I greatly prefer wearing this," said Margarethe.

"*You* prefer wearing it? but I said you were to have your mother's dresses and jewels, and appear as befits a maiden of your rank."

"But, my father, this taffetas trimmed jacket has always been deemed suitable for Else, and me, too; why should you wish me to put on costly dresses now when I am mourning for my sister?" and the tears rose to Margarethe's eyes.

"Mourning for her? She is not dead. What do you mean!"

EXPEDIENT: *appropriate*

"She is dead to me, and all the world is a dreary blank," exclaimed Margarethe.

"My child, you know nothing of the world yet; you have never seen it. Buried in this secluded castle, a mean dress was of little account; but now all this will be changed, of course."

"What do you mean, Father?" faltered Margarethe.

"I thought you understood that when Else retired to the convent to become the bride of the Church, you would enter the world and become the betrothed bride of a noble knight," said her father, thinking this information could not fail to please Margarethe.

"I have no wish to enter the world, or to become anybody's bride."

Her father looked too much astonished to be able to speak for a minute or two; but at length he said, "You do not wish it! That is twice you have been guilty of the unheard-of boldness of stating that your wishes did not accord with mine. Who ever heard of such a thing as this before? Who asked, or who is likely to ask, what a girl's wishes are in such a matter as this? Would she not be grossly immodest if she had any? Go to your own room, Margarethe, and think over all you have heard concerning the ways and doings of noble German maidens, and perhaps you will discover that to obey a father's word in all things is the first duty of every right-minded girl."

MEAN: *lowly*

Her father was too angry to listen to a single word from Margarethe in extenuation of her conduct; but, pointing to the door, commanded her to go instantly to the turret-chamber, and remain there until she was prepared to yield obediently to his wishes in everything.

Margarethe went slowly up to her own room, inwardly chafing at the unwonted restraint thus suddenly laid upon her; for in all her intercourse with her father hitherto he had been very kind, if not exactly affectionate. It was the first time, however, that she had ever ventured to disobey him, or question his commands, his word being the sole law of her life; and she saw now that she was almost as powerless as a bird would be in the hands of its captor. But she was none the more disposed to yield on this account. The castle was her cage, and her father her master now, and she would have to submit to this state of things; but that she would not do as he wished she was determined.

Her wishes should be considered, and respected, at least as to her future life; and so when her aunt came to her room a few hours after, bringing a casket of jewels as a present from her father, with the message that he wished to see her suitably arrayed in them that same evening, Margarethe only turned away and pushed the jewels aside.

"My dear child, I am afraid you will make a great deal of trouble for yourself if you are not careful," said Dame Ermengarde, seating herself on the oaken chest near the little loop-hole window.

EXTENUATION: *an attempt to partially excuse an offense*
UNWONTED: *unaccustomed*

"I cannot help it," said Margarethe.

"But, my dear Margarethe, you can, and you must; your father is not unreasonable, I am sure."

"Not unreasonable, when he wants me to put on fine clothes, as though I was glad and merry, when I am feeling so sad and lonely about Else? Not unreasonable?" repeated Margarethe.

"My dear, what you complain of as such a bitter trial happens almost every day. There is scarcely a noble family in Germany in which one daughter is not sent to the convent, that the others may more fitly enter the world. You are old enough now to know that wealth cannot be picked up like stones, and how is the proper state of a family to be kept up without the expenditure of wealth, to say nothing of the dowry that must be provided for every bride of knightly degree."

"I wish I had been born in a peasant's hut," exclaimed Margarethe hotly. "I think the nobles are the most miserable people in Germany, especially when they happen to be poor, as we are. They spend their time in grumbling about the wealth and abuses of the Church, and yet make over their daughters to her power as bondslaves, that they may increase their own power to crush the growing liberties of the burghers. I wish I was a burgher maiden, that I do!"

"But, my dear, you see you are not a burgher maiden. Sometimes I have wished you were a boy, Margarethe."

INTERCOURSE: *interaction*

"Have you? Thank you, Aunt, for wishing it, although the wish is in vain."

"If you had been a boy, now, you might have gone to this new University of Wittenberg, and become a learned man under this wonderful Dr. Luther, who seems to be turning the world upside down."

"Turning the world upside down! I wish he would. Anything that could happen would be a relief, I think; but nothing ever does happen in these dull times."

"My dear, it seems to me that the world is waking up from a long sleep, and that the times are anything but dull. When I read the wonderful words spoken by this monk, Martin Luther, in the Church at Wittenberg, I almost think Master John Huss must have come back. Not that I ever saw Huss, my dear. He was murdered by the Pope and cardinals at Constance long before I was born; but I have heard my father talk about how he looked, and I have read the very words he spoke in the Bethlehem Church of Prague. And when I read Dr. Luther's sermons, it seems as though that old time had all come back to me."

"Tell me about that old time. I like to hear people say what they think and mean; I suppose the death of Huss was a murder, if he did not deserve it."

"Of course it was a murder, my dear; only you must not repeat anything I say, especially to Father Sebastian."

"He is not likely to question me as he did poor dear Else. Now, tell me something about the old times in Bohemia, or else about this monk of Wittenberg."

"I think if I were to read a little of what is written here you will be able to understand things better than if I were to tell you. Fritz got this from a friend who heard the sermon preached; and by and by such books as these, and, in fact, all Luther's lectures, will be published; then everybody may read them."

As the old lady spoke she drew her precious little book from its hiding-place under the folds of her dress, and Margarethe sat down, looking rather weary. But the first words that were read startled her into listening with eager attention.

"If we will only consider God in His works, we shall learn that He is nothing but pure, unutterable love; greater and more than anyone can think. The shameful thing is, that the world does not regard this, nor thank Him for it, although every day it sees before it such countless benefits from Him, and it deserves for its ingratitude that the sun should not shine another moment longer, nor the grass grow, yet He ceases not, without a moment's interval, to love us and to do us good. Language must fail me to speak of His spiritual gifts. He pours forth for us, not sun and moon, nor heaven and earth, but His own heart, His beloved Son, so that He suffered His blood to be shed, and

SUFFERED: *allowed*

the most shameful death to be inflicted on Him, for us wretched, wicked, thankless creatures. How, then, can we say anything but that God is an abyss of love—endless, unfathomable love? The whole Bible is full of this, that we should not doubt, but be absolutely certain, that God is merciful, gracious, patient, faithful, and true; who not only will keep His promises, but already has kept and done abundantly beyond what He promised, since He has given His own Son for our sins on the cross, that all who believe on Him should not perish, but have everlasting life. Whoever believes and embraces this—that God has given His only Son to die for sinners—to him it is no longer any doubt, but the most certain truth, that God reconciles us to Himself, and is favorable and heartily gracious to us."

As the old lady paused for a moment, Margarethe rose to her feet. "A monk wrote that!" she said—"those words about God loving us!"

"Yes, my dear, and I believe them," said Dame Ermengarde, with a ring of triumph sounding in her old, feeble voice.

"But—but—I do not understand. It all seems just the contrary. Will you read it to me again, please?" and Margarethe bowed her stately head, and stood with clasped hands, eagerly drinking in every word, as the old lady read over the sentences again.

As she concluded Margarethe said eagerly, "Where can I get a Bible? He says the whole Bible

ABYSS: *bottomless pit*

is full of this—I suppose he means the assurances of God's love to us. I must see for myself if this is true; for if it is, we have all been making a mistake in thinking of Him as a hard, cruel master, and are indeed wicked, thankless creatures. Where can I get a Bible?—a German Bible, I mean."

"My dear, no one ever heard of a German Bible," replied her aunt; "Latin is the language of the Church, and so, of course, it is only in Latin that Bibles are written, because it is the exclusive right of the Church to use this holy book."

"O, Aunt, what shall I do then? How am I to know whether this monk is right in what he says? He may speak truly—perhaps he does—but how are poor unlearned folk to know? He tells them the Bible teaches the same thing as he does; but how can we know this if we don't have the Bible?"

Dame Ermengarde shook her head. "You see, the Church in her wisdom has said that if the common and unlearned people had the Bible it would be very perilous."

"Which would be in peril—the people or the Church?" asked Margarethe.

"My dear, I am afraid you speak very disrespectfully of the Church."

"But I haven't murdered anybody yet, Aunt," retorted Margarethe, smiling.

"I said it was the Pope and cardinals who murdered Huss; but the Church—" There the old lady stopped, for she did not quite see how she could explain the fine distinction that existed in her own mind between the deeds of an individual Pope and the doings of the Church.

"You say you do believe these wonderful words of the Wittenberg monk. How can you, Aunt, when you know the Church teaches us, and we all get to believe somehow, that God is a dreadful hard Judge, our owner, but not our Father—not, at least, a father who loves us?"

"Well, my dear, these words of Dr. Luther's are just such words as I heard, often and often, when I was a child. My mother would whisper sometimes that God, our Father in heaven, was as tender and patient with his grown-up children—the men and women in the world—as she was with us little ones; and then you know it fits in exactly with that little scrap out of the Bible that I have been able to remember, 'God so loved the world, that he gave his only begotten Son.' My dear, Dr. Luther is preaching the truth, the truth of God," said Dame Ermengarde warmly.

"Then the Church has been teaching us lies about God," retorted Margarethe. "Does not the Church profess to teach us what is written in the Bible?" she asked.

"Certainly, my dear. The Bible is the revelation of God's will concerning us. I have heard that again and again."

"Well, I want to know what this revelation is—I must know who is right and who is wrong, Dr. Luther or the Church."

"My dear, they are both right. Martin Luther is a monk—you forget that."

"Dr. Tetzel is a monk too; they both belong to the Church; but they cannot both be right," said Margarethe.

"My dear, I would not let this trouble me, if I were you. They may both be right, you know, only we may not be able to understand it, because we are not wise and learned. Of course you may believe these good words of Friar Luther's, because he is a monk, you see, and administers all the sacraments; and, being wise and learned, too, he has read the Bible for himself, which many of his brethren cannot do."

"It seems a pity they don't learn, then," retorted Margarethe. "They are a set of lazy, ignorant, deceitful old foxes; that is what Fritz calls them; and he says the book he bought, 'Reynard the Fox,'[1] makes everybody laugh at their cunning, and nobody will believe in them soon."

"I am afraid Fritz has learned to disbelieve a good many things since he has been away from home," sighed the old lady.

"I think he has," assented Margarethe; "but I will believe in Dr. Luther if I can; that is, if I can get a Bible, to find out for myself that he is teaching the truth."

[1] *Reynke de vos,* printed in 1498 by Hans van Ghetelen

Chapter V

The Brother and Sister

MARGARETHE sat pondering over what she had heard for some time. Where could she get a Bible, to find out for herself whether these new, strange words of Friar Luther's were true?

The contest with her father about the change in her attire seemed a matter of little importance to her now, but she very much wished to be able to see her grandfather. The old count had spent many years in traveling when he was a young man, and he had a store of curious things gathered during his travels, and it might be a Bible was among them—at least she could ask him; and as the only way of escape from her present confinement was by assuming the obnoxious dress her father had commanded her to wear, she resolved to obey him in this.

She smiled to herself when, having laid aside the stuff petticoat and plainly trimmed jacket, she put on the rich velvet dress that had once been her mother's. All the alterations needed had been made by Dame Ermengarde and her maidens, so that, with the help of her own waiting maid, Margarethe soon arrayed herself in the costly velvet dress and pearls; and as she stood before the bright steel mirror she smiled complacently at the reflection of her tall, stately, elegantly dressed figure; and she whispered softly to herself, "I do not think I want to be a burgher maiden, after all; for such common people are not allowed to wear velvet."

Her father looked pleasantly surprised when Margarethe entered the great hall, and he saw the costly jewels he had bought gleaming and flashing on her head and arms. Truly Margarethe was a daughter to be proud of. She would be no despicable bride for a greater noble even than von Schonstein; and it was with a feeling of triumphant exultation that he led her forward, and presented her, with due state, to her aunt and grandfather.

"I shall send for Fritz to return at once, that he may help us in our preparations for the grand tournament I mean to give in honor of this event," said her father as they stood before the old count.

"Ah, ah! send for the lad, and let us hear what the Wittenberg news is by this time."

"Art thou greatly interested in Wittenberg news?" asked Margarethe, rather timidly.

"Why! hast thou heard it? But I suppose Fritz told thee too of this wonderful monk, who hath learned the lessons of the great Italian preacher,

DESPICABLE BRIDE: *bride to be despised*
DUE STATE: *proper ceremony*

Savonarola, whom the Pope slew eighteen years ago for teaching that the Lord Christ could save sinners without the help of the Church. He must look to his ways, or there will be a burning in Wittenberg, as there was in Florence, unless the monks are wary, and shut him up in some monastery dungeon, as they did brave John of Wessel in the monastery of Mainz; for this brave old monk taught much such truths as this young Friar Luther—that God only, and not the Church, or a man's good works, can save him."

"And—and what dost thou think of these new doctrines?" asked Margarethe, twisting the ring on her finger rather nervously.

"Nay, nay; it is not for laymen to think at all upon such matters as these. We leave all that for the learned doctors of the Church; only an old man feels curious when he hears the same thing coming up, again and again, in different places, at different times, and from people who have never heard of each other. At Mainz, in the Rhineland, not far from the home of our kinsfolk, the von Sickengens, there was this John of Wessel preaching and teaching until they shut him up. He died in 1481. Soon afterward an Italian monk, this Savonarola, began his crusades against the corruptions of the Church. I heard him preach, and saw men and women bowed to the ground and crying out because of their sins; but they burned him at last."

"O, Grandfather, why was it? Was the religion he taught a bad one?" asked Margarethe.

LAYMEN: *those who are not members of the clergy*

The old man shook his head slowly. "It seemed to me better than any other man taught. But I am not learned, you see, and the Church burned him for a heretic; and so I suppose he must have been one, as the Church cannot do wrong;" but the old man smiled grimly as he said the last words.

"But where did these men say they got these new religions from?" asked Margarethe after a pause, and speaking in a lower tone, for Father Sebastian had entered the hall, and was looking at her.

"Well, that is the most curious part of it, my child. These men, as well as the Pope and cardinals, all declare the Bible to be the foundation of their doctrines."

This was just the opportunity Margarethe wanted, and with almost breathless anxiety she asked, "Grandfather, have you got a Bible—a German Bible?"

The old man opened his eyes very widely. "A Bible—a German Bible—who ever heard of such a thing? You must be a strange girl, Margarethe, ever to think of such a thing."

"But why should it be so strange? If the Church is right in all she teaches, why does she not say to the people, now that this printing has been invented and books are getting so common, 'See, this is the word of God Himself,' and give them the Bible?"

"But, my child, we could not understand it; we are unlearned," said the old count rather uneasily, "and the Church is most anxious that no one shall learn the language of the unbelieving Jews—the Hebrew tongue. Our Count Palatine himself, Reuchlin, one of the most learned men the world has ever seen, has been sorely persecuted because he has written and published a Hebrew Grammar and Dictionary, so that students may learn this language and read the Bible, as well as the Greek Testament, for themselves."

"Then perhaps somebody will translate the Bible into German, after all," said Margarethe, a little hopefully.

"He would be a bold man, indeed, who should dare to do this. He would soon learn that the Pope and inquisitors have not burned all their fagots yet. No, no, my child; the Church is too wise to let the people have the Bible to read for themselves: you will never see a German Bible."

Margarethe sighed, but she did not resign all hope. She would talk to Fritz about it when he came home, and if it was quite certain that she could never hope to see the Scriptures in her own language, she would ask him to teach her Latin—that sacred language—the language of the Church, for she had heard that in most of the convent libraries there was a Latin Vulgate, or a New Testament; and perhaps some time when she went to Nimptschen to see Else, the superior might give her permission to go into the library and see this wonderful book, that could alone set her mind at rest upon these doubtful subjects.

INQUISITORS: *members of the Inquisition, who sought to destroy all "heresy" in the Church*
FAGOTS: *bundles of sticks or branches*

With this rather vague hope Margarethe was obliged to content herself; only she took care to go and sit with her grandfather every day now, and talk to him about his travels, and also to her aunt, that she might hear more of those wonderful words spoken by Dr. Luther.

Having her mind thus occupied Margarethe witnessed with calm indifference the grand preparations that were being made in and around the castle for the reception and entertainment of their expected guests. Old lumber rooms and dark closets were ransacked for the furniture that had been stored away there. Rushes and sweet herbs were gathered to strew the guest-chambers, and arras hung in various rooms; so that it was a busy time for everybody.

Her father would have been glad to see Margarethe take more interest than she did in what was going on, seeing it so intimately concerned herself; but he thought it wise not to say anything about this. Margarethe had assumed her position as the stately lady of the castle, and he could not but feel proud and pleased that the costly dresses bequeathed by her mother became her so well; but he would have liked to see her smile more frequently, and look less wistfully out upon the terrace, where she seldom walked now, and it pained him to see her glance, now and then, with brimming eyes, at the vacant seat of Else.

LATIN VULGATE: *a Latin translation of the Bible*
SUPERIOR: *head of the convent*
ARRAS: *tapestries*

But this grief for her sister would speedily be forgotten in the gaiety that would last through the next two or three weeks; and when this was over Margarethe should go and visit some of their friends at a distance. While she was gone he could arrange the terms of her marriage with von Schonstein, and there could be a brilliant betrothal at Christmas, and the young couple could be married in the spring.

This was the plan von Ranitz rehearsed to himself, with a few alterations, whenever he saw Margarethe looking so grave and earnest, as she often did now, and he was glad to welcome Fritz back again when he returned from Wittenberg, and privately told him to devote himself to his sister until Count von Schonstein and his son arrived.

"Why, what is it, my lady sister, that is troubling you? I am half inclined to feel offended; for you have never admired my new doublet, or asked my opinion about the transformation in your own dress."

"Well, what do you think of it?" asked Margarethe, rousing herself, as her brother entered the turret-chamber. "I have not seen your doublet yet, if it is a new one."

"It is new, and the handsomest I could buy in Wittenberg; but it seems to be thrown away upon my lady sister. I shall tell Eric von Schonstein not to throw his money away upon doublets for—"

BRILLIANT: *magnificent*
BETROTHAL: *engagement ceremony*
DOUBLET: *a tight-fitting jacket*

"Do you know this Eric von Schonstein?" asked Margarethe quickly.

"Yes, he is at Wittenberg now, but will follow me hither in a few days. I could not persuade him to come with me."

"I am glad of it. I wish he was not coming at all. I do not wish to see him."

"The wish is quite mutual, I can assure you. Schonstein put himself in a fine passion when the messenger came bringing his father's command that he should come hither."

With the perversity common to human nature, Margarethe was not gratified at this announcement, although she said, with calm indifference, "Well, I am glad we are not likely to trouble each other. Now tell me all the news," she added, by way of finally dismissing the subject.

"Would you not like to see what I have brought for you?" asked Fritz.

"Another letter of indulgence, perhaps?"

"No, no; I could not spare any more guilders for Dr. Tetzel. Have you heard what they did at Jüterbog—Tetzel and his Dominican monks—when they heard that Dr. Luther had been preaching against the sale of indulgences?"

"How could I hear it? You know we hear nothing here but the cooing of the wood pigeons and Father Sebastian's droning. Tell me what it is."

"Well, Tetzel was in such a rage that he had a great bonfire made in the marketplace, to 'burn the heretics,' he said; of course, meaning Luther and the Wittenberg teachers who have embraced his doctrine."

"What is his doctrine? Have you embraced it? Do you believe it?"

Fritz laughed. "My lady sister, I have been to Rome, and when a man has been there he is cured of all such weakness as believing anything or anybody again."

"But—but, Fritz, what do you mean?" asked Margarethe.

"Just what I say. I could not say this before our dear little Else, she would have been so dreadfully shocked; but you never were a very dutiful pupil of our poor old confessor, and never professed much love for the Church, so that it will not pain you much."

"I hate Father Sebastian, it is true, and I have little love for religion; but still I do want to believe in something," said his sister.

"That is because you are a woman, I suppose. I have heard learned men declare that the world never would be without a religion of some sort, simply because the women, in their weakness and ignorance, must have one."

The words were spoken in a tone of lofty assumption that irritated Margarethe.

"At any rate, there are learned men in the world who are earnest in teaching religion," she said warmly.

"O yes, of course, it must be so; but I can tell you that few of the wise and learned men of Italy—and they are the most learned in the world—few, very few, believe even in God now."

"And you share in their unbelief?" asked Margarethe sharply.

"What am I to believe? I tell you, Margarethe, if you went no farther than Jüterbog you would doubt as I do; for Dr. Tetzel and his monks, who are preaching the indulgences all day, spend the money at inns and worse places than that when night comes; and this is as nothing compared with the lives of the cardinals and great prelates at Rome. Luxury, rioting, and drunkenness stare you in the face on every side, and the Pope is the greatest unbeliever of all."

"But this Dr. Luther, whose book you brought to Aunt, does he spend his time like Dr. Tetzel?"

"No, no; Dr. Luther is a true man, and believes what he teaches. No man can deny that. If I could believe in anything, it would be the doctrine he teaches and the life he lives. But I have been to Rome, Margarethe, and all faith is gone."

These words were not spoken in the usual tone of gay badinage that Fritz so often used, but there was a touch of sadness in the tone, as though this loss of his faith had begun to press upon him as a loss, and not a gain, to be exulted in.

Margarethe was puzzled, but instead of returning to this question again immediately she

PRELATES: *high church officials*
GAY BADINAGE: *lighthearted banter*

said, "Where did you meet with Eric von Schonstein?"

"At Wittenberg; he is studying at the university."

"Studying at the university! A noble learning the arts and tricks of monks and priests, instead of studying that chivalry that exalted our noble ancestors!"

"But, Margarethe, the world is changing; the days of chivalry are over. If you did not live in this out-of-the-world castle, you would know that this newly invented printing is turning the world upside down, and learning is the new power that will rule among men and nations."

"But—but it seems so strange that a noble, like von Schonstein, should go to the university," said Margarethe meditatively.

"Many strange things are happening in the world, and stranger yet will happen, I doubt not. One thing is certain, it will be useless for the nobles to think of crushing the burghers now. My father's dream about the Erfurt citizens will never be fulfilled, and it would be better to give up the old feud, or, rather, let it die out."

"O, if he would, Fritz, I should be free of this Eric von Schonstein!" exclaimed Margarethe.

Her brother laughed. "I told you you had little to fear from Eric. Let my father please himself about the tournament and all the grand doings he has planned, and you can please yourself. Be civil, and take as little notice of him as you like; the less the better."

"Does he know why he is asked to come?" said Margarethe.

"I suppose he does; for, receiving his father's letter, he drank off a horn of beer to the good burghers of Erfurt; so he evidently understands the object of our grand carnival."

"But, Fritz, if the old feud with Erfurt, that has given occasion for so many chivalrous deeds, should die out, as you say, what will you do by and by?"

"Fight the Turks, perhaps, unless the Pope and Emperor should quarrel; then, perhaps, I should fight for the Emperor, certainly not for the Pope."

"And why not for the Pope!"

"Because I hate priest-craft. I tell you, Margarethe, the Church must change her teaching and her practice speedily, or all religion will be swept from the earth."

PRIEST-CRAFT: *priestly teachings*

Chapter VI

The Tournament

IN the soft September sunshine, that lay upon the forest and gilded the grim-looking castle into something less repellent, visitors began to arrive—knights on gaily caparisoned horses, followed by retainers and servants; ladies borne in litters, or riding gentle palfreys; while in the valley below, fringing the village, was a motley gathering of peddlers, mountebanks, fortune-tellers, and all that nondescript crowd that, by that supernatural sense known to no one precisely, always scent out where and when anything of unusual interest is to take place, and lend their gratuitous aid to turn it into a carnival.

Such a rout and racket had not been heard in those forest glades for many years; but the news of a tournament had drawn many knights and their retainers thither, and, of course, the crowd followed.

Margarethe was not at all pleased when she saw all these preparations for a grand revel. If Else had only been with her she would have entered

CAPARISONED: *decorated*
PALFREYS: *saddle horses other than war horses*
MOUNTEBANKS: *sellers of quack medicines*

as heartily into the fun as any peasant girl in the village; but now it only filled her mind with vain regrets, and she missed her sister more than ever. She would turn away in sadness from the gayest scene with a murmured, "I wish Else was here. If we could only have had this before Else went to the convent I should have enjoyed it so much; but now—" and Margarethe generally concluded her cogitations with a burst of tears.

But, although she often indulged in these little outbursts when alone, she did not neglect her guests. No one could complain that the stately lady of the castle failed to see that his comfort was attended to; for the bustle and confusion incident upon the arrival of so many strangers was too much for Dame Ermengarde, and so the old lady, as well as the aged count, kept a good deal to their own rooms.

But of all their guests no one pleased Margarethe so much as a young lady about her own age who had come with their kinsfolk, the von Sickengens. Perhaps it was because Anna reminded her of her sister Else, whom she was not unlike; although the young Swiss lady was very different from Else in the matter of religion, or, rather, in her mode of viewing it, and soon confided to Margarethe that she would not go to a convent, although she knew that her family—not being very wealthy, and she a younger daughter—expected that she would devote herself to a monastic life.

GRATUITOUS: *voluntary*
REVEL: *festival*
COGITATIONS: *reflective thoughts*

"I should have done so, I daresay, by and by, but two or three months ago I went with my sister on pilgrimage. My father took us to the holy hermitage, to pray to our Lady of Einsiedeln. It is the most sacred spot in all Switzerland, and over the abbey gate is written, 'Here is obtained a plenary forgiveness of all sins.'"

"But we can buy this forgiveness now, without going on a pilgrimage, which is very much cheaper," said Margarethe.

"I daresay it is; for, although they promise forgiveness as the fruit of the journey, rich gifts have to be presented to the monastery as well; for no one could see the wonderful image of our Lady of Einsiedeln, that has performed so many wonderful miracles, if they went empty handed. This year, however, some never went to see the image; for a new preacher who had lately come from Glaris—not a monk, but the parish priest of Glaris—stood up and preached to the crowd, and it was little wonder that everybody listened, and came again and again to hear such strange, wonderful sermons. We stayed in the valley a week, and went every day to hear Master Ulrich Zwinglius, and I was very sorry when the time came for us to go back to Zurich; but my father says we shall be sure to hear of him again."

"What did he say that was so wonderful?" asked Margarethe.

"Well, I cannot remember much—not many words—but I will tell you all I can remember. He

PLENARY: *complete*

startled us first by saying: 'Think not that God is in this temple more than in any other part of His creation. Whatever be the company in which you dwell, God encompasses you and hears you as well as at the chapel of our Lady of Einsiedeln. Can useless works, long pilgrimages, offerings to images, the invocation of the Virgin or the saints, obtain the grace of God? What avails the multitudes of words in which we embody our prayers! What avail a glossy hood or head well shaven, a long robe with its neat folds, and mules caparisoned with gold. God looks to the heart, and our heart is alienated from God.' Another time he said: 'Christ alone saves, and saves everywhere. Christ, who was once offered on the cross, is the expiatory victim, who, even through eternity, makes satisfaction for the sins of all believers.'"

"But this is altogether a new religion from that which the Church teaches. What do these priests hope to gain by it?" asked Margarethe.

"Ah, it is a question of gain to him, I doubt not," said Fritz, who had joined them.

"Nay, nay, it is a loss to him; for Zwinglius is almost dependent upon the offerings of the pilgrims for his support, and there were few gifts left at the shrine this year. It was strange to see how things were changed by these sermons. The first day of the festival bands of pilgrims wended their way up the hill, singing hymns in honor of our Lady, and counting their beads as they went; but afterward

INVOCATION OF THE VIRGIN: *prayers to the Virgin Mary*
EXPIATORY VICTIM: *the victim who is able to pay*

they could do nothing but talk of the strange good news they had heard."

"Strange, indeed," exclaimed Margarethe; "but is it true? Did you hear where this Swiss priest learned such things?"

"From the holy Scriptures—the Bible. My father went to visit his old friend Baron Theobald, of Geroldsek, who is the administrator of the abbey, and shares with Zwinglius in the offerings of the pilgrims, and who, we were told, had invited Zwinglius to come to Einsiedeln."

"I should think he rather regretted having such a preacher," said Fritz, laughing. "He doubtless wanted one who would fill the monastery coffers, not empty them."

"No, Baron Theobald wants to make the monastery a place of learning and study; and he told my father that not only the brethren, but the sisters, in the convent were to be encouraged in reading the Scriptures. The New Testament, at least, in Swiss will be within reach of all the nuns."

"Then, if it is good for Swiss nuns, it must be good for German ones too. O Fritz, I wonder whether Else has got a German Bible at Nimptschen."

But her brother shook his head. "Else would not read it, for the Church does not approve of such learning."

"But this priest, Zwinglius, belongs to the Church!" exclaimed both girls in a breath; and then Anna added: "He is exhorting everyone who can to read the Scriptures for themselves."

COFFERS: *treasure chests*

"Well, that looks fair and honest; for those who can get at a Bible may find out for themselves whether his doctrine is the same as that taught in the Bible."

"And if the things taught us by the Church are contained in the Word of God, why should we be forbidden to read it?" asked Anna.

Fritz laughed. "I think I had better send you both to Wittenberg, to study under Dr. Luther," he said.

"We heard about this Dr. Luther in several places as we journeyed hither. Is he a learned man like Ulrich Zwinglius, or just an ignorant monk, that is making a great stir, like Dr. Tetzel with the indulgences?" asked the Swiss lady. They were walking down the winding road to a level space in the valley that was being prepared for the tournament to be held the next day, when this conversation took place, and Fritz, who was to take part in it, had come to see how the preparations were progressing.

Before he had time to answer Anna's question one of the workmen claimed his attention. Then Eric von Schonstein and two or three other knights and ladies joined them, and, this being a favorable moment for the traveling merchants and peddlers to ply their trade, they were soon besieged, and a nondescript collection of wares spread out upon the grass.

Rosaries, missals, reliquaries, bits of rag and bone—most precious relics of some saint—books,

MISSALS: *prayer books*

silk and satin ribbons, taffetas, knives, toys; there was something suitable for all ages, classes, and tastes. Amid laughter and merry jesting the ladies for the most part congregated round the stall where the finery was to be seen, and knots of ribbon were bought, to be presented and worn by the knights next day. Of course, von Schonstein would wear the colors of the lady in whose honor these festivities were given, but to whom he had scarcely spoken as yet; and now, although he stood near her, he hurried to the spot where the books were being displayed.

Margarethe, having no knots of ribbon to buy, slowly edged her way to the books; for at the sight of them a dim hope had crept into her heart that perhaps this man might have a Latin Testament, or a portion of one.

But the packman shook his head without looking at his collection, when she asked for this. "I have got the 'Lives' of nearly all the saints," he said: "St. Agnes, St. Elizabeth, St. Catherine, St. Ursula, St. Christopher," and he would have gone on through the whole calendar, just to convince the haughty looking lady that peddlers were not such ignorant men after all, only Margarethe moved away before he had got half through the list.

A few minutes afterward Eric von Schonstein joined her, and with courtly grace presented her with a rather shabby and decidedly clumsy looking book. "There is little but rubbish in the whole pack except this," he said, with an apology for its mean binding.

Margarethe was not too well pleased with her present, for it certainly seemed a most unsuitable book to present to a lady. "What is this?" she asked, with a cold dignity, as she opened the heavy black-letter tome.

"It is the *Praise of Folly*, written by Erasmus, of Rotterdam," answered Eric. "You have heard of the great philosopher, who has exposed so many of the errors of our corrupt Church," he said, with a little more animation in his voice.

But Margarethe shook her head. "You forget how secluded life in the castle is! I have heard of the friar of Wittenberg, Martin Luther, who Fritz declares is turning the world upside down."

"He will turn the Church inside out unless the sale of these indulgences is stopped and there is a great reform in both teaching and practice," said Eric, with more energy than he had yet shown in anything since he had been at the castle.

"I should greatly like to hear this Luther preach," remarked Margarethe. "I have read some parts of his sermons from a book Fritz bought for my grandaunt; but—but I am afraid to believe all he says."

"Why?" asked Eric.

"Because if he is right the Church is wrong; and so, before giving up my old faith, I want to be quite sure of the correctness of the new doctrines. I want

TOME: *book*

to read the Scriptures for myself, from which both the Church and Luther profess to teach."

"But I do not think it is needful you should give up your old faith before believing Luther," said Eric.

"Why, Luther teaches that God loves us—is merciful and tender, as a mother to her children; that Jesus Christ saves us, and is willing and anxious to save us. But the Church teaches that God is a hard, angry judge, begrudging us every moment of happiness, and watching to take vengeance upon us; that Jesus Christ, instead of being merciful and compassionate, is unfeeling, and quite indifferent to our sufferings, until the pleadings of His mother on our behalf induce Him to pardon us, not from love of us, but because He would be rid of her importunity; and it is the whole occupation of Mary, the mother of mercy, and of the saints in heaven, to wring our pardon and salvation out of Him who died upon the cross to save us. Now, which is right, Luther or the Church?"

"Luther," promptly answered Eric.

"I wish I could believe it! O, I wish I could believe it!" exclaimed Margarethe.

Eric looked at her usually calm, but now troubled, face in the greatest amazement. "I did not think women—ladies—ever troubled themselves about such things as these," he said.

Margarethe smiled a little scornfully. "I wonder what your thoughts are concerning us," she said.

IMPORTUNITY: *persistent requests*

"Fritz told me the other day that religion is only for women, and you wonder that we trouble ourselves about it."

"I did not mean that you—ladies I am speaking of—but only that you should think so seriously about these theological differences."

"I see we are expected to have a religion, but to accept it ready-made, without venturing to question either its quality or demands," said Margarethe.

The young knight looked at her with a mystified air, but at last he said, "I think it would be better if ladies would consider more seriously the difference between these new doctrines and the teachings of the Church; but few care to listen to such a subject. That is a wonderful book—that *Praise of Folly*," he said, thinking he had better give a turn to the conversation before he offended Margarethe.

"The *Praise of Folly*, by Erasmus!" exclaimed Anna, who joined them at this moment, looking very rosy, while Fritz, who followed close behind, was looking very triumphant.

"Have you read it?" asked Margarethe.

"No, but I have heard about it, and I have wanted to read it ever since I saw the funny little man who wrote it, last year at Basle."

"Have you seen him? who is he like?" asked Fritz and Eric together.

"Like nobody but Erasmus," laughed Anna. "The little fair-haired philosopher looks as though a gust of wind would blow him away; and if you saw him going along the street, stepping so timidly as he does, you would think he was afraid to look round and see what was going on; but they say that nothing ever escapes his bright blue eyes, and he seldom speaks but he says some sharp, witty thing about the monks, whom he is always ridiculing."

"He is not like our Dr. Luther, then, who is grave and earnest, and sets down his foot as though he feared nothing, and he does not, except evil, I am sure," said Eric.

"You greatly admire Dr. Luther?" said Margarethe.

"I do; I would die for him if it were needful, and so would many others whom I know."

"There must be something in a man who inspires such love as this," said Margarethe. "I should be sorry if it were found that he had been mistaken in his teaching."

"Mistaken! that cannot be," said Eric.

"Only, you see, if Dr. Luther is right the Church is wrong," argued Margarethe.

"Dr. Luther does not say the Church is wrong—at least, not all wrong. Of course, the Church needs to be reformed—all men can see that, and there must be a reformation; but Dr. Luther does not talk much about that; he seems more anxious to point out what is right for us to believe and practice than show us what is wrong in the Church."

"Perhaps he thinks if he teaches what is right the wrong will show itself. That is what Zwinglius hopes for Switzerland," said Anna.

"I see he will begin building before he begins to pull down," laughed Fritz, "which is just the reverse of Erasmus' method. He begins to pull the Church down about our ears, which is all very well for men, who are strong enough to do without religion, but sadly frightens the poor women-folk, who cannot do without it, and may not have heard that a better is being provided for them."

Margarethe looked a little scornfully at her brother, as she said, "So you expect all women-folks are to take their religion at second-hand—believe as men order them."

"They always have done so," replied Fritz; "Anyone will tell you that the most devoted servants of the Church are women."

"I am a woman, but I never was a devoted servant of the Church; but I will not give up the little belief I have even for Dr. Luther, much as I wish to believe the good news he is proclaiming, unless I can find out for myself that it is in the Word of God—the Scriptures—which the Church, and every new religion as well, professes to learn its doctrines from."

"Well, we won't quarrel about it, my lady sister; you shall believe just as much or just as little as you like. See, Anna has elected me to be her knight in the tournament tomorrow," and Fritz proudly displayed a little knot of ribbon.

"And I am to be yours, Lady Margarethe," said Eric with a smile.

"I will give you my knot, but 'Luther and the Bible for Germany' shall be your battle-cry in the lists tomorrow."

"Ah, if the Bible could only be won at the point of my lance, I would contend to the very death for it. Thanks, Lady Margarethe, I will not lower my crest, or cry for quarter," he said, as they turned homeward again.

LISTS: *an enclosed area for combat*
CRY FOR QUARTER: *plead for mercy*

Chapter VII

A Visit to the Convent

WHEN Margarethe and Anna could have a few minutes to themselves, after reaching home, Anna asked her friend why she had given von Schonstein such a strange watch-word for the contest in which he was to engage the next day.

Margarethe looked a little confused at the pointed question, for she did not think anyone had overheard her half-whispered communication with Eric; but at length she said: "You, of course, know, dear friend, that this tournament is rather a serious affair to me—to me and von Schonstein, too; for we may offend both our families when—" and there Margarethe stopped.

"Margarethe, what do you mean? I thought it was all settled, and you and Eric von Schonstein were to be betrothed before the guests departed."

But Margarethe shook her head. "I think my father would like it," she said; "in fact, I am quite sure he would; but *I* don't. I don't like being sold like this, and von Schonstein is betrothed already."

"Betrothed already? Margarethe, he would not dare to—"

"No, no, I mean he is wrapped up, heart and soul, in this Dr. Luther and his doings; and if Luther will only give us a German Bible I shall be quite content; and he fully understood what I meant when I said 'Luther and the Bible;' I give him up to these."

Anna looked a little troubled. "I don't know about giving him up," she said musingly.

"Fritz has won your colors, has he not, dear?" asked Margarethe.

"Yes, but I haven't given him the word yet. What shall it be?"

"If Eric had not been so fond of Luther, and I so anxious to get a Bible, I should have given him the word that has been troubling and puzzling the world for the last hundred years, my grandfather says," remarked Margarethe.

"What word is that?" asked Anna.

"'The Reformation.' Grandfather says it has been the dream of all the best and wisest men in all lands for the last hundred years. Men have prayed, toiled, and died for it; and because of this he believes it will come some day; but how it is to come—how it is to be brought about—this glorious time that is to change everything in the world—nobody seems to know or even to guess."

"Perhaps it will come in our time. At least, I will give this word to Fritz for tomorrow's fight," said Anna.

But when her young knight-errant heard the word he rather gravely objected. "No, no, give me anything but that!" he said, with more seriousness than politeness.

"But why? You told me the world needed to be changed—the Church to be reformed," said Anna.

"Yes, yes, but not by such men as I. I have been to Rome, and lost more than the world can ever give me in exchange. I am not worthy of this battle-cry, Anna. Give me another. Will you give me 'Chivalry'—to fight for the right because it is the right, whether victory or loss be the end of it?"

"But I want to see this grand Reformation that your sister has been talking of, and Zwinglius preached about," said Anna. "Will you take this," she added, after a moment's pause, "Chivalry and the Reformation?"

"The Chivalry to be mine, the Reformation yours. Yes, I will take that; and, if ever this great work that Luther is beginning needs the help of knightly arms to defend it, I will fight for it as I will for its watch-word in the lists tomorrow."

"That is spoken like a true knight. But I must go back to Margarethe now, for we have some preparations to make for tomorrow."

Fritz escorted her to the door of the turret-chamber, and then returned to the terrace, to watch the stars come out one by one, and think of the young Swiss lady and the strange word she had chosen to give him. "What is it? How is it? The philosophers of Italy say that the days of

KNIGHT-ERRANT: *a knight in search of adventure*

superstition are over, the reign of the Church ended—except as it is kept alive by the blind devotion of a few silly women; and yet this doctrine taught by Luther, which is in all things quite different from the unbelief of these doctors, seems to have taken hold of everybody, so that the very air we breathe seems charged with it. There is Margarethe, living her lonely life among the pine-trees, almost crazy for a Bible. Here is gentle Anna, from far-off Switzerland, raving about the new doctrine; and there is Eric von Schonstein, forgetting all hereditary feuds and the chivalrous deeds of his ancestors, blind even to the presence of my stately sister, so wholly is he taken up with this new learning and the Wittenberg monk. Most true is it that the world is being turned upside down; but I wonder who is doing it? Not Luther entirely, for Anna is full of this wonderful Swiss preacher whom I have promised to go and hear; and this book peddler talks of nobody but the 'wonderful shoemaker of Nuremberg,' as he calls Hans Sachs, the man who writes such wonderful hymns that even the peasant can understand them and sing them, too, so simple are the airs to which he has set them."

Fritz was soon joined in his promenade by Eric von Schonstein, and the two friends discussed this subject, enumerating all the men they had heard of as contributing, directly or indirectly, to this wonderful awakening in the world.

"First and foremost I suppose we must thank our enemies, the Turks, for driving so many Greek scholars out of Constantinople to take refuge in Italy and teach in her universities. That was about seventy years ago. It seems a long time ago, but the handful of men who left Constantinople have wakened all Europe since, and scholars have been multiplied all around. There is Reuchlin, with his Hebrew grammar and dictionary, for which he had to fight with the Dominicans.[1] Then there is Erasmus, with his Greek Testament; Hans Sachs, with his hymns; and Zwinglius, the Swiss priest; besides our own Dr. Luther."

"And Dr. Luther is the greatest of all," said Eric warmly.

"I will not contest the point with you today, tomorrow perhaps."

"No, no, not even in a tournament will I have you fight against Luther," said Eric quickly.

"Then you are to fight for him, I suppose? Is that my sister's whim?" asked Fritz.

"It is not a whim to me, or her," said Eric. "You will fight on my side, Fritz."

"I thought we were to fight on opposite sides, to settle that point we were disputing over at Wittenberg the other day."

"O, let that be for future settlement; promise you will fight on my side in the *mêlée.* I am sure your sister will not like to see you on the other."

[1] An order of monks founded in the early thirteenth century by Dominic de Guzman (1170-1221)

MÊLÉE: *hand-to-hand fight*

"So you are beginning to understand my cold, haughty sister," said Fritz, with a short laugh.

"I do not think her cold, or haughty either," said Eric, in a half-offended tone, and he turned away and the discussion closed.

The tournament passed off very pleasantly, only Fritz got unhorsed in the *mêlée*, and slightly wounded, which somewhat dimmed the victory won by his side. Eric fought splendidly, like one of the knights of old, rather than a student knight of Wittenberg, who desired to lay aside spear and battle-ax for the new weapons of progress, learning and printing. Jousts and games all came to an end at last, and Margarethe woke up as from a happy dream. The terrible time that she had dreaded so much had come to an end, and she had been very happy; yes, happy, in spite of Else's absence; and she could not but own it, although she hated herself when she thought how happily the last few days had glided away in the familiar converse with Eric, Anna, and Fritz, that had, somewhat, grown quite natural to all of them.

She had been reading Erasmus' *Praise of Folly*, and they had talked of this and Luther's sermons and lectures at the University of Wittenberg, and how the Castle Church was always crowded to hear Dr. Luther preach.

"If I could only hear some of those strange, new words that seem to be waking the world into life, and set men thinking as they never thought

OWN: *admit*

before, I might be able to believe without seeing the Bible for myself," said Margarethe one day; and she spoke so wistfully that Fritz said lightly, "You had better come to Wittenberg with me, Margarethe. I am going back next week."

"So soon!" exclaimed his sister, who had hoped that Fritz and Eric would stay at the castle a few days longer than the rest of the guests. She would not own even to herself that she would sadly miss her brother and his friend after their departure; but it seemed now that the castle would be ten times more gloomy and dull than ever, after the pleasant hours she had spent in discussing not merely the idle chit-chat of the jousts and tournament, but the grave momentous changes that everywhere seemed to be going on around them. So much did she dread this loneliness that she begged that Anna might stay with her and bear her company during the dreary winter, and her father, well-pleased at her behavior lately, not only promised to arrange this, but also to take her soon to Nimptschen, to see Else.

This was sufficient to console Margarethe for the loss of all other friends, and she bade Fritz and Eric farewell quite cheerfully. It seemed that Eric, like Margarethe, was not so full of joy over his departure, although he was going back to Wittenberg and Dr. Luther; and von Ranitz, watching these signs in the two young people, was content to wait.

The day following the departure of Fritz, Margarethe and Anna, with von Ranitz, and a few attendants, set out for Nimptschen. The ride through the woods in the autumn sunshine, under the sweet smelling pines, was very pleasant; but Margarethe was too eager to pass forward to enjoy it as she would have done at another time. She was, however, in high spirits at the thought of seeing her beloved sister so soon, until they came within sight of the high walls that surrounded the convent garden, and caught a glimpse of the gloomy looking building within.

"It is a tomb, not a house," she whispered to Anna, with a shudder, as they drew near the portal that shut out the world, with all its life, and gladness, and sorrow, and shut in young, ardent souls, to be taught that death and not life was God's crowning gift to man.

Anna glanced apprehensively at von Ranitz, and whispered a warning "Hush," but Margarethe was not to be daunted.

"My father knows I hate the sight of a convent," she said aloud, "and if I could carry off Else, I would."

"You must not talk like that to Else," said her father, somewhat sternly; "You must not forget that this convent is Else's home for life. It would have been yours, you know, Margarethe, if Else had been the elder instead of the younger sister."

PORTAL: *door or gate*
ARDENT: *passionate*

"Yes, yes, I know; and sometimes I wish it was reversed—that I was here instead of my dear, gentle sister; for if the nuns were unkind to her it would break her heart; but I—it would take a great deal to kill me," added Margarethe.

The knight looked at his proud, high-spirited daughter, and smiled. "It is best as it is," he said; "Else is happy in the convent, and you will be happy in the world."

As a special favor, the visitors were allowed to see the young novice in the superior's parlor, without the intervention of the *grille* between them; so that for one rapturous moment Margarethe could hold her sister in a fond embrace, and rain warm tears and kisses on her. But after the first moment of surprise and joy Else tried to disengage herself from her sister's clasping arms, and looked round in startled fear at the sister who had brought her into the room, and who had been deputed to remain with her while the interview lasted.

The white, still face of the old nun was as unmoved as that of a marble statue; but the hard, pitiless eyes were fixed upon the girl's, and as Else turned she met their stony stare, and she shuddered as if with sudden cold as she disengaged herself from Margarethe's clinging arms.

"You, you forget I am almost a nun," said Else in confusion.

Margarethe felt hurt. She had scarcely noticed the presence of the nun, and she could not

NOVICE: *someone who has not yet taken his or her full vows as a monk or nun*

GRILLE: *a grating separating the monastery from the world*

understand what seemed little less than a cold repulse. "O Else, have you forgotten me so soon?" she said in a tone of reproach.

If Else could only have forgotten all she had been taught since she had been here about ruling her heart and conduct, more especially in the presence of relatives and friends who might visit her, Margarethe would have seen that her sister loved her as deeply and truly as ever—might have seen a little, too, of the heart-hunger that had already made itself felt. But Else was so fully conscious of those hard, pitiless eyes being fixed upon her, that she could only say, in some confusion, "No, no, Margarethe, I do not forget you; but, but you forget my vocation; that my life is wholly given to the Church now that I am the bride of Christ."

In these last few formal words, in which Else had been well drilled, Margarethe saw that her sister was speaking under some constraint; and then, glancing at the nun, who still sat, like a black-robed statue, in the room, she whispered, "Let us go into the garden, dear; I want to speak to you."

But Else gave a frightened start at the suggestion of such a thing, and, again glancing at her jailer, she said, "You cannot have anything to say to me that Sister Ursula may not hear. We are all sisters, you know, here, and have no secrets from each other."

Von Ranitz saw that there was likely to be some little difficulty through Margarethe's impulsiveness, and so, leaving his post near the door at the opposite end of the room, he said, "Of course, there are no secrets here. Margarethe has nothing to tell you but what everybody might hear. Fritz has been home from Wittenberg, and we have had some visitors at the castle; and this lady from Switzerland is to stay through the winter with Margarethe."

"O, I am so glad!" said Else, once more regaining her equanimity, and speaking in a natural tone. "I am so glad you will have somebody all the time you cannot get down to visit the peasants, for you will not miss me quite so much."

"And do not you miss me, Else?" asked Margarethe, coming again on dangerous ground.

"I-I have so many sisters here, you see," said Else in a trembling voice, and again glancing at the nun, as if mutely asking whether she was repeating her lesson correctly.

Margarethe saw the look this time; saw the tears, too, dimming her sister's eyes, which she bravely struggled to keep back, and a pang, deeper than any she had yet felt, shot through her heart. Her darling sister loved her still; but that which had been the comfort and joy of their lives had been turned to its bitterest agony.

Margarethe now schooled herself, however, to talk upon indifferent subjects: the doings at home; the old peasants' ailments; what Else was learning at the convent school; and from this Margarethe asked about the library, and whether they had many wonderful books there. She would not

EQUANIMITY: *composure*

mention what wonderful book in particular she was anxious to see, for fear of the attendant nun.

But Else had not been into the library. The novices were not trusted with such costly treasures as it contained, and very few of the elder sisters ever went there either, for most of their time was taken up with needlework, embroidering altar cloths or dresses for the Virgin, and making herb tea and various medicines, as well as clothes for the poor. All these things were dilated upon until the time for their visit came to an end, and then, with a hasty adieu, Margarethe tore herself away, scarcely daring to look into her sister's eyes, lest she should cause her fresh pain through her impulsive outbursts of affection.

DILATED UPON: *discussed at length*
ADIEU: *goodbye*

Chapter VIII

At Wittenberg

MARGARETHE was so much depressed after her visit to Else, so firmly convinced that her sister was not happy in the convent, that her father, fearing if she went home to brood over this in the solitude of the forest castle she might be tempted to do something desperate in order to rescue her sister before the irrevocable vows were taken, resolved to pay a visit to Wittenberg, and take Margarethe and Anna with him.

At another time Margarethe would have been overjoyed at the prospect of so soon seeing the wonderful city from which the new learning was arising, and which was already attracting students from all parts of the world, who were drawn thither by the fame of this learned monk, Martin Luther. But now not even the hope of seeing Wittenberg, and Dr. Luther, and Fritz, could dispel the gloom that hung over her spirit; for her heart was full of unhappiness about Else, and it was not until Nimptschen was left far behind, and the great

IRREVOCABLE: *impossible to take back*

Thuringian forest with its pines and castles almost forgotten in the strange land they now had entered, that Margarethe roused herself to notice anything passing around her.

The country around Wittenberg was a flat sandy heath, dotted here and there with villages of mud hovels, and the only relief to the eyes in this sandy waste was the broad, swift-flowing Elbe, with its fringe of willows and pollard oaks.

When they entered the gate of the city it seemed at first as though Wittenberg itself was only a mud village on an extended scale, with a few handsome buildings set down here and there, as though to make the contrast greater; and Margarethe wondered where her father would find accommodation for them; for a noble traveling with two ladies could not put up with such quarters as a student, or even burghers, might do with.

But as they got further into the city they found that the mud hovels grew less numerous, and that handsome, substantial buildings were rising everywhere in their place. The streets were full of people, too—an eager, thoughtful crowd, seemingly intent upon its own business, and having no time to look at the strangers who had come to visit their city.

Margarethe could not help feeling some surprise, and a little mortification, that these good burgher folks of Wittenberg should take their visit quite as a matter of course, and pay no more heed

HEATH: *uncultivated area*

POLLARD OAKS: *oak trees that have been cut back severely to encourage heavy branching* or respect to them, nobles though they were, than they did to each other. Among their own peasantry in the forest a visit from them was hailed with delight, and men and women, as well as little children, greeting them with a low obeisance, stood aside for them to pass. But here they pushed and jostled them with as little ceremony as they did each other, only staring at her father's jewel-hilted sword, which so plainly bespoke his rank.

"I did not think the burghers had grown quite so upstart as this," whispered Margarethe to her companion, when they had reached the inn, and some fresh slight had been put upon them in the choice of rooms.

"Never mind the burghers; let us sit here and watch the students leave the university; we may see Dr. Luther presently," said Anna.

"But we should not know him," replied Margarethe.

"O, I think I should. It seems as though one must know a man like Dr. Luther instinctively."

But the girls soon found that sitting at the window of a Wittenberg inn was very different from watching from the terrace of the castle in the forest; for the students were as rude and unceremonious in staring at the two ladies as the citizens had been, and Margarethe soon moved from the window in hot indignation.

Meanwhile von Ranitz had gone in search of a more suitable residence for himself and daughter;

MORTIFICATION: *humiliation*
OBEISANCE: *bow*

for he was almost as curious as Margarethe to see and hear this Dr. Luther, and he also intended to obtain an audience of the elector, who was now residing at Wittenberg, respecting some rights that his ancestors had enjoyed, but which had lately been greatly curtailed.

As their visit, therefore, would be very uncertain as to its length, von Ranitz was anxious to secure a private residence if possible; for Margarethe and Anna could not reside at an inn.

After some little trouble and delay he at length found a house, already furnished, belonging to a merchant who was going with his family to reside at Nuremberg for the winter, and von Ranitz resolved to rent it of him for this season.

Margarethe was rather surprised that her father should think they could live with such poor accommodation as a burgher's house would afford; but when she saw the mansion, with its costly modern furniture, its large windows opening to the ground, its rich, soft carpets, curtains, and mirrors, she instantly thought that the elector must have heard of their arrival, and sent these things from the castle.

Von Ranitz smiled at Margarethe's mistake; but there was a little trouble in his voice as he said, "No, no, Margarethe; the house is just as this Wittenberg merchant left it. These burghers are growing so fast in wealth and power, and withal learning so much of this new wisdom that has suddenly

CURTAILED: *reduced*

sprung into life, that I sometimes fear the power of the nobles is waning."

Margarethe looked at her father in astonishment. "How can this be?" she said. "The nobles *must* be the more powerful."

"They have been the mightiest power in the land, but I fear now that their power is waning."

At this point the conversation was interrupted by the entrance of Fritz, who had only just heard of his father's arrival in Wittenberg. He was no less astonished than pleased when he saw his sister and Anna, and heard that they were likely to remain in Wittenberg for several months. The following day he brought Eric von Schonstein to pay them a visit, and the question of the power of the knights being on the decline was again brought forward.

"It is too true, I fear," said Eric, rather sadly; "but it is not too late for them to amend this if they will adapt themselves to the new condition of things."

"And what do you imagine the new condition of things to be, young sir?" asked von Ranitz, rather tartly.

"The old order of things is slowly breaking up, I think, and a new day is dawning for the world; the reforming, the readjusting of things, everywhere has begun. The peasants are rising against their lords, and—"

"Did you never hear of peasant wars, and how they have been put down again and again?"

interrupted the elder gentleman quickly. "If you were a few years older you would know that these ungrateful people are always discontented, and so their discontent promises little to the world in the way of a reformation."

"But men everywhere expect and are looking for a reformation," said Eric.

"I am sure the Church needs it," said Fritz.

"Then let the Pope set about doing it," said his father.

But Fritz shook his head. "The Pope will never do it. I have been to Rome, and know too well that no good thing can come from there," he said.

"But the bishops might call a council, and they, with the cardinals, might do something for this," said Margarethe.

"No, no; the bishops have too much interest in letting things remain as they are. Most of their revenues are obtained by the maintenance of some abuse, and so it is not likely they will try to put them down," replied her brother.

"But the princes who grudge the prelates their wealth and power might help to abate this if they helped in the work of reforming the Church," said Margarethe.

"And lose the friendship of those who help them to hold their own against their vassals and the emperor," replied Eric.

"Well, there are the knights," said Margarethe and Anna together.

ABATE: *end*
VASSALS: *subjects*

"Yes, but will they do it?" asked Eric doubtfully. "It will mean loss to them, as well as to the princes and prelates; for where is there a family among us where some son or daughter is not thrown upon the Church for maintenance?"

Margarethe thought of Else, and her eyes filled with tears; while her father looked anything but pleased at the unpleasant truth being thus dragged forth into the light of day. "The little power the knights now have they cannot afford to lose in a contest with the Church," he said. "The monks and priests are a set of ravening wolves, I know, and the Pope is the worst robber of them all; but what would follow if a few poor knights were to set themselves against this mighty power? Why, their few privileges would be wrested from them, and given to their neighbors the prelates, and themselves crushed."

Eric shook his head. "I fear that what you say would be the opinion of most of the knightly order," he said sadly.

"I am sure it would. Mind, the knights would be glad to see the Church purged of many of its abuses; but they are laymen, and it is not for them to throw away rashly the little power that is left them, to do the work of priests and monks. This Dr. Luther is a monk; he is the most fit for such a work," added von Ranitz.

"Luther is but one man, and he is so taken up with preaching the Gospel, and teaching men the

RAVENING: *ravenous*
WRESTED: *forcibly taken*

only way of salvation, that he has no time to spare for the abuses of the Church," said Eric.

"But others have attacked the abuses first; let Luther do this," said von Ranitz.

"My father would have the Church pulled down about our ears, but Luther is for building up men's souls in what he deems the truth of God, leaving alone the forms and ceremonies of the Church," said Fritz.

"Perhaps he thinks this teaching will endue the forms with new life," said Anna.

"Or else convince men that they are utterly worthless. When shall we be able to hear this Dr. Luther preach, Fritz?"

"He preaches next Sunday at the Castle Church, also on the Festival of All Saints."

"We will go to hear him on Sunday, and on the festival, too," said von Ranitz, who was secretly as anxious to hear Luther as Margarethe herself.

The two girls could talk of little else than the treat that was in store for them on Sunday; but they had the gratification of seeing Luther walking down the street before Sunday came, and Margarethe exclaimed, when she saw him, "I can believe in that man."

Her brother laughed, because she could not explain this feeling of trust; but when they returned home after hearing Luther preach on Sunday she said, "This Dr. Luther does not look a bit like a monk. He is no cunning fox, as you say all monks

ENDUE: *fill*

are, Fritz; he is true, and sees the truth, and teaches it, and—"

"And so you are going to take the part of all monks because Dr. Luther is a monk," interrupted her brother, laughing. "Anna, pray be careful what you say of them before their new champion."

"I am not their champion," returned Margarethe. "Dr. Luther is not the least like any other monk I ever saw. His grand massive head and open genuine countenance are not the least like Father Sebastian's foxy face; and then he speaks so plainly, calling everything by names we can understand—so that when he said God would forgive us all our sins out of the great love that He bears toward us, and not because of any store of good works being offered to Him, I felt that I could believe that better than the letter of indulgence you bought for me of Dr. Tetzel."

"Despising my gifts now! What next?" asked Fritz.

"Do you go to the early mass at the Festival of All Saints?" asked his father before Margarethe could reply.

"Eric and I have agreed to do so. You will take Margarethe later in the day I suppose."

"No, no, I want to go to the early mass," said his sister; "I don't mind the cold of the early morning at all."

"I am quite used to it," said Anna, and so it was agreed that the party should go together.

In the early morning, the thirty-first of October, they started for the Castle Church; but as they drew near they saw that a great crowd was gathered round the church door, and von Ranitz was inclined to turn back and take the two girls home again; but Fritz, who was walking in front, soon came to assure them that there was nothing to fear. "This is no common mob of pilgrims and peasants, but most of them are professors of the university and friends of Dr. Luther; and one of them is reading some theses which the doctor has nailed to the Church door."

"O let us get near and hear what they are about," said Margarethe, and she pressed forward as eagerly as the students around them, anxious to hear what it could be that Dr. Luther had said in this public declaration.

They were not able to get near enough to hear the reading. They learned, however, that they were a declaration against Dr. Tetzel's shameless traffic in indulgences. There were ninety-five articles or questions about this doctrine of indulgence, and Luther affixed to his declaration that he should be at the university the following day, ready to answer anyone who questioned these propositions, and he finished by declaring that he was not a heretic.

Beyond these few particulars Margarethe could not hear much of what was written.

The grand event of the day, the exhibition of the relics that had drawn so many strangers and

AFFIXED: *added*

pilgrims to Wittenberg to gain the indulgence granted by the Pope to all who should gaze in pious reverence upon these sacred treasures, seemed suddenly to have been forgotten in the excitement about these theses of Luther. Students and citizens, peasants and pilgrims, were all talking of the bold words Luther had published, not only against Dr. Tetzel, but against the whole system of purchasing the favor of God.

Fritz was delighted. "Luther has thrown down the wager of battle in this," he said, "and Dr. Tetzel and all the monks will oppose him."

"But the Pope may defend him. Leo the Tenth is no ignorant monk, but a learned man, and can appreciate Luther's learning," said Eric.

Fritz looked at his friend with something of a pitying smile. "How often am I to tell you that nobody knows Rome or the Pope unless they have been to Rome! The Pope is a learned man; but, like most of the philosophers in Italy, he believes in nothing but his own power and glory; and as that is, of course, identical with the power of the Church, he will defend it at all costs. But did you hear that these theses had been sent to the elector's printing-press, and would soon be in the hands of all who liked to buy them?" asked Fritz.

"Fritz, you must get me one as soon as possible," said Margarethe.

"I don't know; you did not value the letter of indulgence I bought for you," said Fritz tormentingly.

"I have already asked the printer to let me have one of the first copies," said Eric quickly, and Margarethe with a smile quietly thanked him for his thoughtfulness.

A day or two afterward the theses were in the hands of many besides Fritz and Eric, for they could not be printed off fast enough to supply the demand; and hundreds of others were listening, as Margarethe and Anna did, while Eric read two or three of the propositions laid down by Luther.

"When our Lord and Master Jesus Christ says, 'Repent,' he means that the whole life of his followers on earth is a constant and continued repentance."

"Every Christian who truly repents of his sins has entire forgiveness of the penalty and of the fault, and so far has no need of indulgence."

"Every true Christian, dead or alive, participates in all the blessings of Christ and of the Church by the gift of God, and without a letter of indulgence."

These were some of the propositions upon which Luther had invited discussion, and which were setting men thinking as they had never thought before.

Chapter IX

Eric

LIFE in Wittenberg, with its busy stir and constant change, was so new and pleasant to Margarethe that, as she said to Anna sometimes, she was being totally spoiled for a monotonous life in the castle afterward.

"These burgher merchants are better off than the nobles now," she said, as she looked round the pleasant, richly furnished rooms of their temporary home, and contrasted them with the bare, clumsily decorated, inconvenient chambers of the castle; and once more the old wish arose in her heart that she had been born of well-to-do burgher parents. Her being able to wear velvet and pearls would scarcely compensate for all the inconveniences of her lot; and when Fritz and Eric came in from the university bringing the latest news of the day, or when they sat together of an evening listening to Eric's notes of Dr. Luther's lectures on the Epistle to the Galatians, Margarethe wished this pleasant life could go on and on forever. If Else

EPISTLE: *letter*

had only been with her, her happiness would have been nearly perfect, for she had begun to lose the fear and dread that formerly oppressed her when any enjoyment presented itself, that God hated to see her happy, and would inevitably bring some misery upon her if she ventured to indulge in it, however harmless or even good it might be. Dr. Luther's teaching was beginning to bear fruit in Margarethe, and she could dimly hope now that there was a religion after all that was suitable even for her.

The sensation that the theses made somewhat troubled her friend Anna, who was, of course, inclined to think that everything ought to be done after the pattern of her Swiss teacher, Zwinglius.

"If Dr. Luther had just taught the people in a sermon that the indulgences were not so efficacious as Dr. Tetzel says they are, I think it would have been better, and all this stir would have been avoided," she said one day, when Fritz came in with the news that Tetzel had been preaching a most violent sermon against Luther's theses, and had threatened to issue some himself in refutation of Luther's.

"Have you heard what our elector says about it, Fritz?" asked his father, a little anxiously; for he had been studying these propositions, and saw that they contained more than a mere denunciation of the sale of indulgences.

"Well, I have heard that he is not too well pleased, for a few have left the university through

EFFICACIOUS: *effective*
DENUNCIATION: *condemnation*

it, and you know he has set his heart upon this new university being the greatest in Germany."

"And it is the greatest, too," interrupted Eric warmly; "and for every student that leaves now ten will arrive shortly, I know, for these theses are being translated into all languages, and the printers are still hard at work, and cannot fill all the orders that are received from all parts of the world."

"Dr. Luther says he never intended that the theses should be printed at all. He merely thought they would raise a discussion in the university, and thus check the sale of Tetzel's indulgences," said Fritz.

"The Bishop of Brandenburg has commanded Luther to cease from any more of these exciting proclamations, has he not?" asked his father.

"Yes, but if the bishop and elector do not choose to support Luther, he has only to go to England, where he will be helped by the king. Did you hear the rumor, Eric, that King Henry of England had invited our friar, Martin Luther, to go there?"

Eric shook his head. "I hope it is not true," he said; "for I believe now that Luther has commenced the Reformation here in Germany, and—"

"The Reformation commenced!" exclaimed Margarethe. "How, when, where?"

Eric smiled at her impetuosity: "I think it was commenced here in Wittenberg, only a few weeks since, when Luther nailed his theses to the church door."

IMPETUOSITY: *eagerness*

"That—the—commencement—of—the—Reformation?" slowly uttered Margarethe.

"But people have been thinking as Dr. Luther writes, for a long time—at least, many people have," added Anna.

"Yes; but there is all the difference in the world between thinking quietly and secretly that a thing *may* be, and publicly declaring it, as Luther has done," said Eric.

"Luther himself is half afraid now of the noise these theses have made," said von Ranitz.

"No, not afraid, but the fears of the prior of his monastery have somewhat troubled him. The prior fears he will bring disgrace upon their order, and this touched Luther very deeply; but at last he said, 'Dear father, if the thing is not done in the name of God it will fail, but if it is, let it proceed.' One of the brethren told me of this only yesterday," added Eric. It was not only the elector and the prior of his convent that Luther had displeased, but the bishops, and prelates, and learned scholars of the Church, whom Luther felt sure would have been in sympathy with him, loaded him with reproaches and accusations.

Of course, the opinion of the Pope was eagerly waited for, when it was known that his theses had been sent to Rome; and many expected that Pope Leo would declare him at once to be a heretic, as he had been urged to do. But the Pope was inclined to feel amused at the sensation caused by

PRIOR: *head of the monastery*

these propositions, and only replied, "This friar, Martin Luther, is a great genius; all that is said against him is mere monkish jealousy."

This speech of the Pope encouraged some of Luther's friends to hope that the Pope himself would help forward the work of renovating the Church; while others, hearing of a secret message sent from the Emperor Maximilian to the Elector Frederick of Saxony, hoped that political capital might be made out of Martin Luther's bold theses.

Von Ranitz heard of this in one of his visits to the castle, and was so overjoyed that he could not refrain from telling Fritz upon his return. "Dr. Luther is a great man," he said, "and if need be I will willingly draw my sword on his behalf. The emperor has sent to the elector a message by his ambassador. These are the emperor's words: 'Take good care of the monk Luther, for the time may come when we shall have need of him.'"

"But what could Dr. Luther do for the emperor? He is not a soldier," said Margarethe.

"No, of course not, and you cannot understand such a matter as this," said her father, although the "matter" seemed to afford him immense satisfaction; and he had long talks with Fritz about the knights taking up arms to defend Luther, if ever it became necessary. Before long it was arranged that Fritz should go, by and by, to their kinsman, von Sickengen, and learn all the latest improvements in the arts of chivalry.

RENOVATING: *restoring*

Margarethe was far from satisfied at being put off without any explanation of the subject that occupied so many of her father and brother's thoughts, and at last applied to Eric von Schonstein. "I am not stupid, although I am a woman; but Fritz seems to think women have no business to hear anything that would set them thinking for themselves. The business of the world must be done without their knowing anything about it, and when it is done, of course we are bound to be satisfied with it, whatever it may cost us. We are to take our religion ready-made, while, according to Fritz's opinion, men, who care nothing for it—who do not even believe in it—are to make it for us."

Margarethe had almost talked herself out of breath in her indignation, and for a minute Eric could only smile at her impetuosity; but he said gravely:

"What is it you wish to know? I do not think you stupid; I think it would be better if women did think for themselves more. Now, what is your difficulty? I will help you if I can; but I am afraid I shall fail, for you are so much wiser in many things than I am that I scarcely know what I shall do without your help when you go away from Wittenberg."

"My help!" uttered Margarethe in astonishment; "I am too ignorant to help anybody."

"Indeed you help me to understand Dr. Luther's lectures as I never did before. They possess twice their meaning and beauty and wisdom after I have heard your comments upon them; and I have sometimes been so foolish as to wish that you could attend the university and hear Dr. Luther lecture for yourself."

"I have often wished it," said Margarethe; "It is an old wish of mine to want to be a man."

Eric smiled. "I am glad you are not—that you are not anything but just what you are, wise, helpful, noble Margarethe, who will one day, I trust, brighten my castle home. I tell you frankly, Margarethe, that when I first heard my father's wishes about you, and received the invitation to the tournament, I almost vowed I would not speak to you during my visit."

Margarethe's eyes were dancing with glee now. "How precisely alike we were in our disposition toward each other!" she replied laughing.

"Say *are*, Margarethe; for all that is changed now, I hope," said Eric anxiously; "I have long wanted to speak myself about what we know to be the wishes of our parents. You will consent to our betrothal, Margarethe?"

"But—but I thought we were mutually determined to hate each other," whispered the young lady. "What has altered your determination about this matter?"

"Now, Margarethe, you do not need to be told what has been the bond of sympathy, overcoming our prejudices and drawing us to each other all this time. You know, as well as I do, that Dr. Luther and his teaching have taught us to know each other; and now I ask you to help me live the truth Friar Martin is teaching, and help me raise the peasants to understand something of this, too."

Margarethe lifted her flushed face for a moment and said, "Will you promise me something, if I promise you this?"

"Anything, Margarethe; anything you wish to ask," said Eric, rather excitedly.

"Your father will have to consent to it, too, and he must arrange it with my father; but unless this can be done I—I do not think I can ever be your wife."

Margarethe uttered these words rather slowly, for she knew enough of herself by this time to be quite sure that if she did not marry Eric she would never marry at all; but the proposal she was about to make had grown to be the one hope of her life—Else's rescue from the convent—and she would rather relinquish Eric than leave Else to her unhappy life in the cloister.

"Come, tell me the conditions of my happiness," said Eric, seeing Margarethe hesitated.

"It will be for your father's consideration rather than yours, I am afraid; but, but it is about my dowry. Eric, you must be content with a poor bride, you must refuse half the amount my father has pledged himself to give me, or I can never be your wife."

"Margarethe, I do not want a single guilder with you. What do you mean?"

"O Eric, cannot you understand? Do you not know that our family is poor, and that Else has been sent to the convent because my father cannot portion two daughters as becomes his state as a knight?" and Margarethe burst into tears as she related how unhappy Else seemed, in spite of the high hopes she entertained of the happiness to be found in the convent.

"Margarethe, I do not want any dowry with you; only consent to our being betrothed at Christmas, and I will ask my father to relinquish every guilder he has been promised."

"O no! Else does not want the whole of it. She would be unhappy then, as I am now; but if your father will be content with half, then Else might come home again and have the other half for her little portion. I suppose it will be a very little portion," she added.

"I do not know at all; but I expect my father at Wittenberg in a few days, and then I will ask him about it, and tell him your conditions; you will not forget that we are to be betrothed at Christmas," he added.

"If your father consents to accept only half the dowry."

"I am not afraid. Now let us forget all that, and tell me the difficulty our talk began about," said Eric.

"I almost forget. What was it?"

"Well, you began by assuring me that you were not stupid—which was quite needless," laughed Eric.

"O, I remember! it was this message of the emperor's about Dr. Luther and the elector's taking good care of him, as he might be needed by and by. He is not a soldier, but a monk," added Margarethe.

"But he may be of more use to Germany than a whole army of soldiers," said Eric.

Margarethe still looked puzzled. "I suppose I am very stupid after all," she said.

"Indeed, you are not, but I am not sure that I can make you understand what the emperor means. You see, there has been for many years a sort of jealousy existing between Germany and Rome; between the Pope and the emperor. And now their power is so evenly balanced that they are constantly watching each other lest one should get a slight advantage of the other. The Pope is always trying to grasp more temporal power, and most of the alliances of the emperor with other countries have this in view; but there is one power the Pope possesses which the emperor does not. He is emperor of Germany, but the Pope is head of the Church, and rules the conscience of the German people. He can, and does, make laws for the Church without regard to the emperor. Now, do you not see that if someone among us, like Dr. Luther, should arise, who through his wisdom and learning should

TEMPORAL: *worldly*

discover errors in the Church supported by the Pope, and if he was loved and supported by the citizens and people of Germany, the emperor—"

"Would make him Pope here," interrupted Margarethe excitedly.

"No, no, the emperor could not do that; he would not wish to do that; but the Pope would probably complain that Dr. Luther was weakening his power over the minds of the people in Germany, and would send to the emperor to deliver him up as a heretic. Then if the emperor wished he could refuse to do this, as he probably would, and there would be a bargaining between them as to what the Pope would give up in the way of power, or some advantage he had gained, as the price of Luther being forbidden to preach anymore."

Margarethe opened her eyes very widely. "The elector would not sell Dr. Luther like that, I am sure," she said.

"I do not think the emperor would wish to do so either. He will be quite willing to take good care of Luther."

"Eric, I wish you had not told me about this now. I have only thought about Dr. Luther doing God's work in the world, making men and women so much happier than they ever were before by showing them that God loves them. I never thought about the emperor having anything to do with this."

"Neither does Dr. Luther. He is doing God's work, I believe, and the emperor may help this, too, in a different way; but I think it is well you should know something about this, for suppose we should hear by and by, when we are far away in the Thuringian forest, that Dr. Luther had been forbidden by the emperor to preach and teach any more, we shall understand then that it is not for any fault in the teaching, but because of some political bargain."

"But Luther would preach all the same, I know. He tells us what he believes God has commanded him, not to please the emperor or elector, but because he is the servant of God," said Margarethe.

"But, Margarethe, if the emperor were to forbid him—"

"He would say that God was his Master, and he was bound to obey him," interrupted the young lady.

"If it should ever be that Luther needed the aid of the knights, I am sure they would all rally round him," said Eric.

"My father believes that the day will come, and Fritz is going to Count von Sickengen, in the Rhineland, to prepare for it."

"Yes, he has begged me to go with him," said Eric, looking earnestly at Margarethe to find out what she thought of the plan.

He was not kept long in doubt. "You will go, Eric," she said grandly; "you will fight for Dr. Luther if there be need for it."

Chapter X

A Bonfire

ERIC and Margarethe were betrothed on Christmas day. Solemnly, in the presence of her father, brother, and friend, and Count von Schonstein, Margarethe promised to be Eric's wife, and Dr. Luther, who was also present, prayed for God's blessing on the plighted pair. The time for their marriage was not definitely settled yet; for it had been arranged that Eric should go with Fritz to the Rhineland, and Margarethe was to go with Anna to Zurich in the spring.

The question of the dowry had been settled with less difficulty than Margarethe had anticipated; for von Schonstein had been too well pleased to find his son had taken a liking to the lady he had chosen to be his wife to make much demur about her small dowry. He protested, however, that these two young people were commencing a reformation on their own account; for who besides themselves had ever dared to fall in love with each other until after they were married? while these were plainly

PLIGHTED: *promised in marriage*
DEMUR: *objection*

convicted of this before they were even betrothed. In Eric's opinion, which he afterward confided to Margarethe, a reform in this social custom of parents choosing husbands and wives for their children, irrespective of their own wishes in the matter, was not altogether to be deprecated, and he avowed that he believed the day would come when all the world would see this, too.

Von Ranitz was not so elated over the alteration in Margarethe's dowry as she herself; for he was vexed that von Schonstein had been told of their poverty, a vexation that he might have spared himself, for his brother knight knew perfectly well why Else had been sent to the convent. As soon as Margarethe's betrothal was over, and the question of her dowry thus finally disposed of, Margarethe was anxious that her sister should be removed from the convent without delay; but her father saw no reason for special haste, especially at this season of the year, when traveling was so difficult, and often dangerous; but he promised to fetch Else before Margarethe went to Zurich. They would all go back to the castle in the spring, and Else should go with them thither, he said; and with this promise Margarethe was obliged to be content.

How pleasant this life at Wittenberg was to Margarethe! She was learning Latin and Greek, that she might be able to read the Scriptures for herself in these languages; for the prospect of ever seeing a German Bible seemed farther off than ever

DEPRECATED: *disapproved of*

now; for Dr. Luther, who stood almost alone as the champion of the authority of Scripture being the sole guide in all things pertaining to religion, was too busy teaching and preaching to think of translating this book into the language of the people, however much he might desire they should have it.

Margarethe conformed more strictly to the rules of the Church now than ever she did before; for Dr. Luther had endued the dead, formal ritual with a new life by his teaching; and, so far from the duties of religion being irksome, they were a delight to her. She went regularly to confession again, for Friar Martin Luther was her confessor, and she had no fear of telling him her doubts and fears and difficulties, for he was sure to be able to help her. One day she asked him to tell her the best way of studying the Scriptures, for she hoped soon to be able to read them in the ancient languages.

"It is most certain," answered Luther, "that we cannot succeed in comprehending the Scriptures either by study or mere intellect. Your first duty, then, is to begin with prayer. Entreat the Lord that He will, in His great mercy, grant you the true knowledge of His Word. There is no other interpreter of the Word of God than the author of that Word, according as it is said, 'They will all be taught of God.'[1] Hope nothing from your works, nothing from your intellect. Trust only in God, and in the influence of His Spirit. Believe one who is speaking from experience."

[1] John 6:45

IRKSOME: *troublesome*

Thinking over this advice of her present confessor, and comparing it with what she had often heard from Father Sebastian about the Church alone having the right to interpret Scripture, she began to understand how it was that so many of the priests and monks, not only in and around Wittenberg, but wherever Luther's fame had spread, hated him bitterly, and often warned their hearers against his doctrine. It hardly needed jealousy to fan this flame of hatred with which Luther so boldly undermined the foundation upon which all their pretensions to power and sanctity were built; but the ever-burning jealousy which one order of monks always bore another added fuel to this fire, and the Dominicans, under Dr. Tetzel, were Luther's most bitter foes.

The theses the Dominican indulgence merchant threatened to issue against Luther were shortly published, and some of them soon found their way to Wittenberg, and into the hands of the students. Margarethe was anxious to see them, too, and asked eagerly what her brother thought of them—whether they were at all equal to Dr. Luther's.

"You will see what the students and university think of them this evening," said Fritz significantly; but beyond this vague answer Margarethe could not get a word out of him.

She had forgotten her brother's words when, in the evening of that cold February day, she suddenly saw the sky over the marketplace become lurid,

SANCTITY: *holiness*
LURID: *horribly glowing*

and, throwing open the window, she could hear the crackling of a fire and the dim confused noise of hundreds of voices.

"Father, there is a fire! all the town will soon be in flames," she exclaimed in a tone of alarm.

"They have lighted it, then—foolish boys!" said von Ranitz, coming to the window.

"What is it, Father?" asked Margarethe.

"Only a bonfire to burn Tetzel's theses. Dr. Luther will not be well pleased, however, when he hears of this defiance of his adversary, I fancy; for he is grave and serious about the matter; but—"

"The students love him so much they would fain fight his battles for him," interrupted Margarethe.

"Yes, yes, and I suppose boys' love will be like themselves, often rash and inconsiderate," replied her father. "I told Fritz I did not like this bonfire lighting, and the more I think of it the less I like it. I tell you, Margarethe, it is not the first fire that has been lighted in a marketplace, and it will not be the last, if Dr. Luther does not take care. This defiance of the holy father is not wise."

"But it is not the holy father, only Dr. Tetzel and his indulgences, that Luther has written against," exclaimed Margarethe.

"Your father thinks as I do, that it would have been better to have preached against them only," said Anna; "for many people besides Tetzel say that these propositions of Luther's do contain heresy; and, of course, Tetzel sets himself forward as

WOULD FAIN: *desire to*

the champion of the Pope; so that any defiance of this Dominican is defiance of the Pope and his authority."

"But Dr. Luther expressly upholds the honor and power of the Pope in one of his theses," retorted Margarethe. "He says, 'Cursed be he who speaketh against the indulgence of the Pope.'"

"Yes, but what is the indulgence of the Pope? for in another proposition Luther says, 'The indulgence of the Pope cannot take away the smallest daily sin in regard to the fault or delinquency;' and it is this shearing the Pope of all his great spiritual power that I am afraid of," said Anna.

An hour or two later Fritz and Eric came in, bearing unmistakable signs in their blackened hands and faces, and the odor that pervaded them, of the active part they had taken in burning the theses. They were full of exultation, too, but the grave faces of von Ranitz and the two girls somewhat sobered them; and Eric said, "I suppose we are rejoicing as though a victory had been gained, because our leader has sounded the first note of the battle. But then is it not something gained to have that first war-shout raised in no uncertain tone? The world has been watching and waiting and praying and preparing for this; and it has come at last; and the world is looking to our Wittenberg doctor, and wondering what the next step will be."

"I wonder what it will be," said Margarethe musingly.

DELINQUENCY: *neglect of duty*

"I should not wonder if he were to be declared a heretic by the Pope after all," said Anna. "I am afraid these theses, with the stir they have made, will make the monks so suspicious that others besides Luther may be accused of heresy because they teach the same things that he does."

"You are thinking of your Swiss priest, Zwinglius," said Margarethe; "and you would have every one do as he does; but Luther is not the sort of man, I fancy, to be bound by any such consideration as that. He will speak or write as he thinks God's work can best be done, without thinking of how other people would do it, or whether it will bring danger to himself."

"Or to others either," said Anna, a little tartly. "His best friends say he has been rash in this business about the theses, and you know—"

"Yes, I know that we love each other too dearly to quarrel about Dr. Luther," said Margarethe quickly; and she asked Fritz and Eric to go and change their clothes at once, that nothing further might be said upon the subject just now.

If some feared—as they did—that the rash enthusiasm of the students would bring trouble upon their master, they were disappointed, for Wittenberg soon forgot the fire in the marketplace in the more serious business of everyday life; for the resources of the little town were constantly being stretched to their utmost limit by the influx of students that each week brought to the university. There was less beer-drinking and mad prank-playing among these young men now than when Dr. Luther first came among them, and this army of scholars, who were to go forth, by and by, throughout the length and breadth of the world to teach the truth they were now learning from Dr. Luther's lips, were already exhibiting in their own lives the power of the Gospel to regulate and purify and ennoble them.

When spring blossoms began to peep above the brown earth once more, and the leaf-buds of the stunted oaks began to burst, Margarethe, with her father and Anna, prepared to leave Wittenberg for their home in the Thuringian forest, but Else did not leave Nimptschen to go with them. Margarethe would have been willing to go by herself and fetch her sister away from the convent, but her father said it would be better for Father Sebastian to go and arrange with the authorities for Else's renunciation of a religious life.

Margarethe fretted and chafed against this delay, and against the employment of Father Sebastian as ambassador in the business. She urged that, as Else was simply a novice and had not taken the vows, her father could very easily arrange the matter with the lady superior; but this was just what von Ranitz dreaded above all things, for he knew the representations that would be made to him of the disgrace that would fall upon his family name by the removal of his daughter—a disgrace that would send a thrill of horror through every noble family in Germany; for it would be heard and talked of in every family with whom the sisterhood were connected, and only the daughters of nobles could be received at Nimptschen. Father Sebastian, being himself an ecclesiastic, could manage this affair without causing any scandal, and von Ranitz did not mind talking to the old family confessor, or even ordering him to bring back his daughter from the convent.

It was scarcely likely, now, that Margarethe would be able to see her sister before her departure for Switzerland, for Anna had received news of the death of a distant relative, and his widow, who resided in Zurich, wished Anna to go and assist her in educating her three children.

"It will be better than going to a convent, although Anna Meyer is not of noble birth like her husband's family, but only an innkeeper's daughter," said the Swiss lady, with a little sigh of regret as she told how Meyer had offended his father and all his family by his marriage, and yet never regretted it, although he had lost every prospect of wealth through it.

Margarethe smiled. "I think Eric's words will come true some day, and the world will let people choose for themselves," she said; "for if this burgher maiden was so good a wife that her husband counted the loss of wealth as nothing beside her, she must have been a good and true woman."

ECCLESIASTIC: *member of the clergy*

"Yes, I have heard she was as good as she was beautiful, and Anna Reinhard's beauty had passed into a proverb; but still it is a pity she was not of noble birth," concluded Anna; for in spite of her visit to Wittenberg, and what she had seen there of burgher life and manners, which had so greatly modified Margarethe's opinions, she still retained most of her old ideas concerning the immense superiority conferred upon a person by a noble pedigree.

When they were almost ready to start on their journey westward Fritz announced his intention to take Tübingen in the way, as he was anxious to see its university, and the aged Professor Reuchlin, who had given such offense to the monks by his translation of a Hebrew grammar by means of which scholars could now become conversant with that ancient tongue, and read the Scriptures in that language.

Margarethe was not very well pleased to hear this, for it would hasten their departure from the castle, and she now wished to delay her journey as much as possible, that she might see Else before she went.

Father Sebastian had rather reluctantly undertaken the mission to the superior at Nimptschen, and had promised to return with Else as soon as possible; but Margarethe knew this would not be possible at the rate Father Sebastian would travel, and so she was obliged to content herself with

PEDIGREE: *ancestry*
CONVERSANT: *familiar*

leaving messages with her aunt, and a book and copy of Dr. Luther's theses as memorials of her love; and then they had to set forth on their journey through the forest to the distant Rhineland and Switzerland.

They were quite a large party when all were mounted; for, besides the pages in attendance upon Fritz and Eric, Margarethe took her own maid, and then there were two sumpter mules to carry the baggage, besides a party of retainers who would accompany them the greater part of the journey.

The slow rate of traveling that had to be adopted for safety's sake while they were in the forest was very irksome to Fritz, who would fain have put spurs to his horse, and galloped on ahead with Eric, that they might have the more time to spend at Tübingen; but another petty quarrel had taken place between some of the knights and the burghers of Erfurt, and so, while they were in this neighborhood, the retainers could not be left wholly to their own responsibility.

Margarethe beguiled their slow ride by relating to them various legends of the forest and the spirits who were supposed to inhabit the trees and rocks and dells, and how she used to be afraid to speak of them unless she was sure the gates of the castle were closed against their intrusion; and, truth to tell, even now Margarethe, bold as she was, spoke of them with bated breath and many a glance

SUMPTER: *pack*
BEGUILED: *passed*

behind, as though she was still half afraid they might be following her.

But at length the forest, with its solemn pine trees and ghostly legends, was left behind, and they were traversing one of the highways of the world, with its practical, busy sixteenth-century industry, which put the dreams of their forefathers far away in the background.

Chapter XI

At Tübingen

OUR party of friends had not traveled far beyond the borders of the forest when they were overtaken by von Ranitz, who had felt some misgivings at entrusting his daughter and her friend to two such young champions as Fritz and Eric, although they had a strong party of retainers, some of whom had nursed Margarethe and Fritz when they were children, and were entirely to be relied upon.

Still, this journey was a long one, and the knight began to grow anxious as soon as the cavalcade was out of sight. He could not rest until his horse was saddled and he following them. He could send back all but one or two retainers; and so, leaving the castle in charge of his father and aunt, he was quickly in his saddle. Margarethe was not sorry to see her father join them, for Fritz was so restless and impatient to reach Tübingen that Margarethe feared some accident would happen or some mischance befall their baggage, in his eagerness to press on. Now that her father had joined them, however, Fritz could follow his own inclination about pressing on alone, or continue in their company. He preferred doing the latter, although he grumbled at the slow progress of the sumpter mules; and so, at last, when they were within a few miles of Tübingen, these were left to come on in the charge of the few retainers, while the rest of their party hurried forward as fast as the ladies' palfreys would permit.

This was no new university like Wittenberg, with a town growing up all around, about which no one could say, for a certainty, whether it would grow into a handsome town of substantial houses, or remain a medley of town and village, with its rude, mud hovels. But, then, Tübingen was not on the very borders of civilization as was Wittenberg, but near the beautiful Rhineland, and rich in cathedrals and churches and monasteries, to say nothing of its university and its gathering of illustrious men whose name for learning was of worldwide repute.

"Father, will you take us to see this learned Professor Reuchlin?" asked Fritz.

Von Ranitz shook his head doubtfully. "What account would you give of yourself, Fritz? Reuchlin and I were friends years ago; it would grieve him to hear that my son had only learned enough to disbelieve in everything."

Fritz looked annoyed; and to attract her father's attention from him, Margarethe asked, "Has Reuchlin any children?"

"He has an adopted son—Philip Schwartzerd. He was a little delicate lad when I saw him, quite unfit to learn his father's trade of an armorer, and as he showed great ability for learning, Reuchlin took him as a pupil, and finally adopted him. He must be a year or two older than Fritz—not more—but he has made better use of his opportunities, I doubt not."

Margarethe wondered what Fritz could have said or done to offend his father, for never until the last few days had she heard him find fault with the progress he had made in his various duties, and he had often laughed when his son's disbelief in what had been so generally credited had been brought prominently forward. Fearing there might be some unpleasantness between her father and brother, if they were left alone, she contrived to engage her father in conversation; and from him she learned that this cultivated man, Reuchlin, was a burgher's son who, when a boy, used to sing in the choir of the church, and his sweet voice attracted the attention of the Margrave of Baden, who sent him to the University of Paris with his son. "While he was at Paris," continued von Ranitz, "he met John Wessel, a monk, who was known as 'the light of the world.' From him Reuchlin learned doctrines very similar to those now preached by our monk of Wittenberg; for he said that 'To God alone belongs the power of giving full absolution. There is no necessity for confessing our sins to a priest.

There is no purgatory—at least, if it be not God Himself, who is a devouring fire, and purges away every defilement.'"

"A monk taught this truth before our Dr. Luther," exclaimed Margarethe.

Her father smiled. "Ah, ten years before the monk of Wittenberg was born there was another monk, John of Wessalin, who taught the same, but the Church found means of silencing him, as it will silence Luther. I tell you, Margarethe, it is useless for anybody to contend against the power of the Church; and it will be wiser to give it up at once than lose everything, and then have to give up."

Margarethe looked at her father as it not quite comprehending what this speech might mean, but von Ranitz was looking straight before him, and would not see the look of surprise in his daughter's face.

Presently, however, he said rather abruptly, "Do you think Fritz would like to enter the Church—as a priest, you know—not a monk? He would soon be made a bishop, I know."

"I—I don't understand," said Margarethe, seriously doubting whether she heard aright.

"I spoke plain enough, Margarethe," said her father petulantly. "The fact is, that since I have been to Wittenberg and seen the growing power and wealth of the burghers, I am quite sure that we poor knights cannot enforce our ancient claims and privileges, and without these we shall be poor indeed. It is best, therefore, that Fritz should be provided with a rich living in the Church; and it is not impossible that a bishopric may be offered to him by and by."

Margarethe looked up at her father in dismay. "Fritz is not fit for a bishop," she said hastily.

"He could soon be made fit," said her father.

"But he does not believe in religion at all. He says he has seen and learned too much ever to—"

"To make any use of what he has learned, I suppose," interrupted her father angrily; "he believes in Luther, so he must believe in the Church; and I want you to persuade him to stay here awhile at Tübingen, and study under my old friend Reuchlin."

"But—but there is another reason why Fritz cannot enter the Church. Has he not told you that he desires to wed Anna Geroldsek?"

"How can he do that?" inquired her father.

"She is noble; she is not a burgher maiden; her friends are all of knightly degree," replied Margarethe.

"And her dowry!" demanded von Ranitz. "Fritz cannot afford to wed a dowerless bride." Von Ranitz forgot, in his harshness, how he had himself married without adding a guilder to the family wealth, or gaining anything for the hereditary influence.

Their conversation was stopped here by Anna, who had ridden on a short distance in front with

BISHOPRIC: *position as a bishop*

Fritz and Eric, again joining them. She saw that Margarethe looked anxious and troubled, but, little suspecting the cause, she said, "I have been telling Fritz he had better stay at Tübingen, as he is so anxious to get there."

"I am glad to hear you gave him such sensible advice, Fraulein Anna," said von Ranitz, with more stateliness than cordiality in his tone. Like many another careful parent, he had quite failed to see what was evident to everybody else. His tournament had been a greater success than he desired, or had succeeded in a way he did not desire; and, now that he had been made aware of the fact, he felt offended with Anna as the cause of all this.

The lady noticed the change in the tone, the want of cordiality in the manner, and she had some misgivings that the state of things was about to change for them all.

When she had the opportunity she managed to say to Margarethe, "What is the matter? what has happened? Does your father really wish Fritz to stay at Tübingen?" Anna had her own private reason for expecting that Fritz, and his father too, would accompany her to Switzerland, and, therefore, felt considerably disappointed at the idea of his remaining in Germany.

But Margarethe could only shake her head and whisper, "I will tell you all when we get to the inn;" for her father was close at hand, and Fritz not far off.

SWAY: *influence*

When they reached their destination, which was a comfortable hostelry near the university, Margarethe and Anna retired to have their chat alone, while Fritz and Eric were making friends with some students, and von Ranitz arranging with the host for their accommodation.

It seemed that the noble, learned Reuchlin held but a divided sway here in Tübingen now; for his adopted son, Philip Schwartzerd, although only twenty-one, was so learned a doctor of divinity that the students flocked as eagerly to his lectures as to those of the great professor himself.

"Nothing has been spared by Reuchlin that could help Dr. Philip. His very name has been translated into Greek, because it was so barbarous, and Melanchthon has now so entirely superseded his family name that many do not know him by any other than this Greek translation of it." This information was given to Fritz by one of the older students, and as Fritz was, of course, most anxious to hear this elegant scholar, von Ranitz readily agreed to stay here for a week, that he might have an opportunity of hearing him lecture.

Fritz had seen Reuchlin shortly after his arrival. He had been pointed out to him by one of his student friends, for the professor was a man who could not pass through the streets unnoticed. His tall, commanding figure and noble, genial countenance marked him as a king among his fellows,

BARBAROUS: *uncivilized*
SUPERSEDED: *replaced*
GENIAL: *pleasant*

and, without asking, Fritz had assumed that Dr. Philip Melanchthon was a similar man.

It was, therefore, almost a shock to him when he saw a little, slight-built man, scarcely more than a youth, take the lecturer's place before the crowd of students. He whispered to Eric, "That cannot be Melanchthon!"

But Eric held up his finger. He had forgotten to notice the slight, youthful figure, and was looking at the high expanded forehead, the delicately chiseled, intellectual face; and soon they had forgotten to criticize the man, and were lost in admiration of the learning he displayed, the choice and elegant Latin in which he clothed his ideas, and the clearness with which these were presented to his hearers.

"What a wonderful boy!" whispered Fritz, with a mixture of reverence and fun. The reverence was not sufficient and the fun quite shocking to one or two who overheard the whisper; for to them the youthful doctor was the embodiment of all wisdom and learning. They had grown so accustomed to the boyish figure that they quite overlooked it, and saw only a grave, earnest, learned man.

Von Ranitz went to see his old friend, Reuchlin, but he did not take Fritz; for it was about Fritz he wanted to consult the professor. He thought there would be little difficulty in persuading his son to take up his residence in Tübingen, as he so greatly admired Dr. Philip Melanchthon; but now he heard, to his dismay, that the young doctor was about to leave Tübingen for Wittenberg, whither he had been invited by the Elector Frederick, being recommended by Reuchlin.

"How could you recommend him to leave you?" exclaimed von Ranitz; "he has been—"

"My work and my comfort, dear as a son unto me," interrupted the professor; "but you have not now to learn that to see the Church purified of its abuses and Germany become one of the learned countries of Europe I would give up my beloved Philip even more entirely than I shall have to do by this removal to Wittenberg."

"But why cannot he teach as well at Tübingen as at Wittenberg?" asked von Ranitz, rather impatiently.

"Because Luther is at Wittenberg; and that will be the school for our German youth of the new times that are coming."

"Bother the new times! Why could not the old last for our time at least?" said the knight.

"Because we have helped to get rid of them, made them impossible of return."

"We! I have done nothing. You have been the mighty power in bringing most of this about; and, though I would not let your enemies, the Dominicans, hear me say it, I wish you had left it alone."

"I have done my poor best to help on what I saw was coming, and to give it a right direction; but I tell you, my dear old friend, the change that some call a reformation may prove to be anarchy and confusion for a time, handing the world over to a worse tyranny than ever in the end. I tell you this is not in the minds of a few learned men or true monks, like Luther and Wessel; but in the souls of the people, and it breaks out in such books as 'The Eulenspeigel,' that poem in which the laugh is continually kept up at priests, beasts, and gluttons. Then there is 'Reynard Reinecke,' which every young man reads, and Rosenblat's carnival games; these are all direct attacks upon the abuses of the Church and the evils that have grown out of them."

"It is not of the Church I complain so much, but the insolence of the burghers and peasants. They threaten to throw off all the allegiance they owe to the nobles. What is to become of the knights in this new order of things?"

Reuchlin shrugged his shoulders. "They will not be able to keep down the burghers, or extort as much from them as they have hitherto done," he said.

"The burghers of Erfurt, over whom we have a claim, refuse to acknowledge even their allegiance to us," said the knight. "They dared not have taken this bold step a few years ago; but now what are we poor knights to do?"

"Give up your robber castles, and live useful lives," answered Reuchlin, whose burgher sympathies were all aroused.

ANARCHY: *political chaos*

"But what are we to do? You would not have knights become merchants. I can see, as well as you, that our castles are useless to us now; and if we stay we must starve; at least our children will, for there is no inheritance to leave them but bare walls and poverty; and that is why I am very anxious Fritz should enter the Church."

"Yes, the Church is the refuge for the destitute," said Reuchlin rather sarcastically. "Men who have ruined their fortunes, the sons of knights who have no patrimony, all betake themselves to the Church."

"What else are they to do?"

"Well, you want your son to be provided with a fat living; and, of course, he is anxious about this, too."

"No, I am afraid he is not; but he will have to enter the Church or starve," said von Ranitz gloomily.

"But he is your only son."

"Yes, but he cannot live on bare walls and barren hills, and the little I have will barely last my time."

"But what would you have me do? How can I help you?"

"I want you to tell my son that he *must* enter the Church; that he had better stay here at Tübingen; I don't want him to go back to Wittenberg, for the name of Wittenberg is growing hateful to our bishops."

PATRIMONY: *inheritance*

Reuchlin passed his hand across his head, and considered for a moment. "I will see this young man and tell him what his father wishes," he said; but he would not promise to use any arguments in favor of the plan until he had talked the matter over with him, and heard what he had to say about it himself.

Chapter XII

Confidence

AS von Ranitz was returning to his hostelry after his visit to Reuchlin, he began to think that he might have employed his time better at home in his favorite study of astrology than in listening to Luther's lectures at Wittenberg all the winter. The whole fact of the case was this: His winter at Wittenberg had opened his eyes to the fact that the burghers had begun to break the bonds in which they had so long been held; but he had scarcely envied them their wealth, or the luxuries and conveniences that wealth brought them, until he returned to his bare, desolate castle, and then, like Margarethe, he sorely missed the comforts and convenience he had at first decried. Soon after his return, too, the Erfurt burghers refused to pay the tax levied by some of his ancestors, and sent word that they were prepared to resist any force that might be brought against them, and von Ranitz knew that this was no vain boast.

DECRIED: *condemned*

Of course, the loss of this would make them poorer still, and so it did not need much persuasion from Father Sebastian to make him see clearly that the only way he could provide for the future of his son was by employing his interest to obtain him a good living in the Church; and this was one reason that induced him to follow him to Tübingen.

He had foreseen some slight difficulty in persuading Fritz to view the matter in the same light as he did; but Margarethe's news, that her brother had grown fond of her friend Anna, and wished to wed her, was a difficulty quite unforeseen. If he had only studied astrology for light to be thrown on this dark, intricate future he might have had time to arrange some plan of escape from the entanglement of conflicting circumstances that seemed to be slowly, but surely, drawing everybody into a sort of vortex from which there was, he thought, no escape.

Von Ranitz's perplexities were not lessened when he met his kinsman, von Hutten, a few minutes afterward, who greeted him with great cordiality, and told him he was going to see Reuchlin, to ask his opinion upon a work that had been written, a sort of satire on the Church entitled, "Letters of some Obscure Men;" purporting to be letters of some monks, but in reality holding them up to ridicule.

"A satire on the Church!" said von Ranitz, as he took the book. "It is not the first time you have

VORTEX: *whirlpool*

written against the Church, Ulrich; but be careful; such pastime is dangerous, as you will find to your cost."

Hutten laughed. "It doth not become a chivalrous knight to be over-cautious when there are evils to be attacked and rights to be defended. You have heard of my father's death?" added Hutten with a sudden change in his tone.

"Yes, I heard of that, and how generously you had given up your patrimony to your brother and sisters."

"Of what use was it to me? There is one thing I would have them do, and I will ask you to pray them do it; and that is, change their name, if it be possible, and if it be not, at least never to write to the wandering knight, Ulrich von Hutten, lest they should be involved in some of his troubles."

"Then you think trouble will come of these attacks upon the Church?" said von Ranitz nervously.

"Sooner or later it is sure to come. The very foundations of the Church are being undermined; but she sees no danger as yet, and so, while she deems herself secure, we can carry on the work in this way; but by and by she will arouse, and then we must be prepared to hold all the advantages we may gain now, and oppose force to force as well as argument to argument."

But von Ranitz slowly shook his head. "It will never succeed," he said sadly.

"I thought you were one of us—one of the army of Reuchlinists, as the monks call us. Why, you were one of the first of our order—the knights—to appreciate the learning which Reuchlin introduced, and—"

"And I have made use of it. I have not spent my whole time in hunting and such like pastime, but have devoted myself to the study of astrology, which has helped me to see that such times as these were coming upon us."

"They could be foreseen without the help of any dark art. Has this astrology helped you to provide for it?" asked Hutten, with something of an amused smile.

"I have learned that the Church will be victorious, and it is useless to resist such mighty power as she possesses."

"And so you are about to turn your back upon your friends? I wish I could convince you that we are in the right."

"It may be right, and I could afford to stand up for it, as you do, Ulrich, if I were like you; but the case is just this, I must obtain a good living in the Church for my Fritz. I cannot otherwise provide for him."

"Then let him provide for himself, as I have done," said von Hutten; and at this moment, as though all the astrological calculations were against him, Fritz himself walked up and joined them.

He had seen von Hutten before, and was full of admiration for him; and so when Count Ulrich said rather abruptly, "Why don't you follow me, and serve the emperor, or fight for the right anywhere?" Fritz answered promptly, "There is nothing I should like better, and I am going to the castle of Ebenborg to learn all the latest arts of chivalry."

Von Hutten looked surprised. "I thought you were about to enter the Church," he said.

"I had not told Fritz the good fortune that was in store for him," said his father, wishing von Hutten had been fifty miles away.

"Good fortune? I would not enter the Church if they would make me a cardinal," said Fritz, looking from his father to his friend in amazement. Von Hutten saw in a moment he had made mischief, and thought it better to depart at once, but he contrived to speak to Fritz before he went; and the two arranged to meet the next day, as von Hutten wished to send a packet to von Sickengen at the castle of Ebenborg, and Fritz promised to take it.

After his departure Fritz followed his father, anxious to hear more of what had been such a surprising announcement to him; and as he rejoined him, he said, rather hastily, "What did you mean, my father, when you spoke of my entering the Church?"

"Before I talk to you about it I wish you to see the learned Professor Reuchlin, Fritz; only you must bear this in mind, Fritz: your patrimony is but an empty castle and a few bare hills and trees. Our wealth, such as it was, the dues from the burghers of Erfurt, will never be paid again, I fear, and it is best to look this fact in the face at once."

"I never thought to take those taxes. They were an unjust impost, and we could not expect the burghers to pay it when they were strong enough to defy us."

"Well, they have defied us now, and so I hope you will be reasonable, and let me provide for you in the only way I can."

"Not by getting me a living in the Church."

"Fritz, you can be made a canon at once, almost immediately, if you will—nay, what am I saying? you must—obey me in this matter; it is the duty of children to obey their parents. I suppose you will not deny that?"

"No, I do not; but—but, Father, I cannot obey you in this; for, as you well know, I do not believe in the Church, and, and—" But there Fritz stopped, for he thought it would be better not to mention Anna's name now.

"How many of the bishops do believe in it? I have heard you say that at Rome the highest dignitaries openly ridicule the sacred mysteries, and that the Pope is the greatest unbeliever of all."

"But he professes to believe, and I do not, and will not," said Fritz, doggedly.

IMPOST: *import tax*
CANON: *priest*
DOGGEDLY: *stubbornly*

"Do not speak like that, Fritz. The Church is the only honorable way by which the nobles can be provided for now. We cannot turn merchants, and—"

"For me to think of entering the Church would be most dishonorable," interrupted Fritz, "and I would rather be a peddler, carrying a pack of books from fair to fair, than a canon or a bishop, or even a cardinal. Father Sebastian has suggested this plan of my entering the Church, I suppose."

"Father Sebastian is devoted to the interest of our family, Fritz, and is as anxious to see you well provided for as I am," replied his father.

Fritz smiled significantly. "I am no favorite of his, I know, and he could hardly do me a worse turn than to set me at variance with you, sir," he said.

"Fritz, Fritz, what do you mean? we are not at variance; you will do as I wish, I am sure, when you see the reasonableness of it."

"But I never shall see it to be other than wrong and unreasonable."

"O yes, when you have accustomed yourself to the thought of it. The idea presented to you so suddenly was sure not to please you; but just look round and consider how wealthy and powerful you may become; you will be made a bishop in a few years; and, as you know, their wealth and power is almost equal to the landgrave's or elector's."

AT VARIANCE: *in conflict*
LANDGRAVE'S: *count's*

"Father, I would not be a bishop for all the wealth of Pope Leo himself. Look here: I have been to Rome and seen how these bishops live in what we poor Germans have been taught to think the holiest place on earth, and all the faith I ever had died there; for I thought if there was a God He must have given up His government of the world, or He would never have suffered such wickedness to go unpunished, or allowed such things as are done in His name. I tell you, Father, I would give anything to get back the faith I lost—that Rome has robbed me of; and now you ask me to give myself to the monstrous power that has ruined me, that I may help ruin others! Will you understand now how impossible it is I can ever enter the Church?" concluded Fritz.

Von Ranitz sighed. He began to fear that his dream of wealth and power for Fritz would fade away; but he could not relinquish it all at once. "Before you finally decide this question, Fritz, go and see my old friend Reuchlin. He had promised to tell you my wishes on this point, only von Hutten betrayed the secret beforehand."

"I will see the professor; but I must tell you that it will be quite useless. He cannot persuade me to enter the Church." And, to prevent any further discussion upon the matter, Fritz bade his father adieu for the present, and went in search of Eric, to tell him of this strange whim of his father, and consult him as to the expediency of

EXPEDIENCY: *advisability*

informing him of his wishes with regard to Anna Geroldsek.

Anna was distantly related to Eric, and her young kinsman had been delighted that the choice of his friend had fallen upon her; and now that he heard of the desire to force Fritz into the Church, he said instantly, "But you cannot do this; you are as good as betrothed to Anna."

"And I would not be a priest if I had never seen her. But what do you think about my telling my father of this just now!"

"You must tell him, for he must propose the matter to Count Geroldsek while we are in Switzerland," replied Eric.

"But suppose he should refuse?"

"O he would not do that! He will not forget that the Geroldseks are allied to the Schonsteins," said Eric, who was fully aware of the anxiety von Ranitz had felt to obtain an alliance with his family.

Meanwhile the elder gentleman was revolving in his own mind the very same subject as the younger ones were discussing; but, unfortunately, he arrived at quite an opposite conclusion. He was quite aware of the relationship existing between Eric and Anna; but as it was not very close, and Eric was so devoted to Margarethe, he thought it was very unlikely that the Schonstein family would make my difficulty about the slight that he intended to the girl who had been his daughter's companion all the winter. Fritz might be induced to enter the Church by and by, if he did not at once, if there was no barrier in the way; but if he was betrothed it would be putting it out of the range of possibility almost, and so von Ranitz was quite determined not to yield to any remonstrances from Fritz about this.

He was not greatly surprised that his friend Reuchlin's efforts in this direction were as great a failure as his own, and when he found that nothing further could be done just now, he proposed that they should leave Tübingen and get to the end of their journey as soon as possible.

No one was unwilling to leave, for the time had hung rather heavy on the hands of the two ladies, and Fritz was restless and impatient because he had not been able to speak to his father about Anna. It would have to be done now without further delay, and Fritz gave his sister a hint that as soon as they had left the town, and talking would be possible, he wanted to be left alone with his father.

Margarethe guessed truly for once as to the nature of the "particular business" that was to be discussed, and she whispered, "I have prayed for you both, Fritz; for you, and Anna too."

Her brother started. "Prayed for us?" he said, as though his ears must have deceived him.

"Yes, of course, I know all about this business. I daresay you thought it was a profound secret, but—"

"It is not that—I daresay you have found out my love for Anna; but you said you had prayed for us!"

REMONSTRANCES: *protests*

"Yes, I have. Dr. Luther has taught us that God is our Father, and that we may go and tell Him all our troubles without praying in the Latin words of the missal, or telling a priest what we want. I could not do that, you know, but I could tell God that you did not want to enter the Church, but to marry Anna instead."

"But, Margarethe, how could you, how dared you, pray to God like this?" said her brother, looking at her in open-eyed astonishment.

"It was the truth, you know, and Dr. Luther says that before all things we must be truthful when we pray to God."

"But He would never hear such prayers as yours. You must be daring, Margarethe! you ought to be a man, and go to fight the Turks."

"Why is it so daring to tell God just what you want? I don't want you to enter the Church."

"And so you dare to tell God that you don't want me to serve Him?"

"O no, Fritz; I do want you to serve God, but not the Church."

"And are they not identical? Has not God chosen to link himself to the Church, so that you cannot serve God without serving the Church?" asked Fritz.

But his sister shook her head. "I am sure it is a mistake to think as you do about God and the Church. Dr. Luther made it quite clear to my mind, although I cannot explain it to you, that men and women, and even little children, could serve God in their simple everyday lives, if they would only love Him. Love, he said, must be at the root of all true service; and if we had this love of God abiding in us we could not fail to serve Him, although we might not be able to go to confession, or church, or ever receive any of the blessed sacraments. So you see that although God is in the Church, pardoning what is wrong, and helping all His true servants there, still it is possible to serve Him without serving the Church; and this is the service. I do want you to pray; I want you to love Him, Fritz. Life is so much brighter—so much better—if this love of God is in our hearts."

Looking into his sister's earnest face, Fritz thought that there was little doubt but that she believed and knew what this love of God was, but all the reply he gave was, "How can I love God when I do not even believe in Him?"

Chapter XIII

Friends at Zurich

FRITZ found that his father was as immovable in his determination not to do anything to forward his marriage as he himself was not to enter the Church. Eric was greatly offended, and said that he should at once inform his father of what had occurred, for the honor of the whole family was involved in this matter; and when their roads at length diverged, and the two young men turned toward the Castle of Ebenborg, Eric bade von Ranitz farewell with great stiffness and politeness, but little cordiality.

The journey into Switzerland seemed very dull to the two ladies after the departure of Fritz and Eric, and if it had not been for the constant recurrence of new and strange scenes—new to Margarethe entirely, and new with yet a sweet homelikeness to Anna after her long absence in Germany—but for these diversions of travel they would have been quite depressed by the moody silence of von Ranitz. He was in no enviable position, and yet there were hundreds in the same position just then in Germany.

His father had seen many countries in the different wars in which he had been engaged, but, unlike most of his companions, he began to think less of war as he grew older, and to perceive that a new power was rising in the world; and he had bade his son ally himself to this might that was to conquer the world—the might of intellect—the might of mind over brute force—the might of literature, that was to set the world free from its bonds. Nothing loath, von Ranitz had obeyed the old man to the very letter. He had traveled and seen the principal cities of Europe. He had chosen for his friend Reuchlin, the champion of the new learning. He had been known as a Reuchlinist, although he had taken no active part in the proceedings of the party; but now he saw, to his dismay, that the power by which he hoped to mount to fame and fortune threatened to drag him from his high estate and place him on a level with the despised burghers—his vassals, whom he had looked upon as little better than his slaves.

It was too late now to stem the torrent of this mighty flood that threatened to sweep down all opposition against it. Like a drowning man, von Ranitz could but try to grasp at what seemed his only chance of escape from immediate ruin; and, like many another just now, turned to the Church

NOTHING LOATH: *willingly*

for succor. Nothing had ever been able to shake that. Out of all storms she had come safely with her powers more consolidated and her hold upon men more secure. The Church, and the Church only, could help them to obtain their former grandeur and glory, and so he had bidden his son seek refuge in the Church, and forget all he had been learning to her discredit.

That Fritz should be so blind as not to see that his only hope of wealth and position lay in his taking holy orders, or, seeing it, should not at once act upon it, was a puzzle von Ranitz could not understand, and so he resolved to take Ebenborg on his way home and talk to Fritz again. It would be easy for him to do this, for he had promised to see Lady Hadwig von Sickengen about sending an escort for Margarethe when she should travel from Zurich to see her friends in the Rhineland.

Zurich, nestling in its amphitheater of vine-clad hills, was at last reached, and our travelers were not sorry to reach the house where Anna's friends were now staying. Her father and brother had gone on pilgrimage to our Lady of Einsiedeln, and her mother and two sisters were on a visit to the young widow, Dame Meyer, with whom Anna Geroldsek would continue to reside. Dame Meyer had three children. Gerold, her eldest son, was an engaging and intelligent lad who never wearied of asking the ladies questions about their journey and the learned men of

SUCCOR: *assistance or relief*

Germany. Luther's fame had already reached Zurich, but the Swiss ladies had heard very strange tales about him.

"He may be very learned," said Dame Meyer, "but I do not think I should like him."

"But you would like Zwinglius, the wonderful preacher of Einsiedeln," said Anna warmly.

"Perhaps so. Luther is a German, and the Germans, I have heard, are not used to such independent ways of speaking and acting as we Swiss mountaineers, and so, for a man to say or do anything that is not exactly what other men say or do is thought a wonderful proof of courage and wisdom."

Margarethe felt a little hurt at these disparaging remarks about Luther. Of course, she thought him the most wonderful man who had ever lived, and had secretly believed that he would teach not only Germany, but all the world, the wonderful truth that had so long lain hidden; but it seemed that these proud Swiss were not willing to accept such a wise teacher as Luther because he was not of their own nation.

But, although they might disagree about the merits of Luther, Margarethe was not surprised that the Zurichers were proud of their beautiful city, with its lovely lake reflecting every cloud that sailed across the azure sky, and mirroring and repeating the beauty of the hills, gardens, and terraces that sloped down to its very brink. In the

DISPARAGING: *expressing a low opinion*
AZURE: *clear blue*

distance rose the snow-capped Alps, wearing their diadem of whiteness "in the very presence of the regal sun".[1] "I should never grow tired of Zurich," said Margarethe one day, as she stood on the shore of the lake gazing across at the mountains beyond.

"Then I hope you will stay with us a long time," said the widow, who was walking with her, and who had taken a great liking to Margarethe.

"Thank you, but I am afraid my father will not agree to this—not a long visit—for I have to visit my friends in the Rhineland, and I must reach home again before the winter."

"O no, we cannot spare you so soon; you must spend the winter in Zurich, and go to your friends in the spring," said Dame Meyer, and she would take no denial from Margarethe.

To her surprise, Margarethe found, when the plan was proposed to him, that her father was not so averse to her making a prolonged stay at Zurich as she had expected; and she felt both surprised and disappointed when she heard him say that he would tell von Sickengen that his escort would not be required until the spring.

"But—but you have forgotten Else. She will miss me so much, and I shall want to see her before next summer," said Margarethe, in a half whisper.

"We cannot be sure that Else is at home. It may be that she would not like to leave the convent," said her father.

[1] A line from the play, *William Tell*, by James Sheridan Knowles (1784-1862)

DIADEM: *crown*

Margarethe looked up into her father's face quickly—almost suspiciously. "Have you heard from Father Sebastian?" she asked.

"No. I expected that letters would have been sent before I left Zurich, but they have not come. You see we could not be quite sure that Else would come home, because she did not dislike the idea of going to the convent, as you did."

"But if she should have returned with Father Sebastian she will already have missed me, and felt lonely. I cannot bear that she should be in the forest all the winter with only Aunt Ermengarde for company."

"She will make herself very happy, and you must do the same with your friends here in Zurich. I will give you one word of caution. Do not talk too much about Dr. Luther and our winter in Wittenberg, Margarethe. Count von Hutten can begin to see trouble in the future through this new teaching, and so it is time we had done with it."

"But, Father, I cannot have done with it. I have learned from Dr. Luther that there is a religion suitable even for me," said Margarethe warmly.

"Then you had better stay out of Germany and forget all this Wittenberg monk has taught. I wish we had never gone to Wittenberg," he added.

Margarethe was puzzled. The more so because her father had seemed to be so favorably impressed with Luther's teaching only a short time before. What could it be? what could have happened to make her father so suddenly change his mind? He had not been used to alter his opinion when once it had been formed. Could Father Sebastian have had anything to do with this?

As she thought of Father Sebastian she suddenly recollected how often her father had been closeted with the priest after their return from Wittenberg. She had not thought much of this before, but supposed the business referred to Else, and her return home, and that her father had had some difficulty in persuading the family confessor to undertake the mission to Nimptschen. Now she began to fear that these conferences had a very different object in view, and she felt like a person who had been overreached in a bargain. Else would not be brought home again, she felt sure, and she had been got out of the way that there might be no fuss about it, or at least she had been hurried from home in haste and entrapped into staying in Switzerland for the winter, after which it would be next to impossible to obtain Else's return from the convent, for she would no longer be a novice, but a professed nun; and for her to abandon her vocation, after a public profession, would bring lasting disgrace on the family name.

Margarethe was in no enviable form of mind when she first thought of all this, the day after her father's departure from Zurich. She fretted and fumed, and would have gone after him had such a thing been possible, but, as it was not, she groaned

OVERREACHED: *cheated*

over her own stupidity in not having thought of it all before.

Anna saw that something was amiss with her friend, and after a little questioning Margarethe told her all her fears, adding, as she did so, “I cannot stay long at Zurich now.”

“But, my dear Margarethe, what could you do even if you went home at once? If, as you fear, Father Sebastian has obtained such a sudden hold upon your father’s mind, and is using every effort to prevent him from embracing Luther’s opinions, how could you prevent anything such a clever man as Father Sebastian had made up his mind to do?”

“Clever! he is not clever,” said Margarethe, impetuously. “I tell you, he is a selfish, ignorant old man.”

“But he manages to get round people somehow. You say your dear old aunt is half afraid of him, and your grandfather never cares to offend him; and although your father never seemed to care much for what he said or did, he managed to get your sister sent to the convent earlier than had been agreed upon, when you refused to go to confession and your brother talked so openly of his unbelief.”

“Yes,” admitted Margarethe, “my not going to confession seemed to be the beginning of my troubles—only it was the beginning of the end, I think; don’t you?” she added with a faint smile.

But Anna shook her head. "I am afraid the trouble is not all over yet," she said.

"You do not understand. You know it had often troubled me that I could not be religious; that I hated religion so much, and thought that God Himself hated me as deeply; but now that I find there is a religion in the world suitable even for me, I can never be in such fear and terror about this again."

"But, Margarethe, I heard your father talking to Dame Meyer before he went away; he was saying he was very glad that none of these disturbing influences that were turning the world upside down had found their way to Zurich, and he hoped you would soon forget all you had learned at Wittenberg."

"That is quite impossible. Forget it! I would die rather than forget or give up what I have learned from Luther. To my father the grand noble words might mean only 'disturbing influences,' but to me they were light and life, and have filled the whole world with Easter joy and resurrection hymns; for he has taught me that Christ is risen from the dead; that He is a living, loving Savior, my friend, given to me by God Himself, who loves instead of hates me. Anna, it is this that makes all the difference, to me at least, between the teaching of Luther and the teaching of the Church. Luther teaches that God loves us with the love of a father and mother, but the Church says that

God is a stern, hard judge, who will not relent but for the prayers of the Virgin and saints innumerable, however sorry His poor children may be for their sins."

"Yes, Luther preaches very plainly," admitted Anna, but she was by no means inclined to yield him the first place in her heart. "You see he is not the first man who has taught this—heresy, your father calls it now, for it seems that Father Sebastian spoke of the horrible disgrace of a whole knightly family being heretics."

"Yes, I knew it was Father Sebastian, for he hates Luther, as all ignorant men do hate one who exposes their ignorance and cunning."

"And your father says the Church will soon silence Luther, as it has silenced many others, and then all who have followed his teaching will be brought into trouble."

"This is my father's fear, then, and this is why he wishes me to unlearn all I learned at Wittenberg. This is why Fritz is to enter the Church, too, I suppose."

"Fritz never will do that," said Anna, with a heightened color.

"No, he will not, and if I must be called a heretic for believing Luther, I must bear it; but don't imagine that I shall give up what I hold so dear. But I was forgetting what I wanted to say about Else. Anna, I am so anxious she should leave the convent now, and learn this wonderful truth Dr.

Luther is teaching the world! But unless I return home before the winter it will be too late."

"But, Margarethe, what could you do if you went home? You were at home last autumn, but you could not prevent your sister being taken to the convent, much as you wished to do so, and what could you do now?"

Margarethe shook her head, and the next moment burst into tears. "O, Anna, cannot you help me? Cannot you think of something I might do? The time is getting so short now, and it is for her whole life—poor, dear, dear Else!"

"But, Margarethe, she may be at home. You know Father Sebastian went to Nimptschen before we left, to arrange for her to come home again."

But Margarethe shook her head. "I don't believe it one bit now. Father Sebastian may pretend that he went on that mission, but he will take care Else shall not come near me again, if he can prevent it."

"Then what good could you do if you went home tomorrow? *You* could not take your sister out of the convent."

"O, Anna, what shall I do? I love Else so much; and yet, much as I love her and want to help her, I cannot do a single thing."

"What did you tell Fritz to comfort him just before we parted," whispered Anna. "He told me what you said, and that he knew you believed it; or is it that you can believe in prayer for other people's troubles, but not your own?"

"I forgot that God could help Else even in the convent. I have prayed, and I do pray for her every day, and I am sure God loves her and will help her somehow; but, you see, I want to help Him—help her I suppose," she added.

"And that you cannot do just now; perhaps you may hinder rather than help if you go home too soon; so that it will be better to content yourself here and try to believe that God can do without your help."

Chapter XIV

New Scenes

WHETHER Margarethe was "content" to remain at Zurich or not mattered little; she had to stay; for a lady could not travel alone in those days, and there was no one going to Germany who could be her escort, although there was more communication now between the two countries than there had ever been before.

Luther's fame as a teacher and professor of the new learning had penetrated even to the Alpine villages beyond Zurich, and it frequently happened that a party of Swiss students, on their way to Wittenberg, would pass through or meet at Zurich. These, and the merchants who usually traveled together in large companies for safety, were the principal travelers; and with neither could Margarethe journey, unless she were provided with a suitable escort of her own. Her friends were sorry for her anxiety, and nothing could exceed their kindness and attention toward her; but the children of Dame Meyer were

Margarethe's greatest comfort, especially the oldest, Gerold, who went to a school in connection with the College of Canons attached to the Cathedral of Zurich.

Dame Meyer had many friends among the wealthy citizens of the place, for her husband had been greatly respected, and had filled the highest posts of honor in the government of the city. But it was not for her husband's sake alone that the widow was so greatly liked. Anna Meyer had, because of her gentle, unobtrusive goodness, long since been forgiven, even by her hard father-in-law, for marrying out of her class. Anna Reinhard, the inn-keeper's daughter, was forgotten in Anna Meyer, the unobtrusive, tender, and devoted mother; and, now that she was a widow, her house was a little center where the earliest news of events of every kind of importance were freely discussed.

A few weeks after Margarethe's arrival some merchants brought the news that an Italian monk had arrived in the canton of Schwitz with papal indulgences for all Christians of the Helvetian League.[1] Friar Samson, like his colleague in Germany, claimed the power to pardon all sin; but this power had already been challenged in Schwitz by a priest, one Ulrich Zwinglius.

At the mention of the name of Zwinglius both Anna and Margarethe took more interest in the news, and Margarethe asked eagerly,

"What does Zwinglius say to this traffic?"

[1] An association of the various cantons, or states, of Switzerland

"He is preaching most earnestly against it, while Friar Samson is no less explicit in declaring the power of these indulgences. 'Heaven and hell are subject to my power, and I sell the merits of Jesus Christ to whoever will purchase them by paying in cash for an indulgence.' One of the merchants heard him say these words, and told Zwinglius of them."

"And Zwinglius spoke no less strongly, I am sure," said Anna quickly.

"O yes, he says that Jesus Christ, the Son of God, has spoken thus: 'Come unto me, all ye that labor and are heavy laden, and I will give you rest;'[1] and is it not, then, audacious folly and insensate temerity to say, on the contrary, 'Purchase letters of indulgence; turn to Rome; give to the monks; sacrifice to the priests; if you do these things, I will absolve you from your sins?' Jesus Christ is the only offering; Jesus Christ is the only sacrifice; Jesus Christ is the only way. This was Zwinglius' answer to the merchants; and he is preaching the same doctrine to warn the people against wasting their money and deceiving their own souls."

"He has preached like this before," said Anna, "and Luther himself could not speak more plainly. Margarethe, I believe the Reformation is coming now, and for Switzerland, too, as well as Germany."

Margarethe smiled. "You can believe it because a Swiss priest preaches the gospel, but you were often doubtful about Luther," she said.

[1] Matthew 11:28

AUDACIOUS: *reckless*

INSENSATE TEMERITY: *foolish boldness*

"Of course you love Luther, because he is of your own nation."

"But I think I could have loved your Swiss preacher as well if he taught the truths that Luther did, the truth for which I have been hungering, I think, ever since I first heard that Else would have a vocation and be separated from me, which made me hate religion so much that I fancy I was always secretly groaning because there was no religion in the world likely to suit me."

Anna laughed. "You are a strange girl, Margarethe; I don't believe I half understand you yet, but I don't think you would be so willing to learn what anyone chose to teach you as you profess."

"I was willing to learn from Erasmus," said Margarethe.

"O yes, everybody is willing to learn from the clever little satirical professor, but nobody would ever think of loving him as you love Luther and I love Zwinglius," laughed Anna. "If we could only get him to come here, that you might hear him preach, as you heard Luther last winter at Wittenberg, I am sure you would love him, too."

"Perhaps I should," admitted Margarethe, "although there would never be anyone like Dr. Luther to me."

"Of course not; he is a German, and—"

"But, Anna, do you think if God is going to give the world a Reformation at last, He is going to send a reformer to every separate country?"

"I don't know, I am sure; I have not thought about it in that way at all," said Anna.

"Well, I thought you had from what you have said about Luther and Zwinglius."

"No, but I do think it would be better if it could be so. Of course, Dr. Luther cannot be expected to understand us Swiss. We have fought for and won our independence. Every canton is a little kingdom in itself, and every man feels he is free, free as our mountain breezes; for who could venture to assail us in our mountain homes? and our soldiers fight the battles of the world. Your quiet, plodding German life is different in many ways from ours."

"Yes, I suppose it is," admitted her friend.

"Then do you not see how much better a Swiss could understand the Switzer's thought and feeling about things? He would not be likely to make the mistakes a stranger would; he would understand the people, their ways and their doings, and they would not look upon him with distrust and suspicion if he were one of themselves."

"That is how you look at Luther," said Margarethe quickly.

Anna colored. "He does not seem such a wonderful man to me as to you German folk, but—but—"

"But he is not Swiss," laughed Margarethe. "Perhaps you are right, after all, Anna, and it may be we Germans are just a little ambitious in thinking our Dr. Luther is to be the reformer of the world."

ASSAIL: *attack*

"Well, God knows just what will be best for the world, and it is well that the matter will not be left for such feeble folk as you and I to settle."

"I don't know that wise people would settle it any better. They make dreadful mistakes sometimes; and it is strange that Zwinglius, who has never seen Luther, and could not have heard of him when you heard him preaching at Einsiedeln, should yet be teaching the same truth to Germany and Switzerland."

"Yes, it seems as though God Himself had taught them the hidden secret of His Word, and then given them courage to preach it," said Anna, in a meditative tone; "I am glad you think Zwinglius will be the reformer of Switzerland," she added.

"I wonder what he will do next, after preaching against this Friar Samson's indulgences?" said Margarethe.

"I should not wonder if he came to Zurich; they say he is a great friend of Dr. Myconius, who is at the head of the College of Canons; and so, as he is a learned man, and Dr. Myconius is anxious that Zurich should have schools and a college worth the name, he might ask him to come, if ever he had the opportunity."

"But the opportunity will have to come first," laughed Margarethe.

Dame Anna Meyer had gone to the cathedral service when this conversation took place, and when she came home a little later she looked rather excited.

"What has happened?" asked Anna; "you look quite frightened."

"My dear, you heard the cathedral preacher last Sunday, did you not?"

"Yes, and wished I might never have to listen to him again," said Anna.

"Well, my dear, you never will; for he died quite suddenly this afternoon."

"I did not wish the poor man might die, and I am very sorry; but I could not help wishing that if these canons belonging to the college are too lazy to do the work for which they are appointed, they would choose a man who could preach, and not such a prosy, dozy old fellow as he was."

"Well, you will not have to listen to him again, Anna; but I daresay his successor will be no better. Monks and priests do not expect to have to preach. If they know all the lives of the saints so that they can give the people a change of stories, it is quite enough."

"You would not think so if you had heard the preacher at Einsiedeln, I am sure. I wonder who will get this post of preacher now," and she glanced at Margarethe.

A few days later, and Anna came in from a walk with the children, looking as excited, and far more joyous than the widow had done when she came home from the cathedral.

PROSY: *dull*

"Who do you think is in Zurich?" she asked, bursting into the room where Margarethe and the widow sat at work.

Margarethe had been talking of her brother and her betrothed, and, her mind running still upon these, she said, "Fritz has come, after all!"

But a shadow flitted over Anna's face as she said, "No, it is not Fritz."

"Who can it be, then? Eric would not come without Fritz," said Margarethe in a lower tone, yet half hoping he had taken the daring step.

"I see you will never guess, so I will tell you. It is Master Ulrich Zwinglius. I know I am not mistaken. He is so tall and handsome I could not fail to recognize him."

The widow lifted her eyes from her work, and smiled at Anna's earnestness. "Suppose he has come," she said; "will it make any difference to us quiet womenfolk?"

"I want Margarethe to hear him; and I am sure if he were to be appointed as preacher to the cathedral there would be few empty seats, and fewer people asleep than there are now; for all Zurich would crowd to hear him," said Anna.

"But the canons who have the election in their hands may not like your Einsiedeln preacher," said the widow with an amused smile; and there was a spice of mischief in her tone, as she added, "They may think him something of a heretic, as he has preached against the Pope's indulgences."

But Anna shook her head triumphantly. "I heard my father say that Zwinglius wanted to resign the pension he received from the Pope, but the legate would not hear of it; and while he was at Einsiedeln he conferred on him the honor of being chaplain—acolyte to the Pope—so that he is sure to be preferred to greater honors still before long. O no, he is not a heretic," concluded Anna warmly.

"Very well; since you wish this wonderful preacher to come to Zurich, I must wish it, too, I suppose," said the widow. "I shall certainly go to the cathedral and hear him; but there the matter will end for me, for I am content to let things go on quietly, which they will not do if somebody is constantly finding fault with our old-fashioned ways. Not that it will make any difference to me; O no, I am too old to change my ways now."

Little did Zwinglius' future wife dream of the change the coming of this man to Zurich would make in her life and the lives of hundreds more besides her.

As the days and weeks went on, the ladies heard that Zwinglius had consented to be a candidate for the vacant post, but that others besides him were wishful of the honor, and the canons were by no means unanimous in their desire to gain Zwinglius. The widow grew a little impatient with Anna because she was so anxious for every item of news that could be gleaned touching the result of the coming election.

LEGATE: *an appointed representative of the Pope*
ACOLYTE: *attendant*

While this was pending a party of merchants from Nuremburg brought the news that Luther had been summoned to appear before the Pope's legate at Augsburg, to answer for his heretical teaching contained in the theses against indulgences, and that many of his friends were very anxious for his safety.

"But I heard that he had been summoned to appear at Rome," exclaimed Anna.

"Who told you?" asked Margarethe quickly; "it is strange that I never heard about this."

"Your father did not wish you to know. He told me soon after we commenced our journey, but he bade me keep it a secret as long as possible."

"Well, I think you ought to have told me before this time," said Margarethe in an injured tone.

"But you forget my promise to your father; and then it would only have caused you many weeks of useless anxiety. I wish you had not heard anything about it until it was all over," concluded Anna.

It certainly would have been better if Margarethe could have known either a little more or a little less of what was going on in Germany just now; for all that the merchants knew was that it had been arranged by the Pope's legate, who was a Dominican, and, therefore, one of Luther's most bitter enemies, that the reformer should not reach Augsburg until the emperor and electors had left the diet; by which means Luther would be left entirely to their mercy. The merchants had seen him

DIET: *an assembly of the princes of the Holy Roman Empire*

at Nuremburg, and described him as wearing a ragged old frock, dirty and travel-stained, when he reached the town; but they had heard afterward that a friend would lend him another to appear in before the legate, as he could not afford to buy one.

"The Pope has conferred no pension upon him, although he is the greatest man and wisest teacher in Germany," said Margarethe, rather bitterly.

"Perhaps the Pope thinks he can quiet Luther by harsh means; but as that would not do at all for a Swiss, he will try the plan of coaxing our Zwinglius. I know that is what my father thinks," added Anna.

Anna's anxiety to know whether Zwinglius would be appointed cathedral preacher for Zurich was set at rest at last. The election was declared to be in his favor, and he might be expected to preach his first sermon about Christmas time.

The chapter of the cathedral received their new preacher with all honor; but the charge they gave him must have troubled him not a little at first: "You will use your utmost endeavor to secure payment of the revenues of the chapter. You will exhort the faithful to pay the first-fruits and tithes. In regard to preaching, you may supply your place by a vicar."

Whatever Zwinglius may have thought, he was careful what he said, and, without explaining his views about these money matters, went on to say,

CHAPTER: *assembly of the canons or priests*
SUPPLY YOUR PLACE: *fill your position*
VICAR: *substitute*

"The life of Jesus has been too long hidden from the people. I will preach on the whole Gospel of St. Matthew, chapter by chapter, following the mind of the Holy Spirit, drawing only at the well-springs of Scripture, digging deep into it, and seeking the understanding of it by persevering prayer. I will consecrate my ministry to the glory of God, the praise of His only Son, the real salvation of souls, and their instruction in the true faith."

But this plan was not at all approved by the majority of the electors. No one had ever heard of such a plan of preaching as this, and many began to regret the choice they had made before he had ascended the pulpit steps. There were many worldly-wise people in Zurich, and not a few devout souls as well, who deprecated any novelty in Churchly affairs, and distrusted the "reformation" which was so generally talked of and expected.

Chapter XV

Ulrich Zwinglius

"MY dear, this new preacher from Einsiedeln will never do for Zurich," said the widow when she came in from visiting a friend, a day or two after the meeting of the chapter to welcome Zwinglius.

"Why not?" asked Anna rather anxiously; for she was looking forward to New Year's day, when his first sermon would be preached.

"Why, my child, Zurich is the chief city in Switzerland, the head of the Confederation, and here the wisest and noblest citizens from all the cantons frequently assemble, and, therefore, we cannot afford to have a mere hair-brained innovator as our cathedral preacher."

"He is not a hair-brained innovator," said Anna, rather indignantly.

"My dear, I have just left Canon Hoffman, who was one that voted for him, and persuaded others to do the same, and he has told me what passed at the chapter. Zwinglius proposes to teach nothing but Scripture, and when the canon told him that this was an innovation that would prove more hurtful than useful to the people, he said it was not a new method at all, but that St. Chrysostom[1] and St. Augustine[2] had taught the people in the same manner."

"Well, it will be a change, at any rate, from the legends of the saints drawn out by an ignorant monk, who cannot read, and learns to recite them by heart, and I do not see why we should fear the change for Zurich any more than for any other place," said Anna.

"Only that so many strangers come to Zurich from the other cantons, that all Switzerland will hear of this new way of preaching."

Although the widow thus detailed the grievances of some of her friends, she was by no means disposed to miss an opportunity of hearing the handsome priest, and hundreds of others in Zurich were of the same mind. Several, too, who had given up all attendance at public worship—clever, distinguished citizens, of whom Zurich was justly proud—were curious to hear this new preacher. There was little need for the bystanders to ask what these—the most profound thinkers among them—thought of the strange teacher who had opened the Gospel at the first chapter of Matthew, and, taking it verse by verse, expounded it as he went on.

"We never heard anything like this," whispered one to another, as they began to leave the cathedral.

[1] John Chrysostom, Bishop of Constantinople in the 5th century A.D.

[2] Bishop of Hippo in the 5th century A.D.

"Glory to God! this is a preacher of the truth. He will be our Moses to deliver us from Egyptian darkness," exclaimed another.

But it was not the wise and the learned only that thus rejoiced at the coming of Zwinglius. His preaching touched the hearts of all classes, and the simple and ignorant were as eager to hear him as the great men among the citizens. He extolled the infinite mercies of God the Father, and implored all his hearers to put their confidence in Jesus Christ alone, as the only Savior.

Of course Margarethe could not fail to drink in, with eager joy, such teaching as this, so like to Luther's that, as she remarked to Anna, God's Spirit must have been the teacher of both, since neither had heard the other, and little was known here concerning the actual truths taught by Luther.

The widow, too, quite altered her opinion about the effect this preaching would have on the society of Zurich; and when, after a time, the great preacher began to notice her little boy, she was ready to acknowledge, with Anna, that he was the greatest and wisest man in Switzerland.

But although Margarethe could rejoice with her friends at the coming of this learned man among them, her heart was full of anxiety concerning her sister and friends, and especially the fate of Luther. Anna told her that if any evil had befallen him at Augsburg they must have heard of it; but Margarethe could derive but little comfort from

EXPOUNDED IT: *explained it in detail*
EXTOLLED: *praised*

this. News traveled so slowly in those days, especially in the winter time, when traveling was dangerous and the roads almost impassable, that, as she sometimes said, he might have shared the fate of Huss, or been thrown into some monastery dungeon to linger out the rest of his days, and Switzerland not hear the news until months afterward.

This painful suspense was ended at last. Some merchants arrived in the city, one of whom had seen Luther at Augsburg in the previous October; and Margarethe met him at the house of a friend, who knew how anxious she was to hear all about what had happened at Augsburg.

"Men might well be anxious who knew the monk of Wittenberg, and his honest, fearless character, and how little precaution he would be likely to take for his own safety," said the merchant, who loved Luther almost as deeply as Margarethe, and never wearied of talking about him.

"I traveled with him from Nuremburg to Augsburg. His friend, Link, and another monk also went with him, for Link knew more of those knavish Italians who were to hear Luther than he did, and went to take due precaution for his safety."

"But my father said the emperor would always take care that no harm happened to Luther."

"The emperor had left the diet, and all the electors too, but someone had foreseen the difficulty in which Luther might be placed, and provided for it. On arriving at the Augustinian Convent some friends came to see him, and one of the first questions they asked was, 'Have you a safe-conduct?'

"'No,' answered Luther, 'I have traveled hither in safety, and do not need one.'

"'Indeed! but you must not appear before the Pope's legate until you have obtained one. The Elector of Saxony left express orders with us that you should not trust yourself in the hands of these Italians until you have a safe-conduct from the emperor.'

"Soon after this an Italian came to pay Luther a visit before he should appear before the cardinal-legate. 'I come to give you sage and good advice. Submit yourself to the cardinal; reattach yourself to the Church, and retract all your injurious expressions,' he said.

"But Luther said he had come to defend himself, not to retract.

"'No, no; beware of doing this. What! would you dispute with the legate of his holiness? No, no; retract your doctrines and the theses, and submit to the legate in all things,' advised his visitor.

"But Luther could not promise to do this, or even to attend him, until a safe-conduct should arrive from the emperor.

"'Do not ask for a safe-conduct, it will quite spoil everything,' said the visitor.

"And no doubt he spoke truly, so far as he was concerned," remarked the merchant. "For it was well known that the legate did not intend to let

SAFE-CONDUCT: *a document promising safety and protection*
EXPRESS: *clearly stated*
HIS HOLINESS: *the Pope*

Luther quit Augsburg as he entered it. But Luther protested that he could not offend the elector, who had recommended him to those friends, and who had already sent a messenger after the emperor to obtain the safe-conduct."

"And do you really think the cardinal would have been harsh with him," asked another friend, who, knowing the honors that had been given to Zwinglius, could hardly think that two such different methods would be adopted when the men preached doctrines so similar.

"Harsh!" exclaimed the merchant. "If this Dominican cardinal could have his way, the world would never hear of Luther again."

"Did the emperor send the safe-conduct?" asked Margarethe, who was anxious to hear how the affair had ended.

"Yes, and Luther was told by the legate's messenger how to conduct himself in the presence of this representative of 'the servant of servants,' as the Pope calls himself. 'When you enter the hall where the legate is sitting,' said the messenger, 'you will prostrate yourself before him with your face to the ground; when he tells you to rise, you will get up on your knees, not stand erect, but wait till he bids you. Recollect that it is before a prince of the Church you are to appear.'"

"Dr. Luther must have been somewhat surprised to receive such instructions as these," remarked Margarethe.

PROSTRATE YOURSELF: *lie flat on the ground*

"All this," said the merchant, "was, doubtless, intended to frighten Luther into compliance with the legate's demands, and they so far succeeded that he put little trust in the emperor's safe-conduct as against these Italians. 'Let Jehovah decide,' he said to one of his friends; 'if He requires me to give back my life I am ready to give it joyfully.' The legate had assembled a large number of Italian and German theologians, and he expected to gain an easy victory over Luther. After the preliminary formalities had taken place, the legate said:

"'Here are three articles which, by the order of our most holy father, Leo the Tenth, I have to lay before you: First, you must retrace your steps, acknowledge your faults, and retract your errors, propositions, and discourses; secondly, you must promise to abstain in future from circulating your opinions; and, thirdly, you must engage to be more moderate, and to avoid everything that might grieve or upset the Church.'

"Luther then asked in what particular doctrine he had erred.

"'My dear son,' said the legate, 'here are two propositions which you have advanced, and which you must, first of all, retract: First, that the treasury of indulgences does not consist of the merits and sufferings of our Lord Jesus Christ; second, the man who receives the holy sacrament must have faith in the grace which is offered to him.'

"After a good deal of argument, which the cardinal thought could not fail to convince Luther of his error, Luther replied, 'On the article of faith, were I to yield a whit I should be denying Jesus Christ; with regard to that, then, I am neither able nor willing to yield, and by the grace of God I never shall.'

"'Whether you will or not, you must this very day retract that article; otherwise for that article alone I will reject and condemn all your doctrines,' said the legate.

"'I have no will apart from the Lord,' replied Luther; 'He will do with me what pleases Him. But had I five heads I would lose them all sooner than retract the testimony which I have borne to holy Christian faith.'

"The legate was very angry, and the discussion went on for three or four days, both verbally and in writing, Luther quoting the Scriptures as warrant for his doctrines, and the legate referring to the constitution of the Popes. At last he lost all patience: 'Retract, retract! or if you don't I send you to Rome; I excommunicate you, you and all your partisans; all who are, or may become, favorable to you, I reject them from the Church. Think you your protestors can stop me? Do you imagine that the Pope cares for Germany? The little finger of the Pope is stronger than all the German princes.'"

The merchant related his story with the greatest animation, evidently glorying in the firmness of Luther; but there was one word, one threat, that

A WHIT: *one bit*
WARRANT: *authorization*
EXCOMMUNICATE YOU: *banish you from the Church*

caused the hearts of two or three who heard almost to stand still with horror. He would excommunicate Luther! Who could brave such an awful threat as that? Even Margarethe turned pale with affright, and whispered to Anna, "Do you think they would pronounce such a cruel sentence against a good man?"

Anna was thinking of their own new preacher, Zwinglius, and whether the terrible blighting curse might not be pronounced against him next, if Luther were condemned; and she shivered, and drew nearer to Margarethe, as she replied, "We must pray for them both, my Margarethe."

"Was the curse of the Church pronounced against Luther?" someone ventured to ask aloud.

"No; Dr. Martin was almost driven from the presence of the legate at last, and told not to venture near him again unless he would retract; and he went back to the convent where he had been staying, and waited three or four days, thinking the legate would summon him again. At last his friends grew anxious for his safety, and urged him to leave Augsburg while he could."

"But I thought you said he had the emperor's safe-conduct, insuring his safety, before he saw the cardinal legate," remarked one.

The merchant shrugged his shoulders. "Did you never hear of John Huss and the safe-conduct he had from the emperor. It did not prevent them from burning him at Constance."

PARTISANS: *supporters*

"But the Emperor Maximilian would not surely violate his oath to please the Pope," exclaimed one.

"Not to please him, unless there was something to be gained by it," rejoined the merchant; "but just now our emperor is exceedingly anxious to gain a crown for his grandson, and the Pope could help or hinder his plans very materially; and so what would the condemnation of a single monk be in comparison with the prize to be gained, a crown?"

"But the emperor would not break his word like that," exclaimed Margarethe.

"The friends of Luther thought it would be wiser not to put him to the test, knowing what they did of the emperor's wishes, and having good reason to suspect that the cardinal was making overtures to him with this in view. So at the end of four days Luther wrote a letter to be sent to the legate after his departure, and then before daybreak he, with a trusty guide, stole out of the city, and made their way with all speed to Nuremburg."

Margarethe heaved a sigh of relief. "He was not excommunicated after all, then!" she exclaimed.

"No, he has escaped for the present, and Rome has decidedly got the worst of the encounter; but I greatly fear they will not let him slip through their fingers so easily next time."

Two or three of the little company looked very serious. They were all friends of the new cathedral preacher, and knew that he had spoken as strongly against the traffic in indulgences as Luther had.

OVERTURES: *proposals*

Might they not be visited with a similar trouble when the news of their minister's doctrines should reach Rome?

"They have reached Rome," said one. "They are as well known there as here, but the Pope will think twice before he enters on a quarrel with the Swiss."

"But he is the head of the Church," said two or three together.

"He is, but in all such proceedings as these against Luther he must have the help of the secular arm—the emperor or the elector of the State; but here we have neither emperor nor electors, but are a free, self-governing people; and if any of the cantons like to throw off their allegiance to the Pope they can do so."

Anna glanced proudly at her German friend as this was said, for Margarethe had been apt to boast of the protection the emperor and elector could afford Luther in case of a quarrel with the Pope. Now that the quarrel had taken place, it was seen of how little use this boasted protection was.

"Here in Switzerland, if the people through their councilors choose to hear a new doctrine, the Pope dare not, or at least will not venture, to forbid it. The only power he could bring against us is an army, and when you remember that nearly all his army are hired Swiss from our own cantons, the danger from this is not very great."

"Then you really can do what you like in the matter of religion!" said Margarethe, with a spice of envy in her tone.

APT: *quick*

“We are more free to choose than you in Germany. The only danger I can foresee is, that one canton might choose to stay with the Pope and another to break with him, and then to punish those who had broken their allegiance, or to bring them back to it, he might set the cantons quarreling among themselves.”

“Bring about a civil war! O that would be dreadful! In that case you would be worse off than Germany,” said Margarethe.

But Anna shook her head. “We should still be free,” she said. “We should fight till we died, but we would never take our religion as another chose to dictate, whether he was emperor, elector, pope, or a confederation. No, no, we are free,” she added triumphantly.

Chapter XVI

A Mystery Play

THE spring of 1519 still saw Margarethe at Zurich, but she was daily expecting the escort from her friends in the Rhineland, and doubtless Fritz and Eric would come to conduct her in safety to the castle of Ebenborg, the home of the von Sickengens.

It had been a great relief to Margarethe's mind to know that Luther was safe back in Wittenberg; but it seemed as though the tidings of what had happened at Augsburg had alarmed a good many of the old-fashioned people of Zurich. They did not like the idea of a Reformation at all; or, at least, Switzerland did not need anything of the kind. For Germany it was all very well; they argued that the peasants there were little better than slaves. But Switzerland was free; her peasants were no slaves; the citizens here were not at the mercy of knight, elector, or emperor. They chose their own councilors, and were governed by the Great Council of two hundred, whom they thus elected. What more could they want? What need was there for agitation or for reform?

This was the argument of the priests in the city, as well as of some of the leading citizens; and even the canons who had elected Zwinglius to his post took the part of the monks, who were the most clamorous of all against the new teacher of Zurich.

But Zwinglius was quite unmoved by the clamor. "Whoso would gain the wicked to Jesus Christ must wink at many things," he said, and he kept on his even way, making friends among both rich and poor; for Zwinglius, unlike most of his fellow priests, was not only a true Christian, but a true republican. The equality of mankind was with him not merely a profession, but a living, active belief, and when walking in the streets, or the public squares, he would stop and speak to one and another whom he met, inquiring kindly after their affairs, and saying a word in season for the Master whom he loved. If he saw a party of peasants from the country staring about them as if they knew not what to do, he would at once become their guide, and show them all the sights worth seeing. This was his recreation between the hours of study. Of course, these country folks would not fail to go and hear their guide preach in the cathedral, when they heard who he was, nor were they likely to forget what they heard there, many of them for the first time in their lives.

CLAMOROUS: *persistent in their outcry*

Zwinglius never let an opportunity slip of warning his hearers against the traffic in indulgences; for soon after his arrival in Zurich he heard that the monk Samson, who had come from Rome the year before, had resolved to make that city his headquarters for a time, in his progress through Switzerland, selling these papal indulgences. But before Friar Samson, the indulgence-monger, could reach Zurich, Dean Bullinger, from Bremgarten, arrived in the city, to appeal to the diet of two hundred against the sale of these indulgences in his parish. The dean had forbidden their sale before Friar Samson had arrived; but the insolent monk had defied and excommunicated him, and then threatened to appeal to the Council sitting at Zurich, in the name of his master, Pope Leo the Tenth. Bullinger did not wait for the monk to appeal, but set off at once to lay his complaint before the Council, which Zwinglius' preaching had already prepared to look with suspicion on this vile traffic. Only a day or two before many of them had heard the new preacher say with such a depth of earnestness that the words could not fail to impress them: "No man is able to forgive sins. Christ alone, very God and very man, is able to do it. Go buy indulgences; but rest assured you are not at all forgiven. Those who vend forgiveness of sin for money are the companions of Simon Magus,[1] the friends of Balaam,[2] and the ambassadors of Satan."

[1] Acts 8:9-24 [2] Numbers 22:1-24:25

VEND: *sell*

The envoys from the Bishop of Constance, whom Friar Samson had likewise offended, also arrived to lay complaint against him; and as the Helvetic Council would have neither bishops nor cardinals among them, this complaint against the messenger of the Pope was duly weighed and considered; and when it was known that Friar Samson had reached the neighborhood a messenger was sent to him forbidding his further progress. But the Italian monk would not be kept out of this, the richest city in Switzerland, and so he said he had a message to deliver to the Diet from His Holiness. On hearing this the Council resolved to hear what this message was, and so, with all the stateliness of a great prince, he entered Zurich, to tell the Council that he was entrusted with the Pope's bull authorizing the sale of indulgences.

Knowing what had happened in Germany—that the Diet there could not prevent Tetzel from carrying on this trade, and that money in car-loads was still being sent to Rome—Samson doubtless thought he should soon make good his boast, that he would stop Zwinglius' mouth. But he had altogether overlooked the fact that these Swiss would admit no one who was pledged to support the Pope, who owed any allegiance to Rome, to sit in their council of state; and so, instead of meeting friendly bishops and archbishops, who dared not do other than their master at Rome bid them in his bulls entrusted to this monk, he met only

BULL: *official letter*
CAR-LOADS: *wagon-loads*
BURGOMASTERS: *chief magistrates*

sturdy burgomasters and legislators, who were learning something of gospel freedom from the lips of the hated Zwinglius.

All his Italian art could not disguise the fact that he had nothing more to say than to exhibit the bull of the Pope, authorizing the traffic he was engaged in, and this the Diet would not deign to look at. Before they allowed him to depart they compelled him to retract the excommunication he had pronounced against Dean Bullinger, and then dismissed him in no amiable mood, forbidding him to enter Zurich again.

The defeated monk was in a terrible rage, and did not fail to let Pope Leo know how he had been treated by this brave Helvetic Diet. But the Pope knew he was powerless to alter this. What could he do with a Council that would not admit a cardinal or archbishop? Leo the Tenth was too astute a politician to begin a war where the chances would be so greatly against him. Switzerland could not be dealt with like Germany. He and the German Emperor might engage in a political game of chess, with Europe for the chess-board, and Luther and the Reformation as pawns or castles, as the case might be; but how was this to be done with a council of two hundred sturdy, independent, straightforward Swiss? The thing was quite impracticable. He must use gentle measures; they would brook no threats, and if they would have a reformation they must, only he would take care not to drive

DEIGN: *condescend*
IMPRACTICABLE: *impossible to accomplish*
BROOK: *stand for, tolerate*

them into it by any unwise measures, for fear the whole country would throw off their allegiance to him. So, instead of a bull of excommunication being issued against the brave Council of Zurich, Friar Samson was ordered to return home with what money he had, and not to sell any more indulgences in Switzerland.

It was no small triumph to Zwinglius and his friends when the enraged and crestfallen monk was sent packing out of Zurich without adding a crown to the treasure he had collected; but he was careful not to exhibit this, for he was anxious to conciliate those who were against him, and, like the Pope, he knew he must proceed warily.

Shortly after Friar Samson's departure a peddler came to Zurich, inquiring for Zwinglius. He had a small pack of books slung on his back, and when admitted to the presence of Zwinglius he said he had been sent by a learned man of Basle, one Master Rhenau, who desired him to look over his pack and tell him whether it would be well for him to journey through Switzerland and sell the books in the towns and villages. On looking over his stock he found that most of the books were copies of Luther's "Exposition of the Lord's Prayer for the Laity." He had nothing but the writings of Luther; and on reading the letter he had brought from Rhenau, he found that Rhenau wished him to test the ability and sincerity of this peddler, for he thought the work of spreading the knowledge

CONCILIATE: *gain the favor of*
LAITY: *common people*

of divine truth was too important to be entrusted to an imprudent man.

Zwinglius was delighted with these writings of Luther. "Luther preaches Christ, and he does what I do. Those who have been brought to Christ by him are more numerous than those who have been brought by me. But no matter. I am unwilling to bear any other name than that of Christ, whose soldier I am, and who alone is my head. Never was a single scrap written by me to Luther, or by Luther to me. And why? In order to show to all how well the Spirit of God accords with Himself, since, without having heard each other, we so harmoniously teach the Gospel of the Lord Jesus Christ. We explain the holy book by the help of the Holy Spirit."

There was no jealousy in Zwinglius' mind lest his countrymen should receive the knowledge of salvation from a stranger, and perhaps call themselves Lutheran by and by. Having ascertained that the man was eminently fitted for the perilous task in which he was engaged—for it was more perilous than ever, just now, that Friar Samson had been defeated—he concluded that God had sent this humble messenger to follow in the steps of the proud monk and undo his work. In striving to do this, however, all who had favored and welcomed the Pope's messenger so recently would be the more likely to persecute this poor peddler if he fell into their hands. Before he packed up his books

IMPRUDENT: *foolish, rash*
EMINENTLY: *supremely*

again Zwinglius bought some; for he suddenly remembered the German lady who had told his little friend, Gerold Meyer, so much about Luther and Wittenberg, which the child had repeated to him. So when Gerold went home from school the next day Zwinglius went with him.

Little Gerold was, of course, delighted to take home such an illustrious visitor, and, bounding into the house when he reached the door, he ran to tell his mother who had come to see them. Dame Meyer was not at all disconcerted; for her husband had been one of the deputies to the Great Council, and so she had often received and entertained noble and distinguished guests; but she thought it nonetheless kind that Zwinglius should visit her now. She was also glad of this opportunity to thank him for the interest he had shown in her little son's studies; and so Gerold became the center of interest to them both, and Margarethe and her books were almost forgotten until Zwinglius was about to take his departure.

After he had gone Anna said to her friend, "What a pity it is that Master Zwinglius is a priest, or that priests cannot marry!"

"Why?" asked Margarethe sharply.

"Because—because—but you will not tell dear Anna Meyer what I am going to say. You will laugh, I know, when I tell you what I have been thinking about; but she would feel greatly hurt did she hear me."

DISCONCERTED: *unsettled*

"Of course, it is something quite impossible," laughed Margarethe.

"Yes, quite impossible," repeated Anna; "and yet I could not help wishing it."

"Well, what was it? Let me hear!"

"What a pity it is Master Zwinglius cannot be little Gerold's father!"

"But he said he would watch over him as though he were his own son," said Margarethe.

"Yes, it was that that put it into my head, I suppose, for all at once the thought came—'If you could only be his father in reality;' for Dame Anna looked as beautiful as ever tonight, and Master Zwinglius is so handsome and graceful. Then they seem just as well suited in other things, and I could not help thinking it was a pity priests could not marry; and there might be such a bright, happy home in Zurich."

If Anna Geroldsek could have seen across the vista of a few years she might have had a peep into this, her now imaginary home; might have seen the handsome priest, Ulrich Zwinglius, reading the proof-sheets of his Swiss translation of the Scriptures, and Dame Anna, with another baby on her lap, listening with rapt attention, her beautiful face lifted to watch the earnest reader; and she would have heard from friends and neighbors that he had dared to do what no priest had done before for ages—take to himself a lawful wife.

As the two young ladies talked of this now it seemed not only impossible of fulfillment, but the bare idea of it seemed little short of blasphemy. The two friends agreed never to mention it again, even to each other; and there was little temptation to do this now, for Zurich and Berne were going to celebrate the carnival this year with a mystery play that was exciting the eager curiosity of all the citizens. It was to be called "The Eaters of the Dead," and little boys were to be the actors; but their speeches, which were all mere satires of the greed and luxury of the Pope and clergy, were written by a clever poet of Berne, who had been roused to make this attack upon the Church through the shameless traffic in indulgences carried on in the neighborhood of Berne.

The Lent of the clergy began a week earlier than that of common people, and so on the Shrove Tuesday of the lords, as this carnival day was called, all Zurich turned into the street to see this much-talked-of mystery play; and not a little proud were the boys who had been chosen as actors. Let us glance at them:

One is dressed in gorgeous robes and seated on a showy throne, to represent the Pope, and around him are bodyguards, courtiers, cardinals, bishops, and priests of every degree; behind these stand a crowd of nobles, citizens, peasants, and beggars. Then comes the funeral train of a rich farmer, and the bier is set down in front of the Pope, while one

SHROVE TUESDAY: *the day before the start of Lent*
BIER: *stand built to hold the coffin*
SACRISTAN: *a church official responsible for sacred articles*

of his relatives humbly begs his mock holiness to set his soul free from purgatory, and they will gladly pay a hundred crowns. At the mention of the hundred crowns a sacristan instantly rushes to a curate to secure his share of the booty, the curate then claims his portion, and the bishop at once follows, the cardinals and Pope bringing up the rear. Of course, everyone utters a speech that lays bare the fearful abuses of the Church in words of cutting sarcasm. At last the Pope rises—

"The people now at length believe
That priests can all their sins reprieve
At pleasure—that to them is given
Full power to shut or open heaven.
Preach loudly every high decree
Of him the conclave's majesty;
Then we are kings—the laity slaves.
But if the gospel standard waves
We're lost; for nowhere does it say,
Make sacrifice; let priests have pay.
The gospel course for us would be
To live and die in poverty.
Instead of steeds to mark my state,
And chariots on my sons to wait,
A paltry ass must needs supply
A seat for sacred majesty.
No, I cannot take such legacy;
I'll thunder at such temerity;
Let us but will—the world will nod,

REPRIEVE: *offer relief*
CONCLAVE: *an assembly of Church officials*
PALTRY ASS: *insignificant donkey*

And nations worship us as God;
Slighting their rights, I mount my throne
And partition the world among my own.
Vile laity must keep far aloof,
Nor dare to enter our blest roof,
To touch our tribute or our gold,
Holy water ne'er let them hold."

Some who would not go to the cathedral to hear Zwinglius preach would turn into the streets to see this mystery play acted, and no one could say but that the representation of the vices and greed of the clergy was true. Some who were the sincerest friends of the Gospel shook their heads at the mummery; but others said it would shake the faith of the careless and ignorant in the superstitions they had hitherto trusted in; and, as Margarethe whispered on their way home, if only a few were brought to question the power of indulgences, the boys' fun would not have been in vain.

MUMMERY: *performance*

Chapter XVII

The Journey

WHEN Margarethe reached home, after witnessing the mystery play from the window of a friend's house, she heard from the servants that a stranger had been inquiring for her; and on hearing their description of him she felt sure it was her brother, Fritz.

"Were there not two friends?" asked Margarethe; for she had certainly expected that Eric would come, too.

But the girl had only seen one—a grave looking young knight.

"Grave looking?" repeated Margarethe. "Then it cannot be Fritz;" and she fell to wondering who the stranger could be, and what had happened, that her brother and Eric von Schonstein had not come.

Of course, she gave herself a great deal of needless anxiety—as we all do at times—for an hour later Fritz presented himself again at Madame Meyer's door, and laughed heartily at Margarethe for distressing herself without any cause.

"It is not worthwhile to do that; it is only a waste of strength that may be needed to bear real troubles," he said, with a sudden gravity; and, looking at him again, Margarethe saw that her brother had changed during their separation; that he did look grave, as the servants had said—grave, and anxious too, she thought, as the evening went on and she had the opportunity of watching him more closely, while he was talking to their host and Anna. Eric had not come with him. She had managed to find this out, but there had been no opportunity of a word in private yet. Fritz had come to fetch her to pay her promised visit to Lady Hadwig von Sickengen, and there would be plenty of time for private confidences as they rode along the lonely roads or through the forests.

A party of merchants and pilgrims were going to join them on their way back for the security their armed escort would afford; and, of course, this obligation was mutual, for the larger the party the less danger was there of their being assailed by robbers. There was one drawback to this arrangement, and that was the slow rate of progress they were likely to make each day; but this Fritz did not care so much for now, as Margarethe would be with him.

Knowing this, his sister very generously repressed her anxiety to hear all that had happened while she had been at Zurich, that Fritz and Anna might have an opportunity of talking to each

GRAVITY: *seriousness*

other, while she went to bid her friends in the city farewell, among them Master Zwinglius, for the young lady had made herself very popular with Dame Meyer's circle of friends.

Fritz could only stay a few days, but during these he and Anna went up the slopes of the vine-clad hills, or wandered along the shores of the beautiful lake, talking of the future—the dim, uncertain future—doubly uncertain now, in the present state of Germany.

Margarethe was not sorry when her round of visits came to an end, and they were at last fairly on their journey, for her mind was full of a vague uneasiness concerning Eric. Fritz had seemed so unwilling to answer any of her questions about him that she felt sure all was not as it should be. So on the first opportunity that presented itself for a quiet chat she drew her easy-going palfrey to the side of her brother's more spirited steed, and said, "Now, Fritz, make your horse keep pace with mine, for I want you to tell me all about everything."

Fritz shrugged his shoulders, and gave his sister a comical look, as he said, "A regular catechism, of course—you've been compiling it ever since I came."

"I have been very good, then, not to let you have it as I compiled it," laughed Margarethe.

"Very good," replied her brother. "Now begin, my lady sister. Of course, you want to know how our emperor is."

CATECHISM: *series of questions*

"O no, no; not the emperor. What care I for him? I believe Germany would be better off without one," said Margarethe impatiently.

"Treason, treason!" exclaimed Fritz, laughing; but the next minute he added more seriously, "You must be careful what you say, Margarethe; we are not among the trees and rocks of the Thuringian forest; and even these are beginning to have eyes and ears now."

"Well, I don't care what happens to the emperor; but tell me first about Else. When did you last receive letters from our father?"

"I have not received any for some time. The winter, you see—"

"But you had letters before the winter—after my father went home," interrupted Margarethe. "I feel sure you were somehow connected with Father Sebastian's journey to Nimptschen more than was dear Else. Did she come back with him?"

Fritz shook his head. "I do not know. Her name was not mentioned in the letter."

"Then she did not come—Father Sebastian never tried to bring her back!" said Margarethe quickly, and the next minute she burst into tears.

"Hush, hush, Margarethe; the people behind will think we are quarreling; and, besides, we cannot be sure that Else is not at home, because my father forgot to mention it in his letter."

But Margarethe shook her head. "I know she is not. O, Fritz, what shall we do? I cannot bear to think of her being shut up in that dreadful convent all her life, and yet she will be—she must be! for she will have taken the vows by this time, and no one can help her."

"Don't think it so hopeless all at once, Margarethe; for it may be, while you are grieving, Else is sitting with Aunt Ermengarde, talking about us; and even if it should be as you fear no one can tell what may happen in a year or two—whether the convents may not be thrown open, and the monks and nuns turned out into the world, to work like honest men and women."

Margarethe looked at her brother as if doubting whether she could have heard aright. "What do you mean, Fritz?" she asked.

"Just what I said, my lady sister. The world is changing so fast, and men are beginning to see that it is more of a workshop and less of a stage for a few to idle their time away on, while the rest are ground down to do the work of the whole. No, no, Margarethe, the world is waking up to learn some strange things; and, among the rest, that there is work for everyone to do—not only the peasants and burghers—but the knights and nobles, and monks and nuns."

"But what could knights and nobles and monks and nuns, do?" asked Margarethe, when she could recover from her astonishment.

But Fritz shook his head. "The world will provide work for all in the days that are coming; for the peasants are no longer content to spend their lives for the benefit of their lords without receiving anything for their toil beyond that which will enable them to continue it. They are beginning to feel they have rights to be respected, as well as the burghers—souls that are somehow their own, and not the joint property of the priests and nobles. They, too, are inquiring what this cry for knowledge means, which they hear on every side. Dr. Luther was only a miner's son, they say, and, therefore, their sons may be as great if they have the same opportunities of learning."

"But—but who ever heard of peasants learning anything but how to do their daily work, except they become monks?" replied Margarethe.

"The world does not want any more monks," said Fritz; "there are too many already."

"And who do you think are to teach the peasants?" asked Margarethe, still in open-eyed astonishment.

"Well, that is just the work for the monks—those who can read must become schoolmasters; those who have learned a trade must work at it; and those who can do neither must go back to their friends, or put their hand to any work they can find."

"And whose plan is this?" asked Margarethe, before venturing to commit herself to any opinion about it.

"O, many are thinking about it; the peasants are forcing men to think, whether they will or not, for many fear that they are organizing and preparing for a great war to throw off the yoke of their masters, and Eric and I both agree that they have good cause to complain."

"Where is Eric?" asked Margarethe. She had been watching for an opportunity to ask for some particulars about him ever since she had been out.

"Did I not tell you that he had gone home?" replied Fritz.

"Yes, but—but did he send no messge—no word to me?" said Margarethe. "I certainly thought he would have come with you; he told me last year he greatly desired to see Zurich. Fritz, has he changed?" she suddenly asked, facing round upon her brother, while the tears rose to her eyes and the color to her cheeks.

"Changed?" repeated Fritz slowly.

"Yes, you know well what I mean. Were there ladies at the castle of Ebenbourg, where you have been staying?" she asked fiercely.

"Why, of course there were ladies," said Fritz. "Lady Hadwig could not spend the time alone; but it was not to dance attendance at a lady's bower that Eric and I came to Ebenbourg, and it is little enough we have seen of the fair dames; for Luther's business at Augsburg convinced us that we must prepare to defend our champion against these wily Italians. The Pope must know he has the whole people of Germany to reckon with, as well as the emperor, in this matter."

But Margarethe was not going to be drawn into a political or theological discussion now. She was

BOWER: *a lady's apartment in a medieval hall*

uneasy about Eric, and had a dim suspicion that her brother was keeping something from her. "Is Eric quite well?" she asked.

"Yes, he is looking better than ever he did. He never was very handsome, you know, Margarethe; but I really think he is improving in that particular now. Is there anything else I can tell you, my lady sister?"

"You have told me nothing, yet; but are hiding something from me, I feel sure," said Margarethe angrily; and it was with difficulty that she kept back her rising tears. She left her brother's side and urged her palfrey into a canter, but Fritz was soon by her side again.

"Come, Margarethe, you and I cannot afford to quarrel; or at least I cannot, for you are the only one I have left to me now."

Fritz spoke so mournfully, so sadly, that Margarethe's anger was subdued in a moment; but the next she was saying, "I wish you would tell me all about everything, and not treat me like a baby."

"But, my dear Margarethe, what could you do? it would only be troubling you for nothing."

"Well, perhaps I could not do much in the way of help, but still I have a right to know what the trouble is."

"No, my lady sister, it is the duty of all true knights to spare the weak and helpless from every needless pain."

"But I am not weak and helpless," said Margarethe rather indignantly; "I am as strong as you are, at least to bear trouble, and it would not hurt me half so much to know what the trouble is as to be wondering and surmising, and never knowing anything definite."

"But, Margarethe, ladies have no right to wonder and surmise. They ought to be quite sure that a true knight will ever strive to keep the trouble from hurting them."

"Fritz, I wonder what you think women are made of?" retorted Margarethe fiercely. "You say chivalry is dying out, that knights will soon be a thing of the past; and I am glad of it, for when they have gone, and there are only men and women left in the world, the women may be allowed to do their part—the part that I believe God intended they should do, that their hearts are aching and breaking to perform."

"Well, what is this? what have you to complain of?" asked Fritz, when he could recover sufficiently from his astonishment to speak.

"Well, I will try to tell you what I mean by telling you what I have often thought when I have been in the churches and seen the people kneeling before the image of the Virgin. I have felt I should not like to be the blessed queen of heaven, to be worshiped, but I would rather be a poor woman who could go about helping the poor. I tell you, Fritz, women don't want to be petted and worshiped and made dolls of, but they want to help those they love—to share their troubles and cares, as well as their joys and pleasures; and this is what I want; I

PETTED: *spoiled*

want to know all about you and Eric, and the dear old dull home in the forest."

Her brother shook his head meditatively. He was thinking of what Margarethe had said, and inwardly wondering how it was that not only the ancient faiths and institutions were rapidly changing, but that men and even women—the women were the greatest wonder to him—were making even more rapid strides in a reformation of all their old habits of thought and deed. He forgot that the beliefs and creeds had remained eternally unchanged but for the living spirit of man, and his determination to adapt these to the needs of his soul, instead of binding down his soul to the dead letter of the law that had for ages passed as belief, but the outcome from which had only been the coldest, hardest unbelief, and utter negation of God. He forgot, too, that while women like Margarethe could not travel through the world, and make themselves acquainted with all that was passing in its seats of learning and among the busy haunts of men, husbands and brothers and fathers took home to them tales of what they had heard and seen, and that women, pondering over these things in their quiet homes, or going about their daily duties, were insensibly catching the spirit of the age, and applying it, too, as everyone else did, to their special department of life, and thus were being educated to bear their part nobly in the work God was doing for and in the world.

But it was hard for Fritz, who had been educated

INSENSIBLY: *unconsciously*

at home in all the old-fashioned ideas concerning women, to admit that they had any right to take an active part in the work of life; to know of its troubles and cares where these could possibly be concealed from them—at least, women like his sisters. Of course, it was different with common people, like burghers or peasants. Fritz was not quite sure whether he regarded these as women at all; but certainly for ladies, like his sisters, there could be no doubt of the matter; they had no right to be troubled with the cares and frets of life; and so he said: "Margarethe, I cannot think where you have learned such strange notions; but you must try to put them aside, and believe that we are solely studying your happiness by wishing you to remain in ignorance, at least for the present, of what is causing a little perplexity."

It was Margarethe's turn to be astonished now. How Fritz had managed to get through this set, formal speech without a stop she could not tell. She felt sure it had been carefully conned over beforehand, which, of course, increased her suspicions that the trouble they were hiding from her was a serious one; and yet, in spite of her misgivings could not help laughing.

"Did you and Eric get up that nice little speech between you? I am sure I am greatly obliged. It does you both great credit, but is not of the slightest use, I can tell you, for I mean to find out all about everything; and you know when I say I will do a thing I mean it."

CONNED OVER: *studied*

Chapter XVIII

More News

FINDING that her brother would not tell her anything about Eric or his affairs beyond what she already knew, Margarethe asked whether anything had been heard of Luther lately.

"If you had not been in Switzerland, my lady sister, you would have heard of the gathering of knights at the castle of Ebenbourg, and that our noble kinsman, von Sickengen, has been preparing for the shelter and defense of Luther all through the winter."

"But has Dr. Luther left Wittenberg!"

"Not yet, but we know not how soon he may have to do so, and he knows not whither he shall have to fly. You know he has appealed from the Pope to a General Council of the Church, and by the bull of a former Pope whoever was guilty of such a revolt as this from the Church was to be denounced by excommunication."

"And will they do it, do you think?" asked Margarethe.

"The Elector Frederick of Saxony certainly thought they would, and that his State would be involved in the calamity; and so he sent to tell Dr. Martin he had better leave. Dr. Luther's friends were in sad trouble, and had assembled at supper to bid their teacher farewell, when a second letter came, bidding him hasten his departure."

"O Fritz, and Father said the elector and emperor would be sure to protect him," said Margarethe sadly.

"Yes, as long as it suited their purpose," rejoined her brother, fiercely. "I tell you, Margarethe, that the princes of Germany will stifle the people's cry for freedom if they can, and if Germany is to be saved the old days of chivalry must be revived once more; the knights must fight for this new liberty of the people."

"Well, they have been fighting against it long enough," said Margarethe.

"And, seeing it is useless to struggle longer against the mighty stream of popular opinion, the growing power of the burghers, and the spirit of freedom and liberty that seems to possess everybody and everything, we mean to guide and direct, and specially do we mean to protect Dr. Martin Luther, the brave champion of Germany. I wonder who our next emperor will be, and whether he will take the side of Luther or the Pope?"

"I had forgotten we had no emperor now. The elector of Saxony is the regent of the empire now,

REGENT: *one ruling in place of the emperor*

is he not? When did the emperor die."

"About the middle of January, and, of course, there are several candidates for the imperial throne."

"Who are they?" asked Margarethe.

"The King of France is one; the King of Spain another; and—" but there Fritz stopped.

"Who is the other?" asked Margarethe.

"I will tell you by and by, but—but, Margarethe, I am afraid to hope that he will succeed; it would be such a good thing for us and for Germany if he did!"

"For *us* and for Germany?" repeated Margarethe. "Well, I believe God will control the election, whoever may be elected, and that He will choose the best for Germany, if not for us. But who is this other candidate?" she asked.

"Our kinsman, Franz von Sickengen!"

Margarethe took a long look at her brother. "You are practicing some of your old fun upon me," she said.

"No, I have had little time or thought for fun lately. It is quite true, what I am telling you; and some think he has a fair chance of being elected. He certainly stands a better chance than the King of France, and the Pope is not favorable, I hear, to King Charles of Spain; so that it may be we shall suddenly become great folks, Margarethe. Did I tell you that the Pope has sent our elector of Saxony the golden rose this year?"

But this wonderful honor of receiving the golden rose was quite eclipsed by the thought that they might soon claim an emperor as their kinsman; they, the poor, half-despised, rigidly proud family of von Ranitz might be able to hold up their heads with the highest in the land, to say nothing of the material benefits that would accrue from such an exalted relationship. Of course, Margarethe thought of all this as she rode along by her brother's side; thought of the influence and power this would give them, and the protection they might be able to afford to Luther and others—they, whom no one had thought worthy of any notice, might become a power in the land; and the thought was very pleasant to the young lady, as well as to her brother.

"O Fritz, I hope he will succeed!" she said; "And Eric, how pleased he will be!"

Fritz made no reply to this, but directed his sister's attention to some trees at a short distance, and a little shrine around which a number of pilgrims were kneeling. "That image worship is almost as bad as the traffic in indulgences," he said. "Did you hear that the Pope issued a bull last year, after Dr. Luther left Augsburg, confirming the doctrine of indulgences in every point where Luther has attacked it, so that if he continues to preach as he did before, it must be in direct antagonism to this special bull now."

"Our Diet should have served Tetzel as the Council of Zurich did Friar Samson—sent him packing, papal bull and all," said Margarethe. "But now tell me what Eric thinks of our kinsman's possible elevation to a throne," she said.

But Fritz only shook his head. "He did not say much to me about it," he said; and he shut his mouth as though he were determined not to utter another word upon the matter.

But Margarethe was equally determined that she would find out what this strange reticence of her brother's could mean, and, turning upon him suddenly, she said, "Fritz, you have quarreled with him!"

"No, I have not quarreled with him," answered her brother.

"Then who has?"

"What makes you think there has been a quarrel at all?"

"I am sure there has been something of the kind—a quarrel, or a misunderstanding, or something equally uncomfortable. Now, do tell me, Fritz, what it is."

"I wish you would not ask so persistently about a business you can do no good in," said Fritz shortly.

"You cannot tell what I might do in it. At any rate, it is my business, and I have a right to know all about it."

"Your business?" uttered Fritz.

"Yes, of course; for what concerns Eric certainly concerns me. Are we not betrothed? If my father could have had his way I should have been his

RETICENCE: *quietness, reserved manner*

wife long since," exclaimed Margarethe.

"And now my father says you are never to be his wife. There! the secret is out, although I vowed I would not tell you," and Fritz turned to see what effect his words had had upon his sister.

But in the growing twilight he could see little more than that her hands had dropped almost powerless at her side, and the reins hung slack over her palfrey's neck; but she uttered no word for several minutes.

At last she managed to say, "Did my father tell Eric this?"

"Yes, the letter came about the beginning of February, and was soon followed by one from von Schonstein himself, commanding Eric to return home at once."

"And he went!" said Margarethe, in a mournful tone; "Left me without a word! O, Eric, Eric, I did not think it possible you could be so cruel!"

"Now, Margarethe, don't blame Eric for what he could not help. What could he do when your father and his both wrote saying the betrothal contract had been annulled?"

"Do! Is he not a man, and I a woman? Are we a couple of sheep or oxen, that we can be traded with or bartered at their pleasure? True, we were betrothed at their desire, but our hearts ratified the contract, or I, for one, would never have entered into it; and that my father knows right well. How long is it since Eric left Ebenbourg?" she asked.

ANNULLED: *canceled*
RATIFIED: *confirmed*

"Before I started on my journey to Switzerland. Now, Margarethe, do be calm and sensible; of course, you know well enough that such things as these often occur, and that is why it is so much better for the marriage to follow immediately after the betrothal, and then any little scandal like this cannot happen."

"Little scandal!" repeated Margarethe. "No one seems to think that it may mean the ruin of two lives!"

"Now, you know that no lady—no German lady of knightly degree—ever thinks of disputing the choice that has been made for her; and you, Margarethe—"

"Well, I suppose I am not German at all," said Margarethe, defiantly. "Dear old Aunt Ermengarde said I put her in mind of her father, and he was a Bohemian, you know."

"Hush, hush, Margarethe; don't talk of our ancestors being Bohemians; you know they were heretics and the natural enemies of Germany."

"No, I don't know anything about it, but I believe what Aunt Ermengarde says, for I never could submit to this German fashion of a father selling his daughter; and so I suppose I am a Bohemian heretic who has been dropped by mistake in a respectable German family."

"And, therefore, must follow the German fashions, and conform myself to their rules," remarked Fritz.

"Yes, when it suits me. Otherwise I will follow my own conscience—do what is right at all costs."

"And is it not right for a daughter to obey her father?" demanded Fritz.

"Yes, of course it is, in a general way—that is, when her father's commands do not require her to do anything that would be against her conscience."

"O well, we will leave the discussion of this, and you will act like a sensible girl, I am sure, and not give our father any more trouble than can be helped. I am causing him trouble enough," added Fritz.

"How is that?" asked his sister.

"Well, that meddling confessor—that Father Sebastian—when he went to Nimptschen had the offer of a rich canonry, which, of course, my father desired me to accept by way of a settlement in life, since it is fully certain we shall get little more from the Erfurt burghers."

"And which, of course, you declined," said Margarethe.

"I certainly could not accept it, for how could I enter the Church when I hardly know whether I believe in anything beyond what I can see?"

"Then you think sons may disobey their parents, and that the law about this only applies to daughters?" said his sister.

"Well, of course there is a difference," said Fritz, slowly; "a woman is—well, a woman," he concluded.

"I suppose she is, and, as such, is not supposed to have the privilege of a conscience of her own. Her guardians hold that for her. But you, of course, can follow the dictates of yours, whether disobedience is involved or not."

"Margarethe, would you have me enter the Church," demanded Fritz, fiercely, "when you know I cannot believe in what she teaches? You told me, above all things, to be honest to myself and my own convictions, and now—"

"I tell you to be the same," said Margarethe, stopping the flow of angry words. "I should have despised you had you accepted this tempting offer; but as I am able to appreciate honesty in you, do you not think I have the right to exercise the same honesty myself?"

"Well, no one wishes you to be dishonest, my lady sister."

"Do they not, when I am bidden to break the most solemn vow a woman can make? A nun is disgraced forever for breaking her vows and leaving a monastic life, even though they have been taken for her in infancy, and she finds them so galling that life is a misery to her; and yet a maiden is to break her betrothal vow, and perhaps her heart, at the dictates of mere caprice or worldly ambition. Fritz, if it is not right for you—"

But here Margarethe was stayed by one of the escort joining them to consult her brother about the advisability of putting up for the night at a

GALLING: *grievous*
CAPRICE: *whim*
STAYED: *stopped*

hostelry close at hand, that they might travel by day through the lonely forest road that was the next stage of their journey.

The bustle and excitement of alighting and unloading their weary horses and mules, and finding accommodation for a large party on such short notice, occupied all Margarethe's thoughts and attention for the next hour; but when her brother had disposed of his escort, and she had watched the merchants and their servants unloading their beasts and carrying their various packages into the inn, until the last had been disposed of, her thoughts once more recurred to Eric and the strange conduct of her father, and then she wondered whether she should ever see him again.

She was so overcome with this thought that she burst into tears, and then kneeled down to pour out her heart in prayer to God. She was alone, and there was little fear that she would be interrupted; for everybody was busy downstairs preparing supper, and Fritz had taken care to secure this chamber for her, that she might be free from all intrusion. He had gone for a walk with one of the merchants, and so she was left free to think over this new and unexpected trouble. It was not easy to lay it aside—to cast her burden upon the Lord. She had knelt down, feeling it a burden that was almost crushing her, and thought its weight was somewhat lightened when she at length rose from her knees; yet she still bore it. She had taken it to

RECURRED: *returned*

God, but she could not leave it with Him—could not believe yet that He would carry it, and make her path plain before her face when the time came for her to walk in it.

But she was calmed and subdued, and began to feel sorry for what she had said to Fritz in her passionate anger. "The Reformation must begin in our hearts and bear fruit in our lives, if ever it is to be real and true," she murmured. "But O, what slow progress it makes in me! how proud and angry I am if anyone ventures to cross me. Eric has told me of this in his kind, gentle way, and I have been hoping all along that when he was always by my side to help me I should be able to control my fierce temper; but now—" and the self-communing ended in another burst of tears.

This outburst, however, was soon interrupted by the return of her brother. She heard his voice calling to the landlady to serve supper in their private room, and just had time to dry her tears when he came in.

"What is the matter, Margarethe?" he asked, in a tone of deep concern, seating himself on the long, broad settee beside her.

"Well, for one thing, I am very sorry for some of the things I said to you today. It seems as though I was always to be the same Margarethe."

"And why should you not? I am sure I would not have you changed;" and he stooped and kissed her

SETTEE: *wooden couch*

high, white forehead, and looked lovingly into her dark eyes.

She laid her head on his shoulder as she had been used to do when a little girl. "Fritz, the Reformation Germany needs, and that we all need, must begin here," and she laid her hand on her breast. "The freedom and liberty that we need, the freedom the Gospel offers to us, is the conquest of our own passionate hearts. Of course, I shall always be the same Margarethe in one sense; but I want to be a new Margarethe in another—renewed by God's Spirit; and if I were, I should not have talked in such a passionate, defiant manner as I did today."

Fritz looked down at her thoughtfully for a minute or two. "I don't know, little sister, but I think you are changed from what you used to be. But if such a great change is needed in you, what must be the change I need?"

"The same—a change of heart; a turning round altogether from the old aims and loves and motives, and a new love taken in their stead—the love of God, through Jesus Christ our Lord, constraining us to aim at pleasing Him in all we do."

Fritz shook his head sadly. "I shall never attain to that, Margarethe," he said; "for I cannot even assure myself for a certainty that there is a God at all."

"But you want to believe it, Fritz; you are stretching out weary hands for the old faith that you used to boast of having thrown away. You never boast of that now."

"Should I boast of losing the most precious jewel that was ever entrusted to man? I never knew its preciousness until it was lost, and now my search for it is in vain."

Fritz and Margarethe Nearing the Castle of Ebenbourg

Chapter XIX

Count von Sickengen

THE Castle of Ebenbourg was reached at last—"the hostelry of righteousness," as many of the knights had begun to call it; and Margarethe soon found herself thrown into the midst of a whirl that for a time made her forget her own individual cares—or, at least, they shrank into such small proportions that she was ashamed to mention them. Everybody was so earnest and eager that the good knight Franz von Sickengen should succeed in being elected to rule the empire, that there was a constant coming and going of knights with courtly trains of retainers, messengers being sent hither and thither. To add to the cares and anxiety that pressed upon the chosen band who were gathered here to uphold German freedom, the prince-archbishop of Treves had joined with the two papal nuncios in trying to get Luther into their power; to beguile him into coming to Treves, from whence he would, doubtless, be carried a prisoner to Rome.

NUNCIOS: *ambassadors*

"You know, my dear, that the brave Dr. Luther has again refused to recant, and this time the papal nuncio sent was Miltity, the Pope's chamberlain. He is a German by birth, but his Italian education and long residence at Rome have made him a more dangerous enemy than even the other nuncio, de Vio, who is Italian." Lady Hadwig von Sickengen gave Margarethe this explanation a few days after her arrival, as they sat together in the lady's bower, discussing the departure of a couple of trusty servants who had been sent as spies to Treves.

"They have been trying to convince Dr. Luther of his errors again, I suppose," said Margarethe.

"They had made up their minds," replied her hostess, "that he should recant or be sent to Rome; for Miltity brought seventy briefs with him, which he intended to produce and post up in every town through which he should pass on his way back to Rome with Luther as prisoner, lest the people should attempt to rescue him. Even the Elector Frederick knew not what to do about protecting Luther, when he found how determined the Pope was to silence him; and whether he should take refuge here, in this our poor hostelry of righteousness, or leave Germany for France, was a question hard to decide."

"But he did neither," exclaimed Margarethe.

"No, my dear; God himself upset everybody's plans by the death of the Emperor Maximilian,

CHAMBERLAIN: *personal attendant*
BRIEFS: *official letters from the Pope*

which has given the power of regent to the Elector Frederick, who is now able to protect Dr. Luther. The Pope is trying to win him with the gift of the golden rose to abandon Luther; but if Franz is elected emperor the Pope may spare himself the trouble of sending any more legates to entrap or drive Luther into a recantation; for he will protect the Reformation as well as the liberty of Germany."

"Who else desires the emperor's throne?" asked Margarethe. "Surely no one has so great a right to it as a German knight, unless it were one of the electors themselves."

"The emperor's grandson, young Charles, who is now so great a monarch that my Franz says the sun never sets on his dominions, in Spain and the new, great country of America. Then there is the King of France, and King Henry VIII, of England, each of whom thinks he has a right to rule our German folk."

"And which of these does the Pope favor?" asked Margarethe.

"Neither; for each of them is so powerful now in Europe that the Pope can scarce hold his own, and, therefore, he may favor von Sickengen; although our friend Ulrich von Hutten thinks it is scarcely to be expected."

Lady Hadwig took a keen interest in all that concerned her husband, and when she found that Margarethe was scarcely less interested than she herself in these affairs of public moment, she kept

MOMENT: *importance*

the young lady about her more than she did most of her visitors at this time, and by degrees Margarethe grew to love and trust the stately lady almost as much as she did her dear old aunt, whom, however, she often longed to see.

Lady Hadwig took upon herself the replenishment of her young kinswoman's wardrobe, for she knew that the family were poor—poorer than ever since these changes had set the burghers free; and so, without wounding the sensitive pride of Margarethe, she presented her with two or three new and costly dresses—the first really new dresses Margarethe had ever had; for hitherto she had worn those left by her mother, except one or two plain, homely ones, which she had worn only in the retirement of her own room. The preparation of these dresses, and helping Lady Hadwig with her guests, fully occupied Margarethe's time now, and there was little chance of her being dull in this castle, although it was deep in the forest; for the clatter of horses' hoofs was continually heard approaching or departing along the well-trodden road that led to this hospitable shelter.

News of the intrigue to get Luther to enter Treves was brought by different messengers, and warnings dispatched to Luther and the Elector of Saxony by others; and at last they had the satisfaction of hearing that Luther had refused to go, and the Electors of Treves and Saxony had agreed that the matter should be postponed until the meeting of the diet in two years' time. The Pope himself was too much occupied with the temporal affairs of Europe—the opposing of Charles, on the one hand, and Francis, on the other, in their efforts to mount the imperial throne—to pay much attention to the clamor against an insignificant German monk. Luther could be settled with when the weightier business of finding a suitable occupant for the vacant throne had been settled. So, while the Pope was planning and intriguing, the monk was studying the decretals of the Popes by the light of sacred Scripture. Writing at this time to his dear friend Spalatin, he said, "I am reading the decretals, and I know not whether the Pope is antichrist himself or only his apostle, to such a degree in these decretals is Christ outraged and crucified." These writings were one of the chief cornerstones upon which the papacy was built, and so, while the Pope was carefully guarding his temporal power, looking closely after every outpost of the citadel, the chief cornerstone upon which the whole was based was being slowly but surely struck from its place by Luther. Rumors of the doctor's study and great dissatisfaction were brought by the various messengers that were now continually passing to and from Wittenberg. To Margarethe it was something wonderful, the passing to and fro of so many letters; for she shared in the general news-carrying, and sent letters to her father and aunt, begging them to send her

DECRETALS: *decrees*
CITADEL: *fortress*

letters in reply, especially regarding her questions about Else and Eric. She wrote to her aunt about the former, and to her father about the latter, but from neither did she obtain very satisfactory replies.

Else had not returned, her aunt said, and Father Sebastian had refused to answer any questions about her. Beyond this she knew nothing. She longed to see her dear children once more, and begged Margarethe to return home, that she might see her before she died. Her father's letter was even still more unsatisfactory. After congratulating her on the favor shown to her by the future empress, Lady Hadwig, and the high position she would probably hold at court, he went on to say that, with prudent foresight, and to spare her any unpleasantness, he had broken off her engagement to marry Eric von Schonstein, as she would by and by be in a position to wed one of the wealthiest and most powerful knights in Germany.

Von Ranitz understood very little of his daughter's character, or there would have been far less self-complacency expressed in this letter, and Margarethe would probably have felt far less irritated; but as it was, the letter sent by another messenger a short time afterward was anything but a dutiful epistle. In it she boldly declared to her father that she would wed Eric von Schonstein and no other. He himself had chosen him, and she had learned to respect and love him, and had written to him by the same messenger telling him this, and asking him to return to the Castle of Ebenbourg for a time at least. After the letters had been dispatched and the messenger was beyond recall, Margarethe began to fear that she had acted rather hastily, and at last she ventured to tell Lady Hadwig something of their family difficulties. The lady smiled, but shook her head when she heard of the letters being sent.

"I remember this Eric von Schonstein, a quiet, studious looking young knight, more given to reading and meditation than to the practice of arms, I have heard. Margarethe, I am afraid you have not acted wisely," said the lady, "in summoning this Eric to attend you here."

"Why?" demanded Margarethe, a little resentfully; not that she objected to her own wisdom being questioned, but she thought she detected something like a slight to Eric in the tone in which the lady spoke.

"My dear child, you must not be angry at what I am going to say. I think your father, being a poor man, has a right to take every care that you should not suffer from the restraints and inconveniences poverty must inflict, and which I am sure he has so bravely borne."

Margarethe's eyes filled with tears. "I am afraid I am very hasty, in spite of all my struggles to subdue my temper. I do not doubt my father's love, or question his right to take care of me; but you know, my dear Lady Hadwig, that Eric von Schonstein was his own choice; and, although I was not very willing at first, and would not consent to the betrothal until I had learned to—to like him, yet now that we are betrothed, I do not think anyone—not even my father—ought to interfere between us."

"And you really are betrothed to this Eric?" remarked the lady.

"Yes, we were betrothed at Wittenberg, in the presence of Dr. Luther, more than a year since."

"Then why have you not been married? I think your father was very foolish to be in such haste about the betrothal."

"The von Schonsteins are our equals in birth, and far more wealthy," said Margarethe.

"Perhaps, but they are only von Schonsteins, and you—Well, I think your father has been overhasty," concluded the lady.

Margarethe felt far from satisfied, and yet what could she do. Lady Hadwig certainly was not, from some cause, favorably impressed with Eric, although she had spoken of him as quiet and studious. After revolving the matter in her mind for some time, she resolved to speak to her brother about it, and ask him how he and Eric had spent their time during the winter.

It was not often the brother and sister met now. Fritz had thrown himself, heart and soul, into all the plans of his kinsman, von Sickengen, and he was often away from the castle on some errand for the knight, or joined a hunting party in the forest; so that it sometimes happened that days elapsed, and the brother and sister did not meet, even at meals, when most of the company met in the great hall.

But Margarethe was determined to watch for her brother now, and so she placed herself at a window commanding a view of the castle yard early one morning, where she thought he would most likely appear. To glance across at the fresh green of the forest trees, shimmering and dancing in the May sunshine, brought back to her mind the day when she and Else had stood together watching for Fritz to appear round a bend of the road in their own Thuringian forest. It was only two years ago. "Only two years," repeated Margarethe softly to herself, "and yet it seems like a lifetime, so many strange things have happened and are happening."

As she spoke, the horn at the gate was blown three times, to announce the arrival of some messenger, and the next minute she saw her brother Fritz walk toward the gate that was being opened by the warders. To hear the news in these days, when so many startling things were occurring, was held to be everybody's duty, and Margarethe could see by her brother's varying color that the tidings brought by the stranger were of no common interest, and she longed to hear what it could be; but she could not go down to meet the troops

WARDERS: *guards*

of strangers who would probably be about in the corridors and on the staircases; for this castle of Ebenbourg—palace and fortress in one—was not like their little insignificant castle home in the Thuringian forest, with its handful of peasant retainers, every one of whom she knew. No; here at Ebenbourg were gathered all the foremost spirits of Germany, with hosts of servants and retainers in attendance upon them.

Margarethe did not have to wait long before hearing the news brought by the last messenger from Wittenberg. Dr. Eck, the invincible theologian, who was such a perfect master of the art of disputation that he had borne the palm from eight universities, had made an attack upon Luther respecting his views on the primacy of the Pope, and there was to be a meeting between the two at Leipsic to debate the question, if Duke George would allow it.

"It will be a regular tournament," said Fritz, rubbing his hands with glee. "Dr. Eck is as vain of his powerful tongue as a soldier is of his sword, and thinks his arguments must always continue to be invincible."

"But the subject he has chosen Dr. Luther dare not attack—the primacy of the Pope," said one of his friends, who stood with him in a little alcove, whither Margarethe had retreated.

"He would not twelve months since, but have you not heard what has been said since he began

DISPUTATION: *debate*
BORNE THE PALM FROM: *won victories at*
PRIMACY: *supreme authority*

studying the decretals upon which the primacy of the Pope rests?" inquired Fritz.

"I wish they would leave the Pope alone; to attack him is worse than attacking the indulgences."

"More dangerous, you mean. But, then, what is Dr. Martin to do? Eck has invited the attack."

"Well, I hope Duke George will refuse to let Luther come to debate. I should think, as a descendant from those miserable Bohemian Hussites, he must be alive to the danger of stirring up any more strife between Luther and the Pope. Bohemia was torn to pieces for sixty years through the religious war brought on by those heretics."

"I don't believe they were heretics any more than Dr. Luther is," said Margarethe indignantly, and drawing herself up to her full height as she spoke.

"Never mind, we won't quarrel about the Hussites," said Fritz; "we have enough to do to mind our own business in these days. Have you heard that the electors are to meet next month at Frankfort, and make choice of an emperor?"

His friend nodded. "Have you heard, too, that our party stands little chance—that the crown is to be offered to the regent Elector of Saxony, and that the Pope will support him in preference to either of the other claimants?"

"The Elector of Saxony to be made emperor! Then Luther will be as well protected as though Count von Sickengen won the throne," exclaimed Margarethe.

But Fritz looked rather disturbed. "It may do as well for Luther, perhaps," he said; "but it will make all the difference in the world to Fritz and Margarethe von Ranitz."

"I had forgotten you, Fritz," said Margarethe penitently. "I was only thinking what a noble emperor our elector would make; and then he is so fond of Dr. Luther."

"Yes, he is, and the bringing his name forward as a candidate will ruin us, I fear; for, of course, von Sickengen would have no chance of success beside him. You cannot understand what this will mean to us, Margarethe: it will cut me off from my father completely!" and Fritz sighed as he spoke.

"But why should it? Of course, our father would be pleased if Count von Sickengen should be made emperor; but still I do not see why he should be so greatly displeased with you if it fails."

"Ah, you have forgotten that my father has set his heart upon my entering the Church. He has given up all hope in Luther and the Reformation—that is, that it will ever bring wealth and honor to those who follow it."

"Fritz, I do not care whether it brings wealth or poverty, honor or shame; I will not forsake it," said Margarethe in a low but fervent tone, as they walked along the corridor together toward Lady Hadwig's apartments.

PENITENTLY: *remorsefully*

Chapter XX

At Leipsic

THE month of June, 1519, was an important one in the history of Germany and the Reformation, for at Frankfort were gathered the electors, to make choice of an emperor, and at Leipsic arrived Dr. Eck, the champion of the Pope, and a day or two afterward came Dr. Luther and Melanchthon, and Archdeacon Carlstadt, with whom the disputation was to be held; for Duke George had forbidden Luther engaging in it, and would only give him leave to come to Leipsic as a spectator, as so many other doctors of theology came. With Luther came about two hundred of the students of Wittenberg, armed with pikes and halberds, resolved to defend their master like soldiers, should the need arise; for it was believed that Luther would be drawn into the discussion, and, perhaps, take the place of Carlstadt. It was well known through all Germany that Eck earnestly desired to have Luther for a combatant, feeling sure of victory over him, which would, of course, greatly add to his glory and fame.

The chances of von Sickengen being the successful candidate for the vacant throne had become so small that he retired from the contest before the gathering of the electors at Frankfort; and now, instead of going to that city, he, with Lady Hadwig, Margarethe, Fritz, and some other knights and ladies, with a large retinue of servants, repaired to Leipsic, and reached there in time to be present at mass in St. Thomas' Church, which service was to be the commencement of this famous battle of the theologians as to the right of the Pope to be the head of the Church.

After the service they watched the procession of knights, abbots, doctors, and students, who walked back to the palace in the hall of which the debate was to take place.

Count von Sickengen gained admittance for himself and some of his friends, but Margarethe and Lady Hadwig, after watching the long procession of students and citizens who brought up the rear, had to content themselves with watching from the window of their hostelry the bustle and excitement going on in the streets, after Eric had left them; for Eric von Schonstein had not been long answering Margarethe's letter in person, and one purpose of Count and Lady Sickengen's journey hither was to make peace between von Ranitz and the young people who had incurred his displeasure.

Of course, it had been a great disappointment to all the count's friends to resign the hope of his gaining the throne of the emperor; but it troubled

REPAIRED: *returned*

Margarethe less than anyone else, because she had little doubt but that her father would agree with Lady Hadwig's plan for her, since his own ambitious hopes and schemes had failed; and she hoped that she and Eric would be married shortly, and that Fritz would be allowed to marry her dear friend, Anna Geroldsek.

But although Margarethe and Eric were never weary of talking over their own private plans and hopes for the future, they were scarcely less interested in the public events now going on here and at Frankfort. They knew the imperial crown was to be offered to the elector of Saxony, Luther's friend and protector, and it was chiefly on account of this that Count von Sickengen had withdrawn from the contest; and so of the final result of the election they had little fear now, as the Pope supported his claim in preference to his more powerful rivals. They were thus free to give their undivided attention to this theological contest, now going on at the ducal palace. The ladies knew by the increased stir and bustle in the streets when the discussion had ended, and soon afterward Fritz, with the count and his friends, came in.

"The real discussion has not begun yet, for only Eck and Carlstadt have spoken. Luther with his friend Melanchthon are only spectators," said von Sickengen, in answer to a question from his wife.

"Then it is not over yet," said Margarethe, who hoped their stay at Leipsic would not be a long one, as she was impatient to reach home.

DUCAL PALACE: *palace of the duke*

"It will not be over for a month, at least," said Fritz, who never failed to tease his sister whenever he had the opportunity.

"I do not think it will be over for some days," said the count, answering a look of Margarethe's. "Dr. Eck is determined to have Luther for his opponent; no one else has been able to vanquish the Wittenberg doctor, but he feels certain of an easy victory. I hope it will not last too long," he added, "or mischief may come of it in more ways than one."

"What is the danger, Franz?" asked Lady Hadwig, in some slight alarm.

"Well, it is pretty certain that Dr. Luther and those who favor him will not have fair play here. The pulpits will all be closed against them, but opened to the others, and I hear there is great jealousy among the students here, at Wittenberg taking all newcomers now. Then these Wittenberg students are not the most discreet people in the world, and in their passionate love for their master are not likely to hear him defamed without a protest. I have bid Fritz keep them in order as much as he can. He will go among them, and keep them from going to any excess in beer-drinking, or declamation, either."

Finding that they were likely to be detained at Leipsic for a week or two, Margarethe resolved to visit Nimptschen and see Else before she went home, as Nimptschen was only a few miles from Leipsic, and as so favorable an opportunity might

DECLAMATION: *speech-making*

not again present itself for some time. She was the more anxious to see Else now; and to give her, if possible, a copy of Dr. Luther's work on the Lord's Prayer and some of his lectures, which she had just received from the printer; for she feared that if she waited for her father to accompany her he might object to these being given if he knew it, and she would scarcely have an opportunity of giving them without his knowledge. Lady Hadwig feared she might have some difficulty in passing them to Else without the older nun, who was always in attendance, likewise seeing them; and so she proposed to go with Margarethe, and take one of the wonderful mechanical toys sold at Nuremberg, which would be sure to please and amuse the nuns. By a skillful contrivance of wheels and springs a miller was made to carry his corn, poultry in the yard could crow and fly, and horses draw a loaded team to the barn. This was to be a present to Else from Lady Hadwig, and while the *grille* was open for its admission Margarethe was to contrive to slip her books in as well, after having whispered to Else to hide them in the sleeve of her robe.

Margarethe was so anxious for the success of her plan, and to discover, if possible, whether her sister was happy—whether her life in the convent had satisfied her expectations—that she grew quite agitated before they reached their destination, and Lady Hadwig had to whisper to her to be more calm, or their plans would prove quite a failure, and she might be forbidden to see her sister again.

It was easy to whisper caution, but how could Margarethe restrain her tears when the grating was at last drawn aside from the *grille*, and a still white face appeared on the other side? Surely that face, white as the linen bands in which it was enveloped, could not be Else's, and those listless eyes were never used to dance with fun and glee as hers did. A shiver as of pain passed over the white face as Margarethe uttered, "Is it Else—my little sister Else?"

Lady Hadwig, fearing that Margarethe's impulsiveness would make this meeting an uncomfortable one, drew her away from the *grille* as soon as the words were uttered, and went forward herself to speak to the young nun; and she soon contrived to gain admission to the parlor for herself and Margarethe through the wonderful toy she had brought with her. It was a great favor to be admitted behind the *grille*, but the old nun who had been sent with Else was more curious to see this wonderful toy herself than her young companion was, and after they were admitted she went to fetch the superior and some of the other sisters, and while she was gone Margarethe gave her sister the books she had brought, and also begged her to read the New Testament if ever she had the opportunity.

Else submitted to her sister's embrace—it could scarcely be called more than submission—and it seemed a relief to her when the visitors departed. Margarethe was full of sorrow at her sister's coldness. "They have crushed all the life and love out of her," she sobbed, as Lady Hadwig led her back to the carriage that was waiting for them at the gate. The lady let down the cloth curtains, so that Margarethe could indulge her grief without restraint for a time, but at last she ventured to interfere. "Hush, hush, my child; you have forgotten that God can take care of Else even in the convent—give her the light you had prayed she might receive even there."

"But she is so hard and cold—she does not love even me now," sobbed the sister.

"You forget that poor Else looks upon all human love as sin now. I do not think it is easy for the poor child to maintain that cold appearance; and who knows how many tears she will shed in secret when she recalls our visit, and every word and look that passed?"

"Then it is cruel—ten times more cruel to shut people up and forbid them to—" but here Margarethe broke down again, blaming herself now for thinking hardly of poor Else.

Lady Hadwig was quite glad when they reached Leipsic again, where there would be sure to be some news awaiting them that must arouse Margarethe from her sorrow about Else.

Yes, there was news awaiting them—news from Frankfort, but scarcely such as they had expected!

HARDLY: *harshly*

To the disappointment of every friend of the Reformation, the Elector of Saxony had refused the crown, and the young king, Charles of Spain, had been elected to succeed his grandfather.

Count von Sickengen was angry and grieved, and complained loudly of Frederick's cowardice in refusing to take the helm because the times were perilous. "We have been betrayed," he exclaimed. "The liberties of Germany have been sold; for Charles is more papal than the Pope himself, and we shall yet have to defend Luther with our swords if the Reformation is to be secured."

Many a one besides von Sickengen looked anxious and disturbed when the result of the election was made known; and the friends of Luther hoped he would be cautious in this disputation; and some were more than half sorry that Duke George had at last given his consent to his taking the place of Dr. Carlstadt. Opinions in the town were in such violent opposition now that meetings between the students of the rival universities generally ended in a fight. The monks of the neighboring monasteries had most industriously set afloat the wildest rumors concerning Luther and his dealings with Satan, so that when he one day went into a church where a priest was performing mass at a side altar, the man was so frightened that he took all the sacred vessels he could carry, and ran to hide them, as though Satan in person was after him. But the fears of the ignorant and the superstitious, and the brawling and quarreling of students, were as nothing to the dismay felt by most of Luther's friends when, during the second day's discussion with Eck, he boldly declared that certain of the doctrines of John Huss and the Bohemians were perfectly orthodox.

Fritz and Eric, who were both present and heard Luther say this, came home full of it. "Everybody sprung to his feet and began talking, some crying, 'He is mad!' so that for a time neither Luther nor Eck could be heard," said Fritz.

"But what did he really say?" asked Margarethe.

"Well, in the morning he had spoken of the Bohemians as schismatics and heretics, because they separated from the Church; and so, as soon as the assembly were settled quietly in their places this afternoon, he rose and said clearly and boldly, 'Certain of the tenets of John Huss and the Bohemians are perfectly orthodox. This much is certain. For instance, That there is only one universal Church, and again, That it is not necessary to salvation to believe the Roman Church superior to others. Whether Wycliffe or Huss has declared so I care not. It is the truth.'"

"Did he say that?" uttered Lady Hadwig, and she glanced at her husband, as if asking his opinion.

But the knight only shook his head. "Were it a question concerning the temper of a sword I should know more about the matter, but I only know this, that our Dr. Luther has more wisdom

ORTHODOX: *consistent with traditionally held beliefs*
SCHISMATICS: *those who spread division*
TENETS: *beliefs*

in his little finger than Dr. Eck and the schoolmen in their whole bodies; and so I am not going to be frightened by what he says about the Bohemians, although Duke George may."

"He certainly is frightened," remarked Eric; "and wishes Luther were safe out of his dominions, I know."

"He dreads a civil war, I believe," said Fritz.

Count von Sickengen was sufficiently alarmed to send in secret for a numerous body of his retainers to repair to the neighborhood of Leipsic, that they might be in readiness for any emergency that might arise; for this famous disputation was by no means at an end yet, and what else Dr. Luther might say to offend the Pope and his champion no one could tell. It seemed that Luther's knowledge was growing, and no one could now foresee when or where the advancing strides would end. At first he had only attacked the doctrine of indulgences as taught by Tetzel, but respected the Pope's decrees. Afterward he rejected these, and had appealed to a council. Now he discarded even this, and boldly declared that no council can establish a new article of faith, or claim to be infallible. Thus all human authorities were disowned by him now, and so it can be well imagined with what trembling fear his more timid friends waited, not knowing what daring thought he would next enunciate in this dangerous discussion.

INFALLIBLE: *unable to make an error*
ENUNCIATE: *speak*

At last, to the relief of many others besides Margarethe, the disputation came to an end, having lasted twenty days. It had been sought by Dr. Eck, as the champion of the Pope; but if he had only known that a deadly wound, never afterward to be healed, would then be struck at the whole papal system, he would not have been so eager for the contest. He admitted that he had been, to a certain extent, defeated; for in appealing to authorities and councils Luther had shown himself as apt as his antagonist, while his knowledge of Scripture gave him an immense advantage, although Eck would not admit, as Luther laid down, that the Word of God must be the only standard and authority for the Church.

The discussion over, Luther and Melanchthon, with their friends and the students of Wittenberg, took their departure from Leipsic, and Count von Sickengen, with his train of servants, followed soon after. Everybody felt thankful that nothing more than a few brawls had as yet resulted from Luther's bold declarations; but the end might be more serious yet. When reports of the proceedings had reached Rome, and the Pope, having settled the election of the emperor, would have time to attend to these questions of faith impeached by Luther, some bold step might be taken to silence him once more; and with such an emperor as Charles, how could they expect protection for the Reformer?

IMPEACHED: *challenged*

These were the points discussed by the count and Fritz as they journeyed along the road toward the Thuringian forest; of course, each became more convinced of the need of armed resistance, should the attempt be made to crush Luther and the Reformation.

Chapter XXI

A Living Tomb

AT home once more—at home in the Thuringian forest, with the wind sighing and moaning through the tops of the tall pines!—at home again, with the dear old aunt and grandfather, who were verily as little children!

Margarethe, when she first came back, did not think her aunt had changed much; but when the bustle and excitement of her arrival had somewhat subsided she noticed that Dame Ermengarde grew still and quiet, rarely leaving her room, or even her favorite seat, and that now a fire was kept in her stove, though the days were fine and warm. Margarethe wondered, sometimes, how she could live through the years shut up here, with only her father and their limited household; for the hopes that had brightened their journey from the Rhineland had all faded—Lady Hadwig's kind mission had utterly failed, and she was never to meet Eric von Schonstein again. This had been her father's command, and Margarethe, after a sharp struggle with herself, and a sharper one with her betrothed, had submitted; but she solemnly promised Eric, and assured her father, that she would never marry another.

Fritz had refused to submit to his father's will, and had parted from him in the bitterest anger, vowing he would never come home again unless it was to rescue Margarethe from her imprisonment, when she should find out what that imprisonment was. At present she refused to seize, in disobedience to her father's command, what she believed to be her happiness, and in this dutiful submission she was upheld by Lady Hadwig.

The visitors did not make a long stay. After their departure, when Margarethe was left alone, she began to realize for the first time the change the last two years had wrought in herself. Until Else went away she had not thought it possible that any place or mode of life could be more interesting than was their own, here in the forest; and although she had listened with wondering surprise to Fritz's stories of his travels—surprise that the world should be so large, and wonder what the people could find to do where they had no peasant retainers to visit, and how it was possible to find amusement where there were no pine trees to talk to each other in the summer breezes, no fir cones to be gathered, no flowers to be plucked, and no birds or squirrels to watch—she had never once thought those scenes desirable. It must be a strange, wild world outside of their forest she had thought then; but now that she had been into that world, had mingled in its stirring joys and fears and sorrows, the forest was to her as a living tomb. Nothing broke the monotony of life here now any more than it did when she was a girl; but then the changes of nature, the budding and falling leaves, the blooming and fading flowers, had been enough for her, because she knew nothing of the world beyond; but now—now that she knew all the world was awake, and that great and mighty changes were constantly going on that she could never hear of, to rejoice at or be sorry for—she chafed and fretted and fumed, hour after hour, as she took her solitary walk up and down the terrace where she and Else and Fritz had spent so many of their early days. Then she thought of Eric, and the sorrow and disappointment he was suffering, until she almost regretted that she had not rebelliously followed her brother's advice, and left her father's house.

She wondered sometimes what her father's motive could be for desiring to break her betrothal contract; but, whatever it was, he kept it carefully to himself as yet, and Margarethe was allowed to do as she liked at present—shape her life according to her own pleasure. Father Sebastian did not trouble her either—did not reprove her for not coming to confession—but seemed anxious to conciliate her as much as possible, although he was by no means officious in doing so. At first,

OFFICIOUS: *aggressive*

Margarethe thought she would spend the greater part of her time in her aunt's room, reading to and amusing the old lady; but she soon found that Dame Ermengarde was beyond such attentions as these now. After a few minutes the reading wearied her, and she fell asleep; indeed, the greater part of her time was spent in sleep now, and her maid sat watching her in silence, holding up her finger if Margarethe spoke or entered the room, lest her mistress should be disturbed.

No one wanted her here, it seemed, for her grandfather was even less awake to the world than her aunt, and her father was so absorbed in his beloved study of astrology as to live in a totally different world from hers. It was the wisdom gained from this study that made him see so clearly, as he thought, the ultimate triumph of the Church over this Reformation, and made him so determined to save his children from the ruin that must fall upon those who had followed Luther and this new learning. At home, in the forest, Margarethe was, he thought, safe, and would soon fall back into her old belief; and Else—well—she was certainly beyond all danger from these disturbing influences. Fritz only seemed obstinately bent on his own destruction, and many an anxious hour was spent devising plans by which he might yet be saved; for the omens over which he pored all pointed to some great danger awaiting him in the future.

The feeling that no one needed her—no one's life was the better or brighter for her being here—grew to be such an intolerable thought to Margarethe at last, that she felt ready to run away, and journey back to the Rhineland alone. Why had God shut her up here in this living tomb, where no one wanted her, when she might have been of use to Lady Hadwig and Eric and Fritz? It was hard, it was cruel, Margarethe said in her heart; "I do well to be angry;" and she nursed her anger against God, and her father, too. But this only made the tedious monotony of her life the more unbearable, and, at last, as a refuge from her own weary thoughts, she left off walking on the terrace, and shut herself up to read in her own room.

She had several of Luther's works, but her most precious treasure was a New Testament. As she had learned to read the Latin, she could now read this for herself. Eric had made her a present of it while they were at Leipsic, and Margarethe had read a good deal of it, but now, recalling the plan adopted by the Swiss preacher of Zurich cathedral, and Luther's advice that prayer should always accompany the reading of God's Word, she resolved to begin, as Zwinglius had done, at the first chapter of Matthew, and read the book through, prayerfully and consecutively.

It was certainly the best remedy possible for her unhappiness; but Margarethe soon found that

CONSECUTIVELY: *in order*

she could not study all day, and the thought still oppressed her that her life was of no use to anyone—not even to herself, just now.

At last she resolved to go down to the village again, and see some of the peasants she and Else used to visit. She had shrunk from doing this, because she knew it would remind her more painfully than ever of her sister's absence; but she resolved to do it now, in spite of the pain, and the reward she gained was greater than she could have anticipated.

"Ah, Fraulein, we have been waiting and watching for you ever since we heard you had come home from the strange places beyond the forest," said an old grandmother, who used to nurse Margarethe and her sister when they were children.

"I did not know you would care so much to see me, or I might have come before; but I cannot bring Else now, and it was Else that everybody loved," and the tears welled up to Margarethe's eyes as she spoke.

The old woman raised her eyes and crossed herself devoutly. "The Fraulein Else was always a saint, and it was not to be thought of that she could be long in the world, mixing herself with our common life," she said.

It was just what had been said of her sister again and again, and yet it somehow displeased Margarethe now; and she said hastily, "I think God would rather see His saints helping people to live their common life better, than that they should shut themselves up in a convent."

Of course, the old woman was astonished, and crossed herself again, although she hardly knew why, except that Father Sebastian had taught them that they must reverence all nuns and monks as being next to the saints in heaven. Little or nothing of what was going on in the outside world ever penetrated to this remote, secluded village. Some of the peasants had heard the name of Luther, but they knew nothing about him or his work. Not one among them could read, or even thought of learning to read. Their knowledge of God and religion had been taught them at odd times by Father Sebastian; but their faith in God was far less real than their belief in the demons and forest spirits who were said to inhabit every tree and cave and brook in this forest land. The boldest of them would not venture to talk of these after nightfall, for fear they should be carried off before morning; and although they cared little about going to confession, even when Father Sebastian accorded them the opportunity, they would not dare to transgress any of the traditional laws these lords of the forest were supposed to have laid down for the observance of helpless mortals.

Now, Margarethe had thrown off a good deal of this old superstition during her absence, and the news of her daring the anger of the forest spirits by several things she had done since she had been

ACCORDED: *granted*
TRANSGRESS: *violate*

home had already reached the village, and this the old woman was determined to tell her of, and very soon began.

"Now, Fraulein, you have been away so long, and got so wise in the knowledge of the big world outside our forest, that I hear you have forgotten things that ought always to be remembered by those who live here," said the old woman seriously.

Margarethe smiled. "What have I done?" she asked.

The old woman looked all round the walls of the hut to make sure that there was no chink open by which her words could be heard outside, and then she whispered, "You have forgotten the forest spirits, Fraulein, and how soon they are provoked."

Margarethe laughed. "I don't half believe in them now; at least, I believe if there are spirits they are not what we think."

The old woman would have been less shocked if she had said she did not believe in God; but to look so unconcerned—nay, to laugh, and say she did not half believe in these dreadful enemies of man—was almost past belief, and the old woman told her so.

Margarethe did not laugh again, but she said, "I am sure we have all been mistaken about this, for there is but one God, and He is our Father in heaven, who loves us, and would not let evil creatures have the power to harm us."

The old woman stared at what seemed such strange talk, but Margarethe, nothing daunted by the old woman's wonder, took out Dr. Luther's book on the Lord's Prayer, which, being written for the people, was easy to understand, and read to her for nearly an hour.

They were strange, wonderful words to her, as they had been to Margarethe long ago, but she begged her to come again and read some more, although she hardly knew whether she ought to listen to the news about a God who claimed to be more powerful than their forest spirits.

The next time Margarethe went she found that the old woman had promised to let some of her neighbors come and hear the wonderful news their young mistress had brought home with her, and an attentive little audience was soon gathered to listen to her reading; and from this time it became an established custom for Margarethe to go down to the village once or twice a week, and read the books she had brought home with her, or narrate the accounts she read in the New Testament of the gracious words and works of the Lord Jesus.

Winter somewhat interfered with this work, but before it came to an end she had commenced the daring experiment of teaching some of them to read. She had had some difficulty at first in persuading them that they had any right to learn this clerkly art, and no one, perhaps, but their young mistress could have overcome their scruples about

CLERKLY: *scholarly*

this; but she did it, and set herself steadily to the task of teaching them.

So the autumn and winter passed away, and life grew more tolerable to Margarethe, and she tried to grow content with her work here in the depth of the forest. When spring came again—the spring of 1520—she began to turn her eyes, with longing expectation, to the grass-grown road by which travelers came to the castle. Surely someone would come soon. Fritz or Eric would come back again, for they would know how eager and anxious she felt about Dr. Luther, and whether trouble had followed through the Leipsic discussion.

But spring deepened into summer, and with the first summer heats her aunt died and was laid peacefully to rest; and then in sheer despair of anyone coming to tell her what was going on in the outside world, Margarethe proposed to her father a journey to Nimptschen to see Else, and tell her of her aunt's death.

But von Ranitz hated the trouble of traveling now, and urged, what was perfectly true, that he could scarcely leave his father for more than a few hours; and Margarethe was made to feel that she was selfish and unreasonable in wishing to leave her home.

So the days and weeks went on again, and many a battle did Margarethe fight with herself to gain the patience and submission needful now from day to day. At last, as she was walking one day on

Margarethe and the Peddler

the terrace, she espied a peddler with his pack toiling wearily up the road toward the castle gate, and she gave orders at once that as soon as the man had rested and had had some refreshment he should bring his pack, and let her see his wares on the terrace. She did not have to wait long, and the wares he brought were precious indeed. He had come direct from the castle of Ebenbourg, in the Rhineland, and had been entrusted with a packet of letters for her.

Margarethe eagerly tore off the outer covers, and then saw that there was one from Fritz, one from Eric, and another from Lady Hadwig. But before reading her letters—which she thought it best to conceal for the present—she must examine the contents of the man's pack, and while she was turning over knives and combs, tiny looking-glasses, strips of taffetas, and sundry copies of Luther's books concealed at the bottom, he was telling her the news of the day; for this was the most important part of a peddler's business—to be a sort of walking newspaper, industriously gathering all sorts of items as he journeyed along, and retailing the same or others, according to who his customers might be.

But his news for Margarethe almost made her heart stand still with affright. It was in everybody's mouth now, the man said, and so there could be no mistake about it: the Pope had issued a bull of condemnation against Dr. Luther, by which he was commanded to destroy all his works, cease preaching and teaching, retract all the errors he had taught, or appear at Rome within sixty days. Failing the performance of these things, the most direful maledictions, excommunications and interdicts were pronounced against Luther and all his followers. Bishops were commanded to seize his books and destroy them, and send all who read them, bound in chains, to Rome.

Margarethe shivered as she heard this awful threat, which had never yet been made in vain by Rome; but she managed to say calmly, "You will not tell anyone else at the castle or in the village what you have told me;" and then she made some purchases and arranged for him to come the next day for her letters, that he would carry back to the Rhineland.

Her brother's and Eric's letters confirmed the news brought by the peddler, but assured her that they were preparing to defend Luther.

After this, silence again settled down, and the autumn and winter of another year passed in the stillness of the Thuringian forest.

MALEDICTIONS: *curses*
INTERDICTS: *formal orders forbidding participation in the services of the church*

Chapter XXII

Conclusion

AFTER the visit of the peddler there was a noticeable change in Father Sebastian's manner toward Margarethe, and a few days afterward, meeting her during her walk on the terrace, he said, "My daughter, I am sorely grieved at your continued obstinacy."

"Obstinacy!" repeated Margarethe, with emphasis.

"Yes, my daughter, you are living in open rebellion against the commands of holy Church. You never come to confession now, and, I greatly fear, neglect the duties of penance and fasting."

Margarethe's eyes flashed. "Father Sebastian, you forget a matter which occurred a year or two since. I told you then you should never shrive me again, and you never shall. I can and do confess my sins to God, and I know that He will pardon them."

"Confess your sins to God, without the help of the Church or the priest? Was ever impiety so

SHRIVE ME: *hear my confession of sins*
IMPIETY: *a lack of respect for God*

daring before!" exclaimed Father Sebastian, and he paced up and down the terrace in great agitation.

An hour or two later Margarethe was summoned to her father's room. "Margarethe, you must submit yourself to the instruction of your confessor," he said angrily; "these are troublous times, and I fear I have acted unwisely in suffering you to leave the shelter of your own home. But I do not doubt your love for me, or that you will render all reverent obedience to my command in this, as in other matters; now, my child, go to Father Sebastian, and tell him you are willing to learn all he may desire to teach you."

"I do not desire any of Father Sebastian's instruction. I have already learned such truths as—as—O Father, do not ask me to give up my faith, the faith I learned at Wittenberg!" suddenly spoke Margarethe, and then she burst into tears.

Her father took this as a sign of submission. "Now, Margarethe, it is useless to contend about this matter. I hoped that if you came home, where you could never hear anything about these unsettling doctrines, you would soon forget them, and return to your early faith in the Church. You have had long enough to do this; but Father Sebastian tells me you still neglect one of the chief commands of holy Church: you never go to confession. Now, this must not continue longer. The times are not only troublous, but dangerous, and it is needful, above all things, that we should not be suspected of holding these pernicious doctrines of Luther."

"But, my father, you once hoped they would be believed by all Germany."

"I did, but times are changed. I cannot be expected to know truth from error; that is a matter for the Church to decide, and the Church has decided. This monk Luther is condemned, with all he ever taught, and even his followers are in danger now. So I hope, Margarethe, you will be reasonable, and not bring the disgraceful name of 'heretic' upon your family."

Von Ranitz thought he had said enough, and looked at Margarethe as she stood near. He hoped to see her shudder at the bare mention of that dreadful word; but, instead of this, she said quite calmly,

"My Bohemian ancestors were called heretics, but the world is beginning to find out that they were good men after all, and spoke words of truth; and so it may be with Dr. Luther, although the Pope now declares him a heretic. I do not wish to disobey you, my father. You know I would not if I could help it; but in this matter, I—I cannot obey. Ask me what else you will—I have given up all else to please you—but not this. O, I cannot give up this—the faith that Dr. Luther has taught me; for it is dearer than life itself to believe that God loves me, loves with the tender love of father and mother too!"

PERNICIOUS: *evil and dangerous*

Von Ranitz knew his daughter well enough to understand that it would be useless to press this matter further just now; but from this time she was suffered to have but little peace. Sometimes her father, and sometimes the family confessor, tried all their powers of argument to induce her to give up all she had learned at Wittenberg. But it was in vain. They did not know that when she left them, after one of these arguments, she went to her room, there to read in her precious New Testament words of strength, and hope, and encouragement, and to pour out her soul in prayer to God—not in a meaningless babble of Latin that conveyed no sense to her own mind—*aves* and *paternosters* rattled off on her rosary—but deep, heartfelt prayer; a pouring out of her soul's hopes, and wants, and fears. Her father did not know of this secret source of strength and consolation; and so Margarethe's calmness and firmness was something he could not understand, but which caused so much vexation that he would fain have proceeded to more rigorous measures but for the cautions of Father Sebastian. He had acquired unbounded influence over the mind of von Ranitz, and by his advice it was arranged that Margarethe should be allowed the winter to repent in, and then, if all their efforts failed to convince her, she should be removed to a convent in the spring.

Father Sebastian, now on the alert, soon discovered her visits to the village, and before the winter

AVES: *"Hail" in Latin, the Catholic "Hail Mary" prayer*
PATERNOSTERS: *"Our Father" in Latin, the Lord's Prayer*

commenced they were forbidden. But the seed of a purer faith had been sown in more than one heart there, and Margarethe had already foreseen and prepared for it. Several of her scholars could read now, and so to each of these she gave one of her treasured books, with the command that they should keep it safely, and read it to others for her sake.

So, when the last visit was paid, Margarethe left her little flock, with the assurance that God would keep alive the little torch of pure religion she had lighted; and it was some comfort to her during the dreary days of that winter to think that her work would not be altogether in vain.

But O, the weary days! how slowly they passed, with nothing to break their monotony but an angry argument with her father, or an equally vexatious one with the family priest. She knew her doom now—knew that she was to be sent to a convent as soon as the spring made traveling possible; and, although she prayed that she might be spared this, she saw no hope of escape, for she had no means of communicating with her brother and friends in the Rhineland, who alone could help her in her difficulty. It seemed as though nature itself conspired against poor Margarethe just now, for the snows of winter were gone by the end of January, and early in March spring had decidedly begun, and preparations were soon made for their journey. Margarethe had often wondered where

VEXATIOUS: *vexing, troublesome*

she was to be taken; she could hardly hope that it would be to Nimptschen. It seemed as though this was a matter difficult to decide upon, both to her father and the family priest, but her little maid had heard that her destination was to be Erfurt; and on the first day of April Father Sebastian, with a few retainers, and a couple of maids to attend Margarethe, set out with her, as he had done with Else a few years before.

But Margarethe was no willing victim, as Else had been; and that she could so calmly set out upon this journey as she did was as great a puzzle to herself as to everyone else. She had no hope of escape now, for the authorities of the convent of Erfurt were under obligations to her father, and their well-known jealousy of Luther would only make them the more willing to do as he wished.

She wondered, in a dumb, apathetic sort of way, as she rode through the forest, whether she would ever journey along that road again, or whether the rest of her days would be passed within the convent walls. Poor Margarethe! how could she know that every step that took her nearer to her destined prison took her nearer to the help of friends?

When Erfurt was reached they were surprised to see the streets so full of people, and the bustle and confusion that seemed to prevail. They were not, however, long left in ignorance of the cause of this unusual excitement. Luther was expected

DUMB: *silent*
APATHETIC: *emotionless*

every hour on his way to the diet now assembled at Worms.

It was an intense relief to Margarethe to hear that Dr. Luther was safe still, in spite of the Pope's bull. Father Sebastian was no less annoyed than she was pleased, and he said angrily, "I thought that meddlesome monk was in Rome by this time."

It soon became evident that they could not reach the convent while the streets were so thronged; for, whatever the jealousy of the monks and university doctors might be, the people loved Luther, and, in spite of the storm that the Pope's bull had raised, they were determined to show him every honor; so Father Sebastian led his party aside to the shelter of a quiet hostelry. As they rode up to the door a party of young knights, travel-stained and dusty, also drew near, and, to Margarethe's inexpressible joy, she saw that they wore the colors and device of Count von Sickengen.

In a moment she jumped from her palfrey, and, before Father Sebastian could understand what she was doing, she ran among the newcomers, anxiously asking, "Is Fritz von Ranitz of your party?"

"Margarethe!" called a familiar voice, and the next minute Eric was by her side, and her brother quickly followed him.

"Save me, save me from the convent!" she gasped, as Father Sebastian came up.

Fritz stepped forward at once to meet him, telling Eric to lead Margarethe inside the house. "I will take charge of my sister now, and relieve you of all further troubles," he said.

Father Sebastian looked at him in amazement. "Insolent boy! do you not see your father's retainers. I tell you we have been sent by him to place your sister in safekeeping."

"Well, you have performed your mission," said Fritz, with a grim smile; "she is safe enough now, and you can return and tell my father so." And Fritz turned on his heel, and went away in search of Margarethe to learn more of this strange proceeding.

He hoped that Father Sebastian would not follow him, but in this he was mistaken. Leaving the men to do as they pleased, the priest joined Fritz again as he was entering the inn, and demanded that Margarethe should be brought out at once, as he had decided to go on to the convent without delay.

"And wherefore was my sister to be taken to the convent?" demanded Fritz angrily; "she is not to be doomed to the service of the Church, and you know it. You know that she is the betrothed wife of Eric von Schonstein, betrothed by my father's express wish and desire."

"But your father has changed his mind; and Eric von Schonstein—as much a heretic as Luther himself—shall never marry a von Ranitz," said the priest, now as angry as Fritz himself.

Then followed a storm of angry words and invectives, heartily enjoyed by the retainers, who,

INVECTIVES: *insulting or abusive language*

having disposed of their horses, stood about, looking at their young master, and triumphing in the discomfiture of the priest.

When Father Sebastian at length turned to leave he found that his party had no intention of moving further for the present, and so he had to hasten on alone to the convent, to consult with his friends there as to the best course to be taken in this dilemma. Meanwhile Fritz turned to inquire about his sister and friend, but it seemed that no one in the inn had seen anything of them. The house was searched, but the lady could not be found or the young knight either, and a little later one of Margarethe's maidens discovered that her companion was also missing; her mistress' favorite maid could nowhere be found.

Fritz fretted and fumed, and at last stormed, fearing he had been outwitted by the cunning priest after all; only the absence of Eric as well could hardly be accounted for in this way. But these private cares and fears had to be laid aside, for he had been sent with other young knights and a large party of retainers, to conduct Luther on his way to Worms, for fear an attempt should be made to injure him. He had also been instructed to try and persuade the Reformer not to trust himself in the hands of his enemies, even with the emperor's safe-conduct, as it was feared that he for his own ends would hand him over to the Pope. But Luther had no fear; nothing could

DISCOMFITURE: *frustration and embarrassment*

shake his trust in God, although an interdict had been published against him in every town through which he passed; and the greatest curse of the Church pronounced upon him and all his followers by the Pope himself only a short time before.

After journeying with him for some miles, Fritz left his horsemen under the care of one of his friends, and hastened forward to Ebenbourg, to acquaint von Sickengen with the failure of his mission, and Lady Hadwig with the strange disappearance of Margarethe. But the lady only smiled when she heard his story—a smile that Fritz could not understand until the lady called a little page from an anteroom, and told him to go and ask Lady von Schonstein to come to her.

"Lady von Schonstein!" repeated Fritz. "Eric lost his mother many years ago."

"And he has just had news of the death of his father," said Lady Hadwig.

"Then Eric is here, and Margarethe, too?" he exclaimed.

"No, Eric has gone home for a short time. I wonder you did not meet him; he rode away scarcely an hour since, leaving—"

But at this moment the arras before the door was drawn aside by the attendant page, and Margarethe entered.

"Here is Lady von Schonstein, Eric's wife," said Lady Hadwig, enjoying the surprise of Fritz.

ANTEROOM: *outer room*

"Fritz, we could not help it; Eric said it was the only way he could save me. You are not angry with us?"

"Angry with you? what have I to be angry about?"

"Our marriage. We could not stay to ask you about it, for our only chance of escape was while you kept Father Sebastian talking, and we hurried away to the Augustinian monastery, and asked to wait there until Dr. Luther came; and then—then—well, we told him all about it, and as he had been present at our betrothal he married us, and we hurried out of Erfurt as fast as our horses could travel."

Fritz heaved a sigh of relief. "I am glad, very glad. My poor Margarethe, you have tried to obey. God has saved you, and will bless you," and Fritz hurried away to hide his emotion.

A few hours afterward a party of horsemen were seen riding in hot haste toward thc castle, but only one or two entered. Margarethe and Lady Hadwig, who were walking on the terrace, saw their arrival, and soon afterward saw them also depart with Master Bucer, the chaplain, and a party of horsemen. They rode down the hill together, and then Bucer and the von Sickengen horsemen rode on toward Oppenheim, and the strangers came back to the castle.

The ladies, of course, felt curious to know who the strangers could be, and, meeting Fritz soon afterward, Margarethe eagerly inquired; for they had noticed that they wore the imperial colors and device, and were evidently distinguished personages.

"They have come on a mission from Worms, to warn us of the danger awaiting Luther if he should enter the city," said Fritz.

"But who are they?" asked his sister.

"One is the emperor's high chamberlain, and the other his confessor."

"And they are friends of Luther!"

"They profess to be."

"But what do you think? Are they sincere, or is it only a trick to betray him into a trap?" said Margarethe, anxiously.

Fritz laughed. "This hostelry of righteousness would be a trap in which he could be hidden safely from his foes. Bucer has gone to fetch Dr. Luther here."

"Will he come, do you think?" asked his sister; but the next minute she shook her head. "He has been summoned to attend the diet by the emperor himself, and has his safe-conduct, too; so that I am sure Dr. Luther will think it his duty to go, in spite of everything. Do you not think so, Fritz?"

"I know not what to think, what to hope. The emperor's confessor has persuaded Bucer that if he could discuss the disputed points here with Dr. Luther everything might be arranged without his running into danger, as he certainly will do if he goes to Worms, and he has come back to await his arrival."

A few hours afterward von Sickengen's men returned with the chaplain, but Dr. Luther was not with them. Their errand had been quite fruitless, and, to the evident chagrin of the chancellor and confessor, they heard that he was pressing on his dangerous journey with all speed.

A little later a friend brought the news that another attempt had been made to stop Luther from entering the town; and, though the message came from his dearest friend, he sent back this reply: "Go and tell your master that, were there as many devils in Worms as there are tiles upon the roofs, I would enter."

How anxious his friends were at this time can well be imagined. He had entered the gates that many prophesied he would never leave again; while others protested that the papal party dreaded nothing so much as his appearing before the emperor and princes, and, therefore, *they* had tried to stop him. Others, again, said the safe-conduct would be violated in his case, as it had been in that of John Huss, and that he had ruined the Reformation in going; but a few began to see clearly that the papal nuncio had dreaded his appearance, and wished for nothing so much as that he should disobey the emperor's command, and fail to appear, in spite of the safe-conduct that had been sent to him; and then who could defend him!

Count von Sickengen could not remain inactive while the champion of Germany was in danger; and so, leaving Ebenbourg, he rode away to Worms, to

CHAGRIN: *embarrassment*

watch the proceedings, and send warnings, if necessary, to his garrison, for he was determined that Luther's death should not be unavenged.

Margarethe and Lady Hadwig waited with eager anxiety for news from Worms, and the count, knowing this, rode over a few days afterward to tell them of the progress of the affair. "Luther is as bold as a lion," he said, in a tone of warm admiration. "Many thought that when he stood before all the princes and nobles of Germany he would retract something that he has held so firmly hitherto; but when the Chancellor of Treves stood up, after his address to the diet, and said, 'Will you, or will you not, retract!' Luther replied, without the least hesitation, 'Since your most serene majesty and your high mightiness call upon me for a simple, clear, and definite answer, I will give it, and it is this: I cannot subject my faith either to the Pope or to councils, because it is clear as day that they have often fallen into error, and even into great self-contradiction. If, then, I am not disproved by passages of Scripture, or by clear arguments—if I am not disproved by the very passages which I have quoted, and so bound in conscience to submit to the Word of God—*I neither can, nor will, retract anything*, for it is not safe for a Christian to speak against his conscience. HERE I AM: I CANNOT DO OTHERWISE. GOD HELP ME! AMEN.'"

"And what said the princes and emperor?" asked Lady Hadwig, anxiously.

"They are certainly favorably disposed toward Luther. No one could fail to be impressed; but the Pope's nuncio and his friends are more than ever bent on his destruction, and it is feared that the young emperor will violate his safe-conduct after all."

It was this part of the business, as well as to bring his wife the news, that had brought von Sickengen home just now. He was anxious to see that his almost impregnable fortress was prepared for any emergency, and the knights and soldiers in readiness. He found that his dear friend, von Hutten, was preparing everything necessary either for a siege or assault, but before he went back to Worms he directed Fritz to take his sister without delay to her husband, as it might be unsafe to leave the castle shortly.

Margarethe would rather have waited until Eric could have fetched her, more especially as she was anxious to know the fate of Luther; but since it was necessary that she should leave the Rhineland at once, and go to her new home in the Thuringian forest, she made her preparations at once, and she and Fritz were soon on the road. Fritz promised to let her know all that happened as soon as possible, and, having taken her safely to her husband's castle, he returned without delay to the Rhineland.

Eric was just preparing to set off for his bride when she arrived. His father had been buried the day before, and, his affairs being in order, Eric had

IMPREGNABLE: *unconquerable*

had little trouble with them, and was only anxious to fetch home his wife to help him in the work of teaching and raising the peasantry of the village from the depths of superstition and ignorance in which they had so long been sunk. Margarethe's experience among the retainers at her own home would prove of great service now, and the quietness and seclusion of their forest home would be less irksome, especially in the society of her husband, than it might have been two years previously. If it had not been the uncertainty—the suspense they were compelled to endure—as to the fate of Luther, their happiness would have been almost complete; but when at last news reached them that he had been allowed to leave Worms to return to Wittenberg, there likewise came the report that he had been seized by his enemies on his way, and had not since been heard of. No one had seen or heard of him since, and von Sickengen and his brave knights were gathering all their forces for war in defense of the Gospel.

"If Luther were living he would bid them lay aside the sword, as he has done before," said Margarethe; and she used all her influence to deter her husband from abandoning the little reformation he had begun among their own peasants, to take up the sword with von Sickengen.

Some hoped that before a blow could be struck Luther might reappear, for it began to be whispered that he was in safe-keeping, and might return to Wittenberg at any hour. But the spring and summer passed, and autumn came; but before it was over Eric had seen Luther walking in the forest a few miles from his own castle. He was dressed as a knight, and bade Eric address him as Master Georges, as those in attendance upon him knew him by no other name. He sent a message to some of his friends, and told Eric that he was busy translating the Scriptures into German, and hoped to have it ready for the printers by the time he was released. This was joyful news for Margarethe, and she resolved to journey with her husband as far as Wittenberg, to deliver the message Dr. Luther had sent, and then, if possible, to go as far as Nimptschen and see Else once more.

They had visited their friends at Wittenberg, and were near the gate on their way to Nimptschen when Margarethe saw her father approaching. He did not notice her until she was close beside him—had laid her trembling hand upon his arm. "Father, Father, you will forgive me!" she said in a choking voice. "You bade me marry Eric; will you not bless our marriage now?"

They were in the street, and she could not say more; but she thought her father would ask them to go with him, and hear what they had to say in excuse. But he did not.

"Will you renounce this Lutheran doctrine at once and forever?" he asked, sternly.

"I cannot—O, I cannot do that!" gasped Margarethe.

"Then I disown you, as I do your brother; I have but one child now!" and he pushed Margarethe aside, and passed on without another word.

Eric led his wife away, so much overcome that she could not speak; but after a time she grew more calm. "I can pray for him, and I will hope still," she said, and then they went on their road to Nimptschen, wondering what reception they would meet with from Else this time.

Margarethe had been so disappointed on her former visits, that she would not allow herself to hope for anything better now; but the moment she saw her sister she became conscious that some undefinable change had taken place in her. There was a subdued eagerness and restlessness in her eyes now, instead of the dull apathy she had remarked before; but Else's first words made her almost scream with joy and astonishment. The sisters had scarcely greeted each other when Else whispered, "I want to come home, dear Margarethe; would my father let me come?"

"You shall come to my home, darling, if you can be released from this prison. But tell me why you wish it so much."

Else held up her finger warningly, for the elder nun was not far off. "Some of the younger sisters have been reading Dr. Luther's books—yours and others—and we wish to leave the convent, but know not how to do so. Cannot you help us,

Margarethe? Tell us what we ought to do. You were always wise and clever, and knew just the best way of doing everything. We cannot stay here unless—unless we are brave enough to die," said the young nun in a trembling whisper.

"You, at least, shall not," said Margarethe.

But Else shook her head. "We must stay or escape together; so you must think for us all, Margarethe. Tell us what we ought to do."

Margarethe thought for a minute or two, and then she said, "So many of the nobles have embraced the cause of Luther that it may be the friends of all the ladies may be glad to hear they wish to return home. Else, I think it would be better for each of you to write to your friends first, and then—then—"

"But suppose they should refuse. You know the disgrace, Margarethe," said her sister.

"Then we must help you to escape. But you will write to our father first, and then to me, if he refuses."

Then they talked on indifferent subjects, and Margarethe spoke to the other nun, hoping she should be invited inside the *grille*. But she was not. The sister suspected her of passing some of Luther's books in before, and watched her closely now; and when she asked to be allowed to see her sister again the following day she was told such a thing was not possible; she could not visit her again for some months.

But although Margarethe was disappointed

at this, and knew that the refusal might prevent the letters being sent for some months, still she could afford to wait for months, or even years, with the hope that she should yet be reunited to her sister; and meanwhile she and Eric might be able to devise some plan for their escape, in case their friends should refuse to receive them. They returned home, to wait with eager longing for the coming of Else's letter; but the winter passed before any tidings came. At last a messenger came from Wittenberg with the news that Else was there, and Dr. Luther, too; and as the spring had come, and traveling was less dangerous, Margarethe and her husband set out at once to fetch the young nun home. She had escaped with eight of her companions, and been brought to Wittenberg; and Dr. Luther at once sent to her father, who, refusing to receive her, or even to see her, he sent to Eric, who gladly welcomed the fugitive.

But while they were rejoicing over the escape of Else, sad news reached them from the Rhineland concerning their dear friends of Ebenbourg. Luther had begged the knights to lay down the sword, telling them the kingdom of God could never be advanced by any weapons but the sword of the Word, the Holy Scriptures, which in a few months would be in the hands of the people, written in their own tongue. But von Sickengen was anxious to do his part in the noble struggle against Rome, and resolved to attack Luther's foe, the prince

Archbishop of Treves, and laid siege to that city. Never was there a more disastrous campaign; von Sickengen was driven to his Castle of Ebenbourg, and this "hostelry of righteousness" was taken by the enemy, and the brave count killed. Von Hutten, with Fritz and a few other knights, escaped into Switzerland, and Fritz eventually settled at Zurich, and married Anna, about the same time as Zwinglius was married to her widowed friend. He was the first priest who dared to throw off the galling bondage Rome had imposed upon her clergy; but he was soon followed by Luther himself, who married one of the nuns that escaped from Nimptschen.

For many troublous but happy years Eric von Schonstein and his energetic and noble-spirited wife lived to bless the world by their Christian example and earnest efforts in behalf of the "great Reformation." Many an important message passed between the dark and lofty castle in the Thuringian forest, in which they dwelt, and the spacious mansion which Fritz von Ranitz had purchased in Zurich. The times became increasingly eventful; but neither wars, nor diplomacy, nor theological disputations, ever absorbed the attention of these worthy people so completely as to cause them to forget the days when Eric first met the stately Margarethe, and Fritz exchanged his earliest greetings with the amiable Swiss maiden Anna. And the story of those years, and the no less interesting experiences of the gentle Else within the dingy convent walls, were often repeated to the eager groups of young folks who in time surrounded both happy firesides.

And now, in bringing my story to a close, I will ask the reader to apply its lessons for themselves; for it is not merely a historical tale that I have endeavored to write, but one that shall help us in all high and noble aspirations; that shall teach us that the path of duty, though it may sometimes seem to lead into danger, is yet the only safe one for us to walk in; and that "by patient continuance in well-doing"[1] even in the everyday duties of our lives there is still great reward.

The End

[1] Romans 2:7

ABOUT THE AUTHOR

Emma Leslie (1837-1909), whose actual name was Emma Dixon, lived in Lewisham, Kent, in the south of England. She was a prolific Victorian children's author who wrote over 100 books. Emma Leslie's first book, *The Two Orphans,* was published in 1863 and her books remained in print for years after her death. She is buried at the St. Mary's Parish Church, in Pwllcrochan, Pembroke, South Wales.

Emma Leslie brought a strong Christian emphasis into her writing and many of her books were published by the Religious Tract Society. Her extensive historical fiction works covered many important periods in church history. Her writing also included a short booklet on the life of Queen Victoria published in the 50th year of the Queen's reign.

EMMA LESLIE CHURCH HISTORY SERIES

GLAUCIA THE GREEK SLAVE

A Tale of Athens in the First Century

After the death of her father, Glaucia is sold to a wealthy Roman family to pay his debts. She tries hard to adjust to her new life but longs to find a God who can love even a slave. Meanwhile, her brother, Laon, struggles to find her and to earn enough money to buy her freedom. But what is the mystery that surrounds their mother's disappearance years earlier and will they ever be able to read the message in the parchments she left for them?

THE CAPTIVES

Or, Escape from the Druid Council

The Druid priests are as cold and cruel as the forest spirits they claim to represent, and Guntra, the chief of her tribe of Britons, must make a desperate deal with them to protect those she loves. Unaware of Guntra's struggles, Jugurtha, her son, longs to drive the hated Roman conquerors from the land. When he encounters the Christian centurion, Marcinius, Jugurtha mocks the idea of a God of love and kindness, but there comes a day when he is in need of love and kindness for himself and his beloved little sister. Will he allow Marcinius to help him? And will the gospel of Jesus Christ ever penetrate the brutal religion of the proud Britons?

EMMA LESLIE CHURCH HISTORY SERIES

OUT OF THE MOUTH OF THE LION

Or, The Church in the Catacombs

When Flaminius, a high Roman official, takes his wife, Flavia, to the Colosseum to see Christians thrown to the lions, he has no idea the effect it will have. Flavia cannot forget the faith of the martyrs, and finally, to protect her from complete disgrace or even danger, Flaminius requests a transfer to a more remote government post. As he and his family travel to the seven cities of Asia Minor mentioned in Revelation, he sees the various responses of the churches to persecution. His attitude toward the despised Christians begins to change, but does he dare forsake the gods of Rome and embrace the Lord Jesus Christ?

SOWING BESIDE ALL WATERS

A Tale of the World in the Church

There is newfound freedom from persecution for Christians under the emperor, Constantine, but newfound troubles as well. Errors and pagan ways are creeping into the Church, while many of the most devoted Christians are withdrawing from the world into the desert as hermits and nuns. Quadratus, one of the emperor's special guards, is concerned over these developments, even in his own family. Then a riot sweeps through the city and Quadratus' home is ransacked. When he regains consciousness, he finds that his sister, Placidia, is gone. Where is she? And can the Church handle the new freedom, and remain faithful?

Emma Leslie Church History Series

FROM BONDAGE TO FREEDOM

A Tale of the Times of Mohammed

At a Syrian market two Christian women are sold as slaves. One of the slaves ends up in Rome where Bishop Gregory is teaching his new doctrine of "purgatory" and the need for Christians to finish paying for their own sins. The other slave travels with her new master, Mohammed, back to Arabia, where Mohammed eventually declares himself to be the prophet of God. In Rome and Arabia, the two women and countless others fall into the bondage of man-made religions—will they learn at last to find true freedom in the Lord Jesus Christ alone?

THE MARTYR'S VICTORY

A Story of Danish England

Knowing full well they may die in the attempt, a small band of monks sets out to convert the savage Danes who have laid waste to the surrounding countryside year after year. The monks' faith is sorely tested as they face opposition from the angry Priest of Odin as well as doubts, sickness and starvation, but their leader, Osric, is unwavering in his attempts to share the "White Christ" with those who reject Him. Then the monks discover a young Christian woman who has escaped being sacrificed to the Danish gods—can she help reach those who had enslaved her and tried to kill her?

GYTHA'S MESSAGE

A Tale of Saxon England

Having discovered God's love for her, Gytha, a young slave, longs to escape the violence and cruelty of the world and devote herself to learning more about this God of love. Instead she lives in a Saxon household that despises the name of Christ. Her simple faith and devoted service bring hope and purpose to those around her, especially during the dark days when England is defeated by William the Conqueror. Through all of her trials, can Gytha learn to trust that God often has greater work for us to do *in* the world than *out* of it?

Emma Leslie Church History Series

LEOFWINE THE MONK

Or, The Curse of the Ericsons

A Story of a Saxon Family

Leofwine, unlike his wild, younger brother, finds no pleasure in terrorizing the countrside, and longs to enter a monastery. Shortly after he does, however, he hears strange rumors of a monk who preaches "heresy". Unable to stop thinking about these new ideas, Leofwine at last determines to leave the monastery and England. Leofwine's search for inner peace takes him to France and Rome and finally to Jerusalem, but in his travels, he uncovers a plot against his beloved country. Will he be able to help save England? And will he ever find true rest for his troubled soul?

ELFREDA THE SAXON

Or, The Orphan of Jerusalem

A Sequel to Leofwine

When Jerusalem is captured by the Muslims, Elfreda, a young orphan, is sent back to England to her mother's sister. Her aunt is not at all pleased to see her, and her uncle fears she may have brought the family curse back to England. Elfreda's cousin, Guy, who is joining King Richard's Crusade, promises Elfreda that he will win such honor as a crusader that the curse will be removed. Over the years that follow, however, severe trials befall the family and Guy and Elfreda despair of the curse ever being lifted. Is it possible that there is One with power stronger than any curse?

DEARER THAN LIFE

A Story of the Times of Wycliffe

When a neighboring monastery lays claim to one of his fields, Sir Hugh Middleton refuses to yield his property, and further offends the monastery by sending his younger son, Stephen, to study under Dr. John Wycliffe. At the same time, Sir Hugh sends his elder son, Harry, to serve as an attendant to the powerful Duke of Lancaster. As Wycliffe seeks to share the Word of God with the common people, Stephen and Harry and their sisters help spread the truth, but what will it cost them in the dangerous day in which they live?

Emma Leslie Church History Series

BEFORE THE DAWN

A Tale of Wycliffe and Huss

To please her crippled grandson, Conrad, Dame Ursula allows a kindly blacksmith and his friend, Ned Trueman, to visit the boy. Soon, however, she becomes suspicious that the men belong to the despised group who are followers of Dr. John Wycliffe, and she passionately warns Conrad of the dangers of evil "heresy". He decides to become a famous teacher in the Church so he can combat heresy, but he wonders why all the remedies of the Church fail to cure him. And why do his mother and grandmother refuse to speak of the father he has never known?

FAITHFUL, BUT NOT FAMOUS

A Tale of the French Reformation

Young Claude Leclerc travels to Paris to begin his training for the priesthood, but he is not sure *what* he believes about God. One day he learns the words to an old hymn and is drawn to the lines about "David's Royal Fountain" that will "purge every sin away." Claude yearns to find this fountain, and at last dares to ask the famous Dr. Lefèvre where he can find it. His question leads Dr. Lefèvre to set aside his study of the saints and study the Scriptures in earnest. As Dr. Lefèvre grasps the wonderful truth of salvation by grace, he wants to share it with Claude, but Claude has mysteriously disappeared. Where is he? And is France truly ready to receive the good news of the gospel of Jesus Christ?

EMMA LESLIE JUNIOR CHURCH HISTORY SERIES

HILDA THE BRITON
Or, The Golden Age
The Story of a Roman Slave Girl

When their tribe in Britain is conquered by the Romans, Bran and his young sister, Hilda, are taken to Rome and sold as slaves. Filled with anger, Bran grows to hate everyone except Hilda. Meanwhile, she hears stories of the Roman god, Saturn, and longs for the day when he will rule the world in a Golden Age where everyone will be happy and free. One day, an elderly slave takes Hilda to hear a prisoner named Paul and she learns of another God, a God who made the heavens and the earth and who loves slaves. What will it cost Hilda and Bran if they decide to follow this new God?

THE MAGIC RUNES
A Tale of the Times of Charlemagne

One day, in 782 A.D., young Adalinda is startled to come upon a Saxon family in the forest where she lives with her father. The family is in desperate need but the husband, Godrith, is suspicious of Adalinda's offers of help, especially when he learns that she is a Christian. He well remembers how Charlemagne's "Christian" soldiers burned his village and killed or captured so many of his people because they refused to convert to Christianity. Will Adalinda and her father be able to show Godrith a different picture of Christianity?

FOR MERRIE ENGLAND
A Tale of the Weavers of Norfolk

In the fall of 1357, a Flemish weaver travels around the countryside in England, at the request of the king, seeking apprentices to learn his trade. Along the way he meets a prosperous wool merchant with two sons—big, strong, sixteen-year-old Roger and small, crippled, thirteen-year-old Tom. The merchant is eager to advance his elder son but the weaver feels drawn to the intelligence of young Tom who is seen only as a burden and a curse. When Roger suddenly disappears one evening, the weaver sees his opportunity to help Tom, but will Tom's father agree to his startling plan?

Emma Leslie Junior Church History Series

SOLDIER FRITZ

A Story of the Reformation

Young Fritz wants to follow in the footsteps of Martin Luther and be a soldier for the Lord, so he chooses a Bible from the peddler's pack as his birthday gift. When his father, the Count, goes off to war, however, Fritz and his mother and little sister are forced to flee into the forest to escape being thrown in prison for their new faith. Disguising themselves as commoners, they must trust the Lord as they wait and hope for the Count to rescue them. But how will he ever be able to find them?

THROUGH STRESS AND STRAIN

A Story of the Huguenot Persecution

These are difficult times for the Huguenots in France when Jules Marot comes to visit his brother's family and brings bad news about their young son, Jacques. Huguenot schools and churches are being torn down and these faithful Christians are forbidden to gather for services. The Marot family watches in dismay as many families who were once fervent in the faith give in to the pressure to convert to the "king's religion." As the persecution intensifies, can the whole Marot family, including their sons, Jacques and François, learn to trust God more than ever before?

Additional Titles Available From

Salem Ridge Press

DOWN THE SNOW STAIRS

Or, From Goodnight to Goodmorning

by Alice Corkran

Illustrated by Gordon Browne R. I.

On Christmas Eve, eight-year-old Kitty cannot sleep, knowing that her beloved little brother is critically ill due to her own disobedience. Traveling in a dream to Naughty Children Land, she meets many strange people, including Daddy Coax and Lady Love. Kitty longs to return to the Path of Obedience but can she resist the many temptations she faces? Will she find her way home in time for Christmas? An imaginative and delightful read-aloud for the whole family!

YOUNG ROBIN HOOD

by George Manville Fenn

Illustrated by Victor Venner

In the days of Robin Hood, a young boy named Robin is journeying through Sherwood Forest when suddenly the company is surrounded by men in green. Deserted in the commotion by an unfaithful servant, Robin finds himself alone in the forest. After a miserable night, Robin is found by Little John. Robin is treated kindly by Robin Hood, Maid Marian and the Merry Men, but how long must he wait for his father, the Sheriff of Nottingham, to come to take him home?

Fiction for Younger Readers

MARY JANE – HER BOOK
by Clara Ingram Judson
Illustrated by Francis White

This story, the first book in the Mary Jane series, recounts the happy, wholesome adventures of five-year-old Mary Jane and her family as she helps her mother around the house, goes on a picnic with the big girls, plants a garden with her father, learns to sew and more!

MARY JANE – HER VISIT
by Clara Ingram Judson
Illustrated by Francis White

In this story, the second book in the Mary Jane series, five-year-old Mary Jane has more happy, wholesome adventures, this time at her great-grandparents' farm in the country where she hunts for eggs, picks berries, finds baby rabbits, goes to the circus and more!

Historical Fiction for Younger Readers

AMERICAN TWINS OF THE REVOLUTION

by Lucy Fitch Perkins

General Washington has no money to pay his discouraged troops and twins Sally and Roger are asked by their father, General Priestly, to help hide a shipment of gold which will be used to pay the American soldiers. Unfortunately, British spies have also learned about the gold and will stop at nothing to prevent it from reaching General Washington. Based on a true story, this is a thrilling episode from our nation's history!

MARIE'S HOME

Or, A Glimpse of the Past

by Caroline Austin

Illustrated by Gordon Browne R. I.

Eleven-year-old Marie Hamilton and her family travel to France at the invitation of Louis XVI, just before the start of the French Revolution. There they encounter the tremendous disparity between the proud French Nobility and the oppressed and starving French people. When an enraged mob storms the palace of Versailles, Marie and her family are rescued from grave danger by a strange twist of events, but Marie's story of courage, self-sacrifice and true nobility is not yet over! Honor, duty, compassion and forgiveness are all portrayed in this uplifting story.

Historical Fiction by William W. Canfield

THE WHITE SENECA

Illustrated by G. A. Harker

Captured by the Senecas, fifteen-year-old Henry Cochrane grows to love the Indian ways and becomes Dundiswa—the White Seneca. When Henry is captured by an enemy tribe, however, he must make a desperate attempt to escape from them and rescue fellow captive, Constance Leonard. He will need all the skills he has learned from the Indians, as well as great courage and determination, if he is to succeed. But what will happen to the young woman if they do reach safety? And will he ever be able to return to his own people?

AT SENECA CASTLE

Illustrated by G. A. Harker

In this sequel to *The White Seneca,* Henry Cochrane, now eighteen, faces many perils as he serves as a scout for the Continental Army. General Washington is determined to do whatever it takes to stop the constant Indian attacks on the settlers and yet Henry is torn between his love for the Senecas and his loyalty to his own people. As the Army advances across New York State, Henry receives permission to travel ahead and warn his Indian friends of the coming destruction. But will he reach them in time? And what has happened to the beautiful Constance Leonard whom he had been forced to leave in captivity a year earlier?

THE SIGN ABOVE THE DOOR

Young Prince Martiesen is ruler of the land of Goshen in Egypt, where the Hebrews live. Eight plagues have already come upon Egypt and now Martiesen has been forced by Pharaoh to further increase the burden of the Hebrews. Martiesen, however, is in love with the beautiful Hebrew maiden, Elisheba, whom he is forbidden by Egyptian law to marry. As the nation despairs, the other nobles turn to Martiesen for leadership, but before he can decide what to do, Elisheba is kidnapped by the evil Peshala and terrifying darkness falls over the land. An exciting tale woven around the events of the Exodus from the Egyptian perspective!

Historical Fiction by Charles W. Whistler

A SEA-QUEEN'S SAILING

Illustrated by W. H. C. Groome

Early one summer morning in 935 A.D., Malcolm the Jarl's home in northern Scotland is attacked by Viking raiders led by Heidrek the Seafarer. Struck down during the brief battle that follows, Malcolm is taken captive and imprisoned on what was once his own ship. Refusing to join the murderous Vikings, he manages to escape with two of the other prisoners, only to end up lost at sea. Through a strange series of events, the three young men come upon the young queen, Gerda, who is alone and desperately in need of help. Together, the three friends, Scottish jarl, Irish prince and English thane, pledge themselves to protect Gerda and seek to restore her kingdom which has been usurped by her evil cousin Arnkel. But first they must escape from Heidrek who is pursuing them across the northern seas. Adventure and danger abound in this exciting tale of brave manly men fighting to uphold the honor of a woman.

Adventure by George Manville Fenn

YUSSUF THE GUIDE

Being the Strange Story of the Travels in Asia Minor of Burne the Lawyer, Preston the Professor, and Lawrence the Sick

Illustrated by John Schönberg

Young Lawrence, an invalid, convinces his guardians, Preston the Professor and Burne the Lawyer, to take him along on an archaeological expedition to Turkey. Before they set out, they engage Yussuf as their guide. Through the months that follow, the friends travel deeper and deeper into the remote regions of central Turkey on their trusty horses in search of ancient ruins. Yussuf proves his worth time and time again as they face dangers from a murderous ship captain, poisonous snakes, sheer precipices, bands of robbers and more. Memorable characters, humor and adventure abound in this exciting story!

Biography by George Manville Fenn

GEORGE ALFRED HENTY
The Story of an Active Life

G. A. Henty was one of the most popular boys' authors of the 1800's, a "grand influence for good" who "taught more lasting history to boys than all the school-masters of his generation." This biography, written by a friend and colleague shortly after Henty's death, offers a rare look at a fascinating man! From his early life as a sickly child, to dodging bullets in the streets of Paris as a fearless war correspondent, or tramping through the jungles of the African Gold Coast, Henty's life reads like one of his stories. A must read for all Henty fans!

www.ingramcontent.com/pod-product-compliance
Lightning Source LLC
Chambersburg PA
CBHW030339310726
48979CB00001B/111

* 9 7 8 1 9 3 4 6 7 1 4 6 7 *